The Woman Upstairs

The Woman Upstairs

Mary Walters Riskin

For Bill,

with best wishes,

Mary

April 16/87.

NeWest Press
Edmonton

First Edition

Canadian Cataloguing in Publication Data

Riskin, Mary Walters, 1949-
The woman upstairs

ISBN 0-920897-20-7 (bound). — ISBN 0-920897-18-5 (pbk)

I. Title.
PS8585.I84W6 1987   C813'.54   C87-091161-9
PR9199.3.R58W6 1987

The author gratefully acknowledges the financial assistance of Alberta
Culture during the preparation of the manuscript.

Credits:
Cover design: Ruth Krahn
Printing and Binding: Friesen Printers, Altona, Manitoba

Financial Assistance:
Alberta Culture
The Alberta Foundation for the Literary Arts
The Canada Council

NeWest Publishers Limited
Suite 204, 8631 - 109 Street
Edmonton, Alberta

Manufactured in Canada.

For Bronwyn

Prologue

I find it easier to land in darkness than in light. It's less difficult to trust the pilot and the plane when there's no possibility of measuring descent against an upward rush of ground. My apprehension about flying is as much a sense of helplessness as it is a fear of death, and it's ridiculous and futile. But still, my heart is pounding faster than it should as we grind down through the night toward the runway in Toronto.

People land at airports every day, thousands of them, without incident. Not many hours ago I worried that there might be no available seat at such short notice, on the Friday evening of a long weekend, and now I should be feeling grateful and relieved to be here. The flight attendants take their seats. I close my eyes, tighten my grip on the arm rests. Landing becomes even less pleasant when you don't want to get to where you're going.

The huge jet bumps down at last, and slows itself with an urgency that pulls me forward in my seat.

Immediately, the plane is transformed. It seems immense and dependable, its cabin a well-lit and comfortable place to be. From my row near the back, I watch the aisles fill with passengers, keeping my eyes forward to avoid meeting those of the slightly-older-than-middle-aged man who's also been sitting alone, across the aisle from me.

Over Saskatchewan, one double gin already inside him, he called, "Excuse me, Miss . . . ?" I thought he was speaking to the flight attendant until I glanced across and saw him smiling at me, patting the seat beside him. I shook my head and looked out my window as though there were more to see in it than night, avoiding even his reflection in the glass.

Now, my remembered abruptness seems ruder than it did up there, and unnecessary too. Madelyn would have smiled, shaken her head, and had it done with, easily and graciously. Or else she might instead have joined him and reported later, "I met the most interesting man on the flight: a priest from Baffin Island." Things tend to turn out that way for her.

When he, too, is part way up the aisle and a young couple with a baby have joined the line behind him, I stand and get my pale green all-weather coat from the overhead storage space.

He doesn't look like a priest from Baffin Island—more like a drug salesman from Calgary. What did he see in me, a woman little more than half his age, wearing blue jeans, a plaid cotton shirt and running shoes, looking tired and nervous? Did he see someone with whom he might pass an hour or so in conversation, to ease the time and tension of the flight? Or did he see a prospect for something more than that?

Men of an age I once considered old, and therefore sexless, have begun to show signs of interest in me, and even to assume that I might be attracted to them as well. And other men—not boys but men, full-grown and out of college for quite some time, well-established in careers and even, in some cases, with whole marriages behind them—have become, in spite of all that time and experience, too young to be of interest to me.

She's dying. She's sixty-two, my mother.

I'm thirty-three, about the age she was when she had Mitchell. In my hair there's a strand or two of grey and near my eyes, fine wrinkling. I don't mind these signals that time is passing, but I am amazed sometimes at the haste with which my life unwinds itself, leaving most of the things that women do in their lives as yet undone in mine.

In the airport, I confirm that the next flight south won't leave until long after I can get to Donellon by car. I carry my suitcase out to the Rent-A-Car row in the parking lot, where I've been told I'll find a dark blue Toyota.

Inside the terminal building, even inside the landed plane, I was aware of the warm mugginess of the Ontario air, but outside I feel enveloped in humidity. It's almost one in the morning by my watch, two fifty-five by the clock on the dashboard of the car. When the sun is up, the heat will be heavy and unpleasant, inescapable. I can't imagine how I stood it for almost nineteen years.

Near the airport, in the soft illumination from lamps high above the road, the highway south seems civilized, fast, direct. The asphalt is smooth and richly black, the median a gentle hollow of close-cropped grasses, the shoulders wide and paved. Cities and towns ahead will give it a respectful berth, distributing and collecting vehicles through elaborate systems of rampways and concrete cloverleaves.

I ease my foot a little on the gas pedal, not quite comfortable with the speed the signs allow me. Those who use this highway regularly must come to believe in it, to trust that it will take them quickly and safely to their destinations. When the road betrays them, as it sometimes must, with a truckload of lumber splayed across two rain-slicked lanes or a stopped car concealed by falling snow, people must die with as much incredulity as fear.

I think of death in all its guises, when I don't want to think of it at all.

I assumed that when I came back here, if I ever did, that I would drive from Edmonton. I would have taken my time across the prairie, through Calgary, Regina, Winnipeg, and then around the northern rim of Lake Superior. Still stopping where I wanted to, I'd have pushed my way through and out of the miles of jack pine and rock and water, and down into Southwestern Ontario, all the time anticipating the tiny personal dramas I would fashion when I reached my mother's house.

I assumed that the time of my return, and the fact of it, would be up to me. But the clergyman, Westmoreland, called at seven last night and by nine I'd packed, driven myself to the airport, and was waiting with a ticket for the next plane east.

She has cancer. She didn't reveal the lumps to Dr. Whittick until late last fall, long after she'd discovered them, long after it was possible to do anything about them. She insisted no one tell me.

I move my left hand from the wheel to rub one eyelid then the other, to run it flat open across the perspiration above my lip and down to break the seal of humidity on my neck where skin meets skin. I'm tired, and the farther I drive the more reluctant I am to reach my destination.

The impetus, the shock of purpose and direction that sent me out of Edmonton recedes as I drive mile after mile of highway. The hum of the engine is steady, lulling me. The damp press of night seeps warmly into me and weighs me down with the urge to sleep.

I blink, deliberately, and then again. By controlling that one reflex, I can keep myself awake. There isn't much oncoming traffic and there's only one set of headlights, far behind, when I glance in the rearview mirror.

When he phoned, Westmoreland told me that even now he'd called without her knowledge or permission, as though this action on his part would itself convey the gravity of the situation. He was doing what he knew was best, he said. He knew I'd want to be there, at the end. He's a master of ponderous tritenesses.

He's also wrong. I don't want to be there, here, at all. But his misplaced assurance and Madelyn's too when, putting aside our recent estrangement, I went upstairs and told her, are why I'm here right now: driving this sleek highway in the middle of the night, twenty-five hundred miles from home. Unanchored by the news, I looked outside myself for the direction I would take and saw that it would have been unthinkable to have stayed in Edmonton.

I wish he'd followed her instructions. I wish he'd called me after it was over.

At Margaret Corner, I turn off the main highway and onto the secondary road that will take me, in another hour or so and after other towns, into Donellon. The night pushes against me softly, firmly, coaxing me to slow, to sleep. Thick-leaved trees, black against the sky, are closer to the road here: in places, their branches reach over me. From the cool open space and daylight that I left in Edmonton, I've entered a tunnel that gradually narrows and darkens, drawing me in with a stifling compression. Yawning, I shift to a lower gear to take a curve. On the straightaway I shake my head and force my eyes gritty wide again . . .

Mother sits in a lawn chair in the shade from the large silver maple behind the house, wearing a pastel dress of yellows and pale pinks. Her hair is softly pinned on top of her head and bright yellow daisies and flaming asters, which she has cut for the tall vase in the living room, are strewn across her lap. Her arms are crossed, her hands tucked under them, covering her small breasts. I am sitting on the lawn beside her, carefully pulling blades of grass from their sheaths. She is turned away from me.

Open on the grass between us is the sharp-pointed pair of scissors that she used to cut the flowers. I lean forward, put my hand out for them

. . . brake, and swerve, slamming myself awake against the seatbelt.

The car is full of the ripping squeal of tires on pavement and in an instant the headlights skim from tree to tree, stab emptiness, arc over underbrush, and stop.

The engine is silent, stalled, the tires still. The headlights beam against a pine, night dampness streaming through the melded shafts of light.

Saturday Morning

Chapter One

Donellon after twenty years away: it's so exactly the way it was and at the same time so astonishingly small.

I've grown used to Edmonton, which Madelyn refers to as the City of Perpetual Transformation. Impatient with itself, Edmonton tears down buildings and installs parking lots, wipes out parking lots and adds new buildings, reroutes roads and rolls up parks, and moves historic structures piece by piece to more convenient locations. It adds whole neighbourhoods, landscaping and all, between one winter and the next and then solves, in great confusions of dirt, machinery, and orange detour signs, the traffic problems that result.

But here—if someone dug up that bank of forsythia and replaced it with trellises and morning glory, the change would be a novelty for years.

The houses which line this street are set far apart and well back from the road. They're old, over a hundred years some of them, and made from red or yellow brick that age has softened, smoothed. From the outside, with their spacious lawns and wide verandahs, the houses look bigger than they are. Inside, the effect is reversed by dark and clutter, by excesses of furniture, by stairwells with oversized bannisters and newel posts. Bedrooms are papered in heavy florals and ferns; their windows are small and covered in white lace that is stretched between two thin brass rods to prevent the lace from fluttering.

The large house with the screened verandah, its brick exterior barely visible through the ivy, used to belong to the Carroll sisters, but now it belongs to Mitchell. He's maintained it well—the wide lawn is trimmed and very green, from the fresh white lattice-work right down to the row of maple trees which lines the street. He understands Donellon, and has made no visible improvements or changes to the house, although he could afford to do so.

He says he bought the house because it's near his office, but he belongs on this side of the river, where Grandmother grew up. This is elegant Donellon, haughty and well-rooted Donellon, a place to which families transplanted themselves after centuries in the British Isles, with the appropriate growing media packed in their steamer trunks: damask tablecloths, woollen cardigans, and tea services of sterling silver wrapped in embroidered tea-towels.

His telling me about the house was intended to underscore the fact that he chose to settle in Donellon, when he might have established a more lucrative practice elsewhere, so that Mother wouldn't be alone. He's clever at finding ways to convey his sense of filial responsibility and, by contrast, my own lack of it.

Except for the gift at Christmas, a hand-printed silk scarf with a box around it that was more impressive than the scarf, I haven't heard from Mitchell since August of last year. Months have often gone by when I haven't seen nor heard from him, even years sometimes, but my conversation with Westmoreland has explained this recent silence. Mother asked that no one tell me she was sick, and Mitchell didn't tell. Mitchell is a dutiful son. He always has been that.

Maybe she's dead already. If I knew that she were dead, I might feel something more than this uneasiness, this nervousness, which increases as my surroundings become more and more familiar; I might be better able to prepare myself for what I'll find when I reach the house. I know about funerals, the progression of the ceremony, and what is expected of the mourners. I know what is done for the dead, but not what to do for the dying.

I packed a black dress, folded it into the bottom of the suitcase and put my black shoes on top of it, then covered them with a large plastic bag from Zellers. They are cached in my bag, these preparations for the funeral, and on top of them are other pairs of jeans besides the ones I'm wearing, other shirts and blouses, underwear, the things I'd take with me if I were travelling anywhere for a few days. I was uncomfortable with the assumption of those black things even as I packed them, and I don't like their being in my suitcase now. I should have come back sooner, when she was well, or I should not have come at all.

I drive slowly through the small business district which follows the residential area. The stores aren't open —it isn't eight-thirty yet— and the quiet street looks orderly, secure and picturesque. The grocer and the owner of the hardware store, the druggist and the barber, compete for the cleanest sidewalks, the most highly polished windows, the least dusty awnings, and each year on Donellon Day the mayor presents these civic-minded entrepreneurs with Certificates of Appreciation which he distributes along with the trophies for the quilts and summer squash.

I saw the ceremony once, standing next to Jenny Haultain near the bunting-woven stage in Leavenworth Park. Jenny's golden hair that summer, when we were ten, was braided into long plaits that hung to the middle of her back. My hair, pale brown, straight, too short for braiding, was pulled into two pigtails. As Dr. Haultain stepped forward and up the wooden steps to accept his framed certificate, I wished he were my father, and that Jenny's hair were mine.

Mother said it was not important that Father got no certificates. His factory might not have have won awards for cleanliness but it contributed to the economy, which was even more worthwhile. I ought to be more than satisfied, she said, that the presentations took place in a park that was named after my great-grandfather. Why would anyone want a certificate when there was a whole bronze statue erected in the family's honour, right beside the stage?

But the statue was Leavenworth, and I was Diana Guthrie.

After the red brick civic buildings, square and ornately trimmed in white, there is a gentle, well-treed bend and a long curved hill and then, directly across the sluggish brown waters of the Pengelly River, like a dingy secret that's been saved for last, the textile factory that won Father no certificates.

Two stories high, the walls of the main building of Guthrie Textiles are pocked with rows of small-paned windows and there are three high, round chimneys which tower above the complex. They're empty and quiet now, but for years they smudged the air with heat and yellow smoke and spilled further layers of grey onto the sallow brick walls below.

The sign on the building still says "Guthrie", although the lawyer, Mr. Quince, managed to find a buyer for it soon after Father left Donellon.

It is unsettling to see the factory so still, so comfortable with its stillness. All summer the dark leaves of the trees surrounding the buildings used to contrast with the mottled jades and brilliant greens of the foliage farther out, but now there's no such contrast. The whole river valley looks cleaner than it used to, its sky washed bright.

I'm not surprised that Guthrie Textiles is no longer in operation. It's small by today's standards, old-fashioned, out of the way. And today, even factories need certificates for cleanliness. But its ease with emptiness is an eloquent sign: a great deal of time has passed since I was in Donellon.

The dark, the heat and noise frightened me when I was very small, and Father rarely took me there even as I grew older. When he did, he left me in his brighter office, the desk piled high with papers, a place where the noise was muffled and the air was a little cooler, while he took care of whatever brief matter he'd dropped by to attend to.

Mother was tolerant of Guthrie Textiles, although she never expressed any enthusiasm for it, nor do I recall her visiting it. But she was practical, mindful that the Leavenworths might have had a statue and a park in Donellon, but they did not have money.

It was Grandmother who really objected to the textile factory, actively and persistently. I suspect that the rest of Donellon, with the possible exception of those who worked for Father, agreed with her. She was usually a practical woman too, but she ignored all financial considerations and focussed on aesthetics when it came to the Guthrie Textiles. To her, the complex was an eyesore, a disgrace and even, on occasion, a scourge. Her family had made a nice clean little city, and the Guthries had come along and coated it in filth.

For all of the years that she visited us, and for the several years that she lived with us, she never once missed an opportunity to look away, deliberately, her eyes lowered in disapproval, when she came anywhere near the factory.

Grandmother would be staying for a week or so, Mother said in the car on the way to the station. After the funeral was over and a little time had passed, she'd go back to her home in Toronto.

"I expect you to behave yourself, Diana. Remember that this is a difficult time for her." She straightened in her seat, and looked over at my father at the wheel. "For all of us. No running, and not a lot of noise."

After a moment she glanced back at me. "All right?"

I nodded.

"I don't imagine she'll stay in Toronto long," Father said, taking his pipe from his mouth and holding it in his hand against the wheel. "There's nothing to keep her there now."

"We'll come to that when we come to it," Mother said quietly. She'd been thinking about it, too, it seemed. "Donellon is her home. It is right, appropriate, for her to be here."

"Here. But not here. If you get my drift."

"Wallace. This is not the time . . . ."

I was afraid that she would start to cry again, but she swallowed and when she spoke again her voice was steady.

"The last thing she'd want would be to live in a house full of children."

Father patted her shoulder, his eyes still on the road. "You're right," he said. "This isn't the time to talk about it."

To Grandmother, the train was the only dignified means of transportation. Railways meant dining cars with uniformed waiters, knives and forks that glistened like well-used tracks, linen tablecloths and sleeping coaches.

That day when she arrived in Donellon with Grandfather Wishart's casket, she'd taken the day coach down from Toronto, which brought her to Donellon station just after noon. She stood in the doorway of the train car, which had shrieked to a reluctant halt in front of us, her back straight and her shoulders even as though a book were balanced on her head. She found us in the little crowd and gave a nod before she looked down again at the steps she'd have to descend to reach us.

Mother was round with Mitchell but her legs and arms were slim, her throat white and smooth, and wisps of short hair had loosened themselves from the soft roll on top of her head and were curled against her temples in the heat. She wore a navy maternity suit with white collar and cuffs, silk stockings with straight black seams, and thick-heeled white shoes. I was proud of the way she looked, and relieved that she didn't appear to be on the verge of tears as she had been for several days.

I would far rather have been with Father down near the luggage compartment than with two newly-bereaved women, but Mother's hand was firm on my shoulder so that I wouldn't wander off. Tears in an adult frightened me at six, and I worried that Grandfather Wishart's death might have affected Grandmother as it had Mother, making her quiet and uncommunicative, and inclined to suddenly leaving rooms with a handkerchief pressed against her mouth.

I didn't remember Grandfather Wishart well enough to feel any real sense of loss myself: he'd always seemed a thin, slightly less than adequate shadow with a pipe, who stood away from Grandmother and nodded when she spoke to him. Except at Christmas, he usually stayed in Toronto when she came down to Donellon.

Grandmother was wearing a collar of bone lace; otherwise she was dressed entirely and imposingly in black, and her thin hair was pulled away from her face. Her expression was one of such extreme displeasure that it seemed that the skin had been pulled back with the hair. The black porter set the portable steps in place and then reached up to assist my grandmother, smiling gently, apologetically.

Without looking at him she held out a folded dollar bill and when he'd taken it, she put her hand on the cloth of his uniform just above the wrist and, as though he were a railing, she descended to the platform.

I was prepared to be kissed by her as I was often, unwillingly on my part, kissed by adults, but she ignored me.

"They asked me if I wanted to be with him. Can you imagine, Edith? Four hours in a baggage compartment? In this heat? I've never heard of such a thing."

Mother touched her shoulder in an attempt to pacify her, but the words had made her wince with pain and I turned away, giving my attention to a plump woman with bright red hair and a dark purple dress cut very low to expose the tops of her immense breasts. She was standing where Grandmother had just been in the doorway of the train car, and once I'd seen her I couldn't take my eyes from her. She seemed to come not only from no generation I could place but from an entirely different civilization. She wore high-heeled shoes of the same deep purple shade as her dress, shoes totally unlike the sensible ones the women in my family always wore.

She was nervously scanning the crowd and ignoring the command of the porter, who'd stopped smiling altogether, that she clear the doorway for those who were waiting behind. At last she caught sight of the person she'd been looking for and she waved frantically, her large white purse banging against her thick hip. Then she stepped down and I couldn't see her any more.

With one hand still on my shoulder and the other on Grandmother's elbow, Mother steered us through the crowd. As we moved toward the baggage compartment, we passed the woman in the purple dress half a train car down, almost totally enveloping a small, thin man in shirtsleeves and trousers. He had a grey suitjacket over his arm. He was backing away from the woman's embrace, clasping her hands to hold her away from him and looking at the faces in the crowd as though he feared someone might know him.

His eyes slipped over us, not noticing us, but I was very aware of him for he looked so much the way that Grandfather Wishart had, small and grey and uncertain of himself, that I almost pointed him out to Mother. She was saying not to dawdle so I went, skip-running to keep up but glancing back to see that the man was pulling the woman away from the train, toward the baggage sheds. His shirt was damp and yellowed beneath the arms, as Grandfather Wishart's never were, and the woman was pointing at her watch, at the train, as I lost sight of them again.

There was some problem with the hearse, Father told us when we reached him. The train was almost ready to depart and there was a big wooden box half in and half out of the baggage compartment. Nobody seemed to know whether to pull it out and set it on the platform or whether to leave it where it was until the hearse arrived. A group had gathered to offer advice and sympathy, and everyone referred to the box as "him".

He hadn't been born in Donellon. He was from Toronto and probaby would have preferred to have been buried there. But Grandmother was a Leavenworth no matter what her last name was and, to her mind, people married into the Leavenworth family, not out of it.

When she said the word, it reverberated. "You are a Leavenworth, Diana. You must never forget that." The name was sacred, not in the sense of the Reverend Westmoreland's lowered, respectful tones, but resoundingly sacred, jubilantly and boomingly sacred, like the gods of Noah and Job.

Her roots were the ones the family would adopt no matter who ever married whom from where, and the entire family was headed for the graveyard in Donellon, for the family plot with its six-foot marble marker to be exact, if she had anything to do with it.

"You can't just dump him on the platform for Lord knows how long until the car arrives," she said. "It isn't dignified." She glared at Father as though he'd arranged this.

His face was red beneath his straw hat and he removed his glasses to wipe his brow with a handkerchief. "They've got a flat, Mother," he said, his teeth clenched, his tone unsuccessfully attempting to hide that fact. "We can't hold the train up any longer."

"You can't just leave him on the platform as though he were a piece of furniture. The train will wait."

Grandmother's major objection to my father was that he was not a true son of Donellon nor of any city or town in Ontario. He was a foreigner: his parents were from the United States. To Grandmother's mind, everything else was a corollary strike against him, explained by this first grave lack.

Father thought Grandmother a snob, and everything she said and did was interpreted by him as pointless affectation. But she was not a snob: snobbery is superficial and self-conscious. Grandmother's haughtiness was mighty, marrow-deep, and had reached its magnificent level of refinement only after passing through several generations of Leavenworths.

Mother was always in the middle then, defending Grandmother with Father, and Father with Grandmother. Later, she took one side and stuck with it. "There weren't the men around then that there are now," she told me when I was about ten, by way of explaining her marriage to my father. "Because of the war." It was as though she'd taken whatever she could get.

With the coffin suspended between Donellon station and the train and no one certain what to do about it, I crossed unnoticed to the door of the train sheds and found it open a crack. Over the hissing of the train I heard sounds: whimpering, a groan. I stood near the gap in the grey, slatted door to listen and then pushed my index finger out to give it a little nudge, to open the door like a breeze I hoped, just as the train emitted a blast of steam and the porter called "Board!", his voice rising through the word.

The man who looked like Grandfather Wishart was leaning back against the duffel bags of mail and the forgotten suitcases and the card-board boxes, his pants down around his ankles and his wrinkled shirt-tails against the bare flesh of his pale white thighs. The woman in the tight purple dress was on her knees before him, her heels toward me and her hands cupped up as though she knelt at the communion rail. His fist rested on her head, and his hand was full of dollars.

His eyes opened slowly and, before he caught sight of me and they widened in shock, I saw in them the helplessness, the weakness: the limpid, stupid eyes.

I fled and was back beside Mother, rubbing my hands against my skirt before anyone there had noticed I was missing. I kept my head down, fearful until we finally got in the car and followed the hearse from the station, that the man would come and find me.

I told Madelyn about the train sheds about five years ago, as one of my offerings in the hurried exchange of reminiscences that marked our transition from acquaintances to friends. I started quickly, hesi-tantly, with the sense of shame that I'd always associated with the incident, shame for the man and woman as well as for myself. But Madelyn listened with such amusement that I finished off slowly and dramatically, adding all of the detail I could remember, drawing out the humour she'd detected.

I recalled the weakness in his eyes, the abject succumbing to a pleasure that he could not control. The woman kneeling at his feet, fully dressed and so uncompromised from where I stood, and no doubt pos-sessing a full complement of teeth which good business sense dictated she not use, held absolute power over him. I wondered whether the woman ever thought of that.

"I doubt it," Madelyn said. "Women weren't taught to think that way."

Madelyn didn't know my Grandmother.

At the bottom of the hill I pull aside to let a yellow school bus, its windows full of students, or campers more likely on July the second, lumber across the bridge. When it has passed I cross the narrow span, barely wide enough to accommodate two cars.

The T-intersection is at the top of the hill before me, and the house is less than a mile west of that.

Chapter Two

There was no stoplight at the T-intersection when I was here before, but there is one now, and it is red. There isn't another car to be seen, but I stop dutifully and wait for the green signal, pulling yet another cigarette from the nearly empty pack on the passenger seat beside me. The ashtray is full, and the inside of my mouth feels coated in sludge. I was going to quit smoking last summer, last winter, in the spring. I'm as tired of making resolutions as I am of smoking. The lighter in the dashboard pops out and I light the cigarette.

When the stoplight changes I move my foot to the gas, but as I ease out the clutch the car stalls in the middle of the intersection. It did that once before this morning as I was pulling out of the motel in Tamwell, where I'd stopped to try to draw my shaking self together. Something in the car must have been knocked loose when I went into the ditch last night.

It's reluctant to start again and I take my hand from the key and my feet from the gas and clutch and wait for a minute in case I've flooded it, grateful that there aren't any other cars around.

A tall thin man has appeared, it seems from nowhere, and is walking down the shoulder of the road toward me, wearing grey bib overalls and a red cap with the brim pulled down so I can't see his face. But I know from the gaunt frame, the casual swinging gait, that it is Noel's father and that he's been drawn in this direction by the sound of a motor that won't start. Fletcher's good with machines and proud of it.

I try the engine one more time and, mercifully, it turns over. I spurt out of the intersection and up the slope, averting my face as I pass him.

By the time I'm past his laneway, the adrenalin has lessened and my whole body shakes. I imagine his astonishment, or his horror, had he realized that he'd almost played good samaritan to me: the person to whom he must certainly have attached some of the blame for Noel's death. It was Mother, not me, who precipitated that terrible event, but I'm sure Noel's father doesn't know that.

Fletcher and I: the two people who knew Noel best and loved him most but we could offer nothing to one another that might have healed. I could learn of his grief only by extrapolating from my own, and I wonder if it even crossed his mind that I was grieving too.

He continues to live with the Guthrie home permanently embedded, thornlike, in his property. I'd have thought he'd have moved away.

The house is exactly as I remembered it, big and square and formidable, presenting its haughty spine to those who approach from the drive. It's an attempted reproduction of the homes on the other side of the river, which fails because its red brick firmly resists all efforts to make it look any older than it is.

I drive through the semicircle of gravel in front of the verandah and pull up next to a small black Porsche which is parked against the garage. If that is Mitchell's, then practising in Donellon has been less hard on his pocketbook than he would have had me believe.

The house looks quiet and empty. It has always looked deserted, even when everyone was home, and I think that's because everything about it is so orderly and tidy, both inside and out. It's also because the front of the house is really at the back.

The car shudders a little as I turn the engine off. I climb out and again check the front end of the Toyota, as I did at the motel earlier this morning. There are a few scratches on the bumper and the grill. No real damage. Nothing so noticeable that I'd have to pay for it.

The trip into the ditch seems less frightening now than it did when it happened. Then, I thought of all the worse things that might have happened when I dozed off at the wheel, but now I'm certain that I closed my eyes for only an instant, if I closed them at all. There may have been something in the road that I can't remember now, something that I swerved to miss.

It was a minor incident. I wasn't hurt and the car wasn't damaged, and I backed out of the shallow ditch immediately, before anyone came along. It frightened me into two restless hours of sleep and a shower in the little motel in Tamwell, which did little to refresh me in this heat. But now I think I let it worry me too much.

I watch myself carefully for signs of impending paranoia, and hypochondria, too: people who live alone are prone to despicable fears.

There is a noise behind me, and I turn to face the house.

Mitchell is standing on the porch, wearing white tennis shorts and a t-shirt, and it's even more obvious today how carefully trim he keeps his body than it was when he visited Edmonton, when he usually wore a suit. He's almost twenty-eight. His hair is dark and curly, and he's grown a moustache again. The last time I saw him, his face was clean-shaven. Madelyn thinks he's attractive and I suppose he is, if you can look at him objectively. I still see the fat.

He's tanned, but his face is paler than the rest of him and there are dark circles under his eyes. He looks unwell. He also looks astonished as he realizes, after a brief moment of puzzlement, who he's looking at. Obviously Westmoreland didn't tell him that he'd called me, and I have the sensation that I had sometimes as a child when, coming in from playing outside too long, certain that there would be trouble, I discovered that no one had noticed how late it was but me. Perhaps I needn't have come here, after all. Perhaps even Westmoreland didn't expect that I'd show up. But it's too late for retreat.

I answer him before he asks: "Westmoreland called. Last night."

My presence assimilated, he starts down the steps toward me. "He can never leave well enough alone."

He crosses the gravel and I wait, expecting one of his perfunctory hugs, which are loose and have no feeling to them, but he stops just short of me and slides the tips of his hands into the pockets of his shorts.

I stand still, my thoughts on the house and on the woman in it.

"How is she?"

He glances back, up toward the second storey where her room is on the far side, and sighs. "She's dying. Westmoreland must have told you that. You wouldn't be here otherwise."

"Is she . . . ?" I pause. "There must be a lot of pain." I hate the way I've said the word "pain". There was something insincere about it.

"The drugs she's being given help a little. It comes and goes." He shrugs, as though to say, "You understand".

I don't, but I nod anyway.

I can smell his cologne: light, expensive, pleasant. He looks down at his tennis shoes and I do too. They look as though they've never been worn before, and his mid-calf-length socks are extraordinarily white against his tanned legs. How did Mitchell ever turn into such a conscientious dresser? From whom did he learn, and why? Perhaps he's been in love with someone I don't know about.

He says, "You've come a long way. And I'm sure it's cost you a lot of money to get here." Now he looks up at me. His eyes are brown and they always remind me of Father's. "But I don't think you ought to see her."

I take another deep breath. "I'm not afraid of seeing . . . ." I gesture uncertainly. "I think I can handle it." As I say this, I'm wondering if it's true. I'm pretty certain that it's not.

"That isn't what I mean." He takes my wrist in his hand. He has a bracelet on his wrist, a thick gold chain. "It would only hurt her, to see you. Bring back painful memories. She doesn't need any more pain than she's got already."

I stare at him. "Mitchell, you've been trying to persuade me to come back here for years."

"Not now. It's too late. If I thought you should come, I'd have called you. I wouldn't have left it to Westmoreland." He looks up again at the house. "She has some quiet times now. It's almost done with. You just can't start anything now. Please."

He squeezes my wrist as though we're comrades, then lets it drop. "I know her better than you do. I know what's best for her. You have to go."

I don't say anything.

He seems to take this as assent, for he pulls a set of keys out of his pocket and his expression has lightened somewhat when he looks up at me again. "You can stay at my place until you're ready to go back. I'm staying here, so my house is empty." He's trying to pry one of the keys off the key-ring.

"No."

He stops and looks at me.

I turn and unlock my trunk.

"I'm staying here."

I look down at my suitcase, then close the trunk again because I don't know where I'm going to put the suitcase when I go in the house. I turn and lean against the car, feeling the heat from the metal through my jeans.

The situation has become bizarre, my not wanting to go in and see her, his not wanting me to go in and see her, my refusal, anyway, to leave. But I can't. I've come this far.

His face has reddened. "I'm asking you to go for her sake. Can't you ever do anything but hurt her?" He glances at the house. "We're not playing games here, you know."

"I've as much right to be here as you do." I'm trying to sound reasonable.

He stares at me for a long time before he speaks again. When he does, the words come in tiny, measured, furious sentences, whispered.

"No," he says. "You don't. She hasn't got a daughter. She has a son. That's all."

He turns and walks up onto the verandah, pulls the door open, goes into the house, and closes the door quietly behind him.

I stand in the driveway and stare at the place where I saw him last. Before I follow him in, I toss my cigarette on the ground and step on it. I hadn't considered that I'd have to confront him as well as her. Each time he came to see me he pleaded with me to come back, to make things up with her. I'm sure this was his motive for visiting Edmonton, that his trips had nothing really to do with business, nor even with establishing and then maintaining contact with his long lost sister. He had a mission, and his trips were for her sake, not mine, nor even his. I assumed that when I got here, he'd be relieved I'd come, even at this late date.

The house is dark. The curtains are drawn to keep the cool inside, but it's uncomfortably warm in spite of that. There's no sign of Mitchell. He must have gone upstairs.

I close the door quietly behind me and stand in the wood-grained vestibule, where Father built the elevator up the stairs for Grandmother and her wheelchair. I blink as my eyes adjust, barely breathing. The house is palpably silent, thick with her presence. Mitchell won't have to worry about my going up to see her for a while: I'd no more set foot on that bottom stair than I would yell, "Anybody home?" as I used to do when I came though this door.

I, who deliberately accomplish those things first which I find most difficult and distasteful, am dammed by the unexpected accumulation of debris I've acquired since I stepped off the plane in Toronto. I've lost the clean edge of determination I had when I left Edmonton last night.

I tiptoe into the living room, the "drawing room" as Grandmother used to call it, and walk more easily on the carpet. The room's unchanged: the stiff-backed chesterfield and chairs still stand on the polished dark oak flooring, toed against the deep maroon pattern of the rug. The heavy curtains across the french doors are closed, but they often were that way when the days were hot. That's not why the room looks dead and empty, despite the excesses of furnishings, long-legged end tables topped with ornamental lamps, lace antimacassars on the backs of the chesterfield and chairs, the tea caddy in the corner.

There is not one plant in here, nor has there ever been, aside from the poinsettias and lilies which were accepted as gifts at the appropriate times of the year. I'm amazed that I grew up in a house where there were no plants. My basement apartment's now so full of them that Madelyn has accused me of turning a perfectly civilized suite of rooms into a jungle. I love the smell of them, the way the air is made deep and rich with the scent of their moist earth.

Plants grow in dirt, and change, which makes them unacceptable to this house. Unless they're dead: there's plenty of wood in the furniture, well-sealed with varnish so that nothing can leak into or creep out of it again.

In the dining room I pull open the bottom doors of the sideboard, aware that it's not yet noon and Mother is right above me. Her room is immediately above where I am standing: I'm that close to her. But there's only sherry, nothing hard enough to knock my throat loose. I'd forgotten the humidity: it drags you down so that you don't ever want to move. It's filled my throat.

This dining room is huge. It easily accommodates the high and solid sideboard, the table at which eight can sit quite comfortably— twelve when the leaves are in—and the china cabinet on the opposite wall beside the door. This room must be half the size of my entire apartment, this house four times the size of Madelyn's.

James Leavenworth, my great-grandfather, bequeathed the Leavenworth family home, which is on the other side of the river, to Donellon—"for the enjoyment and edification of its future generations". I suppose he assumed that with Grandmother living in Toronto there'd be no future family need for it, and so he left it and all of its furniture to the town, and Donellon responded as he'd expected it would: by immediately declaring it an historic site.

I can only begin to imagine Grandmother's dismay when she learned what her father had done with her house. She wouldn't allow us to visit it ("We will not be seen touring our own home") so it wasn't until I was old enough to go alone that I saw it, and I went back several times. The floor plan's a lot like this one.

I don't think she ever really accepted that she no longer had an official home in Donellon, and when she came to stay with us, even before Grandfather Wishart died, it was less as a visiting relative than as a conquering head of state.

Before she came to live with us, Mother and Father and I used to come back from Sunday drives to the table that Hilda had prepared, with a linen tablecloth, and table napkins with silver rings around them. What was coming from the kitchen didn't matter. The Sunday evening meal was distinguished by the grandeur of its setting. Mother and Father brought crystal glasses in with them when they came to sit for grace, and before each of our places there was Leavenworth silverware that I'd helped Hilda polish. I liked to guess what form the dinner would take from the numbers and shapes of the knives and forks and spoons we had been given.

After Grandmother came, every day became the same. Place-mats disappeared completely from the dining room and we had Sunday table settings every evening of the week.

She was here to collect her strength after the funeral, but she'd seemed stronger the day she arrived at the station than she did the night she fell, which was nearly a month afterward. She'd grown pale and shaky and had taken to walking with a cane, which Father had purchased for her in town, because of her fear of falling.

I prayed for her recovery. Her interminable naps interfered with my jumping my bicycle off the ramp I'd made out of small logs and pieces of flat wood, and her presence at the dinner table meant that I wore a dress. Mother seemed determined that I should learn all of my table manners at once, even obscure ones that made no sense at all, like leaving the last cookie on the plate when no one else wanted it.

We waited at the table for her to come down, me itching to get it done with and out to play again, and Father growing more irritated as his wait for dinner lengthened every day. But her determination had been unimpaired by widowhood: she brooked no offers of assistance. We waited.

Mother suggested that perhaps it was a blessing. If she were here when the baby came, it would save her another trip.

"Don't suggest it, Edith," Father said, his voice hard with warning. "That's another three weeks at least."

They were increasingly impatient since Grandmother had come, and I was careful of what I said because they snapped as easily at me as they did at one another.

Mother was wearing a pale blue maternity dress that night; Father wore the dark suit he'd worn to work. Her cheeks were pink, as they'd been more often than usual during her pregnancy, but Father looked really hot. There was perspiration on his forehead and under his sideburns and he kept wiping his face with his big white handkerchief. Until Grandmother came, he'd usually changed before dinner, before he read the paper, into a short-sleeved shirt and pale cotton trousers.

"This afternoon," Mother said, leaning forward to whisper, "she was knitting in the sunroom. A sweater she'd started for Father the last time I was in Toronto. It's harder on her than you give her credit for." She straightened, primly.

Father looked down at the drink in his big pale hand. "Maybe she didn't want the wool to go to waste."

"That isn't funny, Wallace."

Mother looked icily away from him and snapped her eyebrows at me. "Sit up straight, Diana."

My shoulders had hunched and stiffened with the need to laugh.

"I'm sorry," he said, looking up. "I didn't mean it."

"Of course you meant it. You wouldn't have said it if you didn't mean it." Mother brushed brown curls from her forehead and refused to look at him.

He sighed and added, almost in a whisper, "I'm sure she'd get better faster if she went home."

We heard her on the stairs then and waited silently as the cane tapped down them one by one, waited for Grandmother and grace. I felt I could put my finger out and ping the membrane of tension at the table.

The meal was eaten in almost complete silence until at last Grandmother asked my father how his day had been, asking it as though it were the proper thing to do even though she had no interest at all in the response, and Father responded in kind: briefly, telling nothing, inviting no additional questions.

"And yours?"

She shrugged straight shoulders. "It's hard to rest with children in the house."

"Perhaps you'd be more comfortable at home."

She ignored him.

Mother pursed her lips.

Hilda brought a pitcher of ice water and put it on the table, and everyone watched her do it.

Grandmother sat across from me, her back to the sideboard and the three long windows that looked out over the wide green lawn and the flowerbeds. Her expression was unclear in the shadows. She was cutting her meat into such tiny pieces that she barely had to open her mouth to get them in.

Mother silently finished the last of her dinner and Father, his plate empty first as it always was until Mitchell was old enough to wield his own fork, was looking over her shoulder at the brandy bottle in the china cabinet. He was waiting for Grandmother and me to finish the first course so that Hilda could bring dessert.

But I could not finish my first course. There was a brussels sprout on my tongue, cold and intact, which I could not bring myself to bite into, and which, I knew, was far too large to swallow whole. My hands twisted the linen table napkin in my lap and my throat was closed and painful. I was concentrating very hard on the white wooden lawn swing beyond the windows to stop myself from throwing up.

On my plate there were two more of them. I'd left the brussels sprouts to the end, hoping they'd disappear before the roast beef and potatoes were all gone, or that Father would spear them with his fork and save me as he'd sometimes done before.

"It's very fancy to have roast beef on Tuesday night," Grandmother said. "At home, we have it only on a Sunday, and then infrequently. I suppose this is an American custom." She looked at Father.

"Wallace is not American, Mother," my mother said. "You know he isn't. He was born right here in Donellon like you were."

"My father was American, though," he reminded them. "And Mother, too. Although that has nothing that I can think of to do with roast beef on Tuesdays."

Mother wanted to say something to Father but she changed her mind and looked at me instead.

"Good grief, Diana. Don't tell me you've still got that in your mouth? Just chew it up and be done with it. We'll never get dessert at this rate." She looked apologetically at Grandmother. "She's usually very good about eating dinner."

It was mushy, green, and cold, and it squatted on my tongue.

"She should be excused," Father said. "She looks pale."

I looked hopefully at Mother.

"Just the one in your mouth," she said, glancing again at Grandmother. "We'll see about the other two afterward."

"It doesn't hurt to try new things. That's how we acquire a taste." Grandmother edged a sliver of sprout into her own mouth.

Father clenched his fist tight around his table napkin and put it down hard on the table. "I can't believe that we're discussing the contents of someone's mouth. Where is Hilda? I want a cup of coffee."

No one moved. I sat a minute longer looking at all of them, all of them looking at me. Dinner was rising in my throat and I was trapped by the thing in my mouth.

And then it seemed quite simple. If I had something in my mouth that I didn't want to be there, I would have to take it out. My throat loosened with relief as I leaned forward.

I ought to have raised my fork and put the sprout politely on it as I'd been taught to do with gristle. I might even have gently opened my mouth and let it drop, and have been forgiven in time. But instead, the sprout seemed to have taken propulsion from my loathing of it and I spat it directly at my plate.

It skidded off the rim, and sat on the shiny white tablecloth, looking as bad as it had felt when it was sitting in my mouth.

The three adults in a single sound drew in their breaths.

I felt my face grow red as I looked from Mother to Father to Grandmother. There was no hint of warmth in any of their expressions.

"I hate you." I muttered at my plate. "I wish you were dead," I said. "All of you."

I stood up, terrified.

Mother looked at Father, and both of them began to stand. Grandmother was pulling herself up as well. I had one moment's vision of the three of them descending together in rage upon me, when Hilda came through from the kitchen, with the coffee.

Grandmother turned, startled, toward the door and reached out to grasp the edge of the table to steady herself. She missed, and I watched wide-eyed as she fell, slowly, one crack of sound as her cheek hit the table's edge and then she collapsed out of sight, silently, on the far side of the table.

"Mother!"

My mother's scream was terrible in my ears. She bent, awkward with her pregnancy.

"Don't move her. I'll call Whittick," Father said, and hurried from the room.

I stood for a moment, staring at the place where Grandmother had disappeared, too frightened to kneel and look, to go around and look, sure that all that silence must mean that she was dead.

I glanced at Hilda who stood still at the door, the coffee pot in her hand, her mouth agape. Then I turned and ran.

Chapter Three

I'd never had occasion to run away from home before, so I was ill-prepared for it. I became more organized, a better planner, as I got older, and my skill continues to increase with age so that now I may be considered an expert at making escapes from unsuitable situations: of both short and long duration. Already, I'm planning my move from Madelyn's basement suite, developing a course of action that will leave room for no argument or discussion from either her or Sonny, but will merely take effect before they're aware of what I'm doing.

But when I was six, I had no favorite hiding places, no well-tested routes over which I'd traditionally made escapes, and my flight from the dining room had been unrelated to the possibility of arriving somewhere else: I'd just wanted to be gone. When I reached the mailbox at the end of the laneway I paused, uncertain, panting hard.

The highway was bare and waiting, mottled with light by the late sun through the maples and the elms. Behind me the drive was quiet and empty, the tops of the trees moving a little as though they'd been disturbed by my passing. There were crickets somewhere, and far off the rippling of frogs. These usual sounds of evening seemed unnatural to me, as though by listening to them I was failing to hear the sounds of my pursuers.

I was sure I'd been pursued: it didn't occur to me that, with Grandmother lying on the dining room floor, no one might have noticed, or cared, that I was gone.

I went left, the road to Donellon more familiar than the road away, and down into the grassy ditch. My mind was full of Grandmother's fierce blue eyes, never leaving my face, accusing as she fell, her pale cheek cracking against the table's edge before she disappeared. She was fallen, surely dead. But even after she'd dropped from sight those same eyes, those Leavenworth eyes, had sparked their accusation at me—from my mother's face.

I stumbled on rocks, my breath coming in short hard gasps, but still I didn't stop. Since the day of the funeral, everything I'd done had been unsuitable, in need of adjustment by either Grandmother or Mother. I'd been consistently noisy, clumsy, and inconsiderate of others, and I'd felt increasingly uncertain of the reactions my actions would produce.

That feeling, however, had been amorphous and dilute compared with what I felt now. What I'd done tonight was entirely different because this time I'd known what I would do and say, and known that it was wrong before I did and said it.

I found a pathway leading deep into the woods and took it. Now they couldn't find me, and the dim light comforted for its concealment. But as I ran, panting, tripping, into the darker woods my mind formed the immensity of my wrongdoing and created the forms that could make me adequately pay.

I imagined pursuers who were shrouded and indistinct, huge enemies who, as I ran, became increasingly divested of all that was familiar.

At last I could run no farther and when I came to a large flat stump, waist high, I climbed up on it to catch my breath. My bare knees scraped the bark and the moment I stopped moving the mosquitoes formed around me and began to bite in earnest. I slapped at tiny needlepricks on arms and legs and face, and then I felt tears start as my determination to run away shivered and fell around me.

It seemed darker and the fear shifted again, and grew. Darkness would release the flaps of owls and bats and sounds which bore no physical form at all, would smudge the edges of light and dusk which kept things in their proper places. Without the benefit of a Hansel, I'd have to spend the night alone in these deep woods unless I moved immediately. But where? I could not go back.

I heard a rustle and a low laugh from the direction I'd just come.

I froze.

"If you're moving, they don't bite so bad." It was the voice of a boy and I let my breath out slowly. I could see a bit of red behind a bush.

"What are you doing there?"

"Who's there?" I asked.

He stood and I recognized Noel Fletcher, the tall lanky boy from the farm which surrounded our property on three sides. He wore blue denim coveralls and a red plaid flannel shirt, and around his neck there hung a set of binoculars on a black leather strap. His thick curls stood up on one side of his head as though he'd been sleeping on them.

"That's our stump you're sitting on. I should call the police."

"Trees don't belong to anyone," I said.

"Sure they do. That one was my dad's favorite, until he had to cut it down. Matter of fact, he just sent me down here to make sure no one was sitting on it."

He moved through the underbrush until he was standing on the path in front of me. "Aw, hell. I'm teasing. What're you doing here anyway, all alone? You're too little to be here by yourself."

I bristled and tucked my fear away: he was only a year or two older than I was. "I just felt like a walk, that's all."

"You know your way back?" He was suspicious of my non-chalance.

I looked back at the path. "Of course I do."

"There's a shorter way to your place. Bet you don't know that one."

I looked at him, his brown eyes so dark that the pupils and irises seemed to be the same shade, and shook my head.

"I'll show you."

Slapping at mosquitoes, I climbed down and followed him deeper into the woods.

I'd seen him once before when Father took me over to borrow an axe. The house he lived in with his father was small and untidy, the yard littered with pieces of automobiles and tractors, the once-yellow paint of the house now cracked and peeling and the porch concave and totally without paint where it had been walked on.

Mr. Fletcher was a quiet man who rolled cigarettes as he needed them. While he and and my father had been inside, Noel had come running from the barn, his pants muddy to the knees and a hand up to keep his cap on, but he'd stopped when he saw me on the porch and had disappeared back into the barn. When the men came out there was no sign of him and when Father asked after him, Fletcher grumbled that the boy was never around when he was needed.

Low branches of wild raspberry scratched at my legs and I wished I were wearing overalls like Noel's. The sound of frogs grew louder and at last we came to the clearing and the pond. Noel continued down the path which veered away to follow the edge of the water but I stopped and called to him.

"I don't have to go back yet."

He shrugged and went to sit on a low grey rock near the water and raised his binoculars to his eyes. He seemed to have forgotten me.

I sat on another a distance from him and tucked my skirt under me so it wouldn't trail on the soggy ground. My shoes, polished white by Hilda only that afternoon, had acquired a coating of thin brown muck but I felt by then that I was so enmeshed in trouble that dirty shoes weren't going to make any difference at all.

I looked out at the pond. The light was brighter out there, reflected cool grey-blue from the water, and deep green near the edges where it caught the shadows of the trees. The water was still but as I watched its surface broke near the centre, sending out concentric ripples toward the edges. Then another and another, and circles met circles, meeting to form new patterns. I remembered a painting I'd seen on the wall of Father's office of a man in a small rowboat, casting into a lake that seemed almost as small as this.

"Fish," I said.

Noel said nothing.

"Do you fish here?" I said more loudly.

"Sometimes."

He lowered his binoculars to one knee and looked at me. "How come you ran away?"

"I didn't run away," I said and stared at him for a moment. "How do you know I ran away?"

"Done it myself before."

"How come?"

He shrugged and raised his binoculars again, directing them now at the woods behind us and turning his back to me. "Lots of reasons."

I began to tell him, speaking slowly at first so I could leave out the parts I wanted to, but by the time I was finished I'd told him all of it, hoping that he'd be impressed with my wickedness.

He didn't say anything for a long time after I was done and then he turned around, looking thoughtfully at me. "I've never had brussel sprouts. Guess my dad don't like 'em."

I stared at him in amazement. I'd never heard of an adult who didn't eat things he didn't like. Until the episode at the train station, all adults had seemed to me to follow exactly the same set of rules. Now it appeared that all of them were different: even my parents' identities had separated themselves from one another since Grandmother came to stay.

I felt better, safe, and the air was cool and peaceful. I was content to sit and watch the wisps of mist curl over the surface of the pond. I envied Noel his coveralls and long sleeves as I rubbed away mosquitoes from my legs, my arms, my neck.

"I doubt she's dead," he said suddenly. "I know about dead, and a little fall like that isn't going to do it." He toyed with the focussing knob between the lenses. "But you're going to catch hell. No doubt about that." He said it almost respectfully and my back straightened.

"What do you see through those things?" I asked, nodding at the heavy-looking binoculars.

"Same as with your eyes, only bigger. Clearer."

"Can I try them?"

"No."

As I eyed them enviously, a small breeze came across the water and I shivered.

"They'll be hunting for you," he said, standing.

"I'm not going back."

He laughed. "Don't be dumb. You can't stay here all night."

I followed him dispiritedly around the border of the pond and felt mud and water creep into my shoes, wetting my socks and feet. I ached with fatigue and cold and my legs and arms stung where they'd been scraped and bitten.

"What happens to you when you go back, after you run away?"

"The strap, sometimes. Depends on if he notices. Sometimes he doesn't notice."

There was a clearing and the lawn and the house beyond it, yellow at the windows. Light tangled across the grass, a counterfeit of welcome.

"Noel?" I said at the trees when I reached the grass, but he was gone.

Instead, I heard Hilda's voice a little distance from me.

"She's here!" she shouted. "Diana's here! I've found her!"

Father acknowledged her from somewhere around in front of the house, and behind the glass doors to the living room I saw the silhouette of my mother.

Hilda came to live with us on a temporary basis, to help with the house and with me while Mother was pregnant with Mitchell. She'd worked for us before, a full day and two half days a week, but it wasn't until I was six that she took up residence in the basement room that Father'd made into a bedroom for her. It used to be his den.

Her temporary job's lasted twenty-eight years so far, and in this shining spacious kitchen, a room that a lot of people probably associate with their mothers, my mother's presence is diminished. This is Hilda's territory and in this spotless room with the swinging door closed, white in here and dark wood on the dining room side, I'm able to breathe more easily. There's even a small breeze from the screen door at the back entrance.

Hilda herself is nowhere to be seen, and I didn't notice her little car in the drive when I came in, but I can tell by one glance around the room that her absence is only temporary. There's a *National Enquirer* on the table: her favorite, and probably only, reading material—aside from the Bible. She studies each article carefully and then emits a grunt of disgust or surprise or approval at the way the world is going. That this paper bears no resemblance at all to the world that comes to her through that radio on the fridge, or through her senses, a paler world where there are no two-headed cats, or chimps giving birth to humans, or nuns impregnated with satanic sperm, doesn't seem to bother her.

Having checked every cupboard in the dining room and found no hard liquor at all, I've settled for a cup of instant coffee and am turning pages through the tabloid (a radio announcer in Edmonton calls papers like this one, "The Supermarket News" and reads headlines like, "Man watches in horror as wife explodes at breakfast table", which make me laugh while I'm getting ready for work. When I lived with Brian we listened to news-related programs, but I've discovered I'd rather be entertained than educated first thing in the morning), when I hear the familiar sound of Hilda's Volkswagen Beetle chugging to a stop beside the house. That little car must be almost twenty years old by now for we bought it, or Hilda did, just after Father left.

Mother never learned to drive, preferring to offer the guidance of a second set of eyes to the person at the wheel, and when Father left Hilda was instructed to learn to drive immediately, which she did, without complaint or hesitation, somewhere in her late forties. She drives the same way she works, carefully enough but fast, with sudden unexpected stops to reaffirm her bearings. Although I've always been nervous when Hilda was at the wheel, there probably isn't a single dent in the body of her car.

She drew the line of acquiescence at driving the large black Chrysler which Father had left in the garage. Eventually Mother, in an act she probably still regrets, told Hilda to sell the big car and buy something more to her liking. She doubtless expected something as grey and unobtrusive as the woman with the brand new driver's license, for when the small red Beetle drew into the driveway many hours later and came to a sudden halt, Mother closed her eyes.

"It was the cheapest car available," Hilda said proudly, producing a thick wad of change and handing it to Mother. "Had to take the bus all the way to Harding to get it."

"I can't go out in that!"

Hilda coloured and whispered, bowing her head, "It was the only colour they had."

She'd put a hundred miles on it already in the return drive from the dealership so there was no question of returning it, though Mother tried for half an hour or so on the phone. When it became apparent that the car would stay, I noted a glimmer of something like joy in Hilda's eyes which surprised me because of her frequent and eloquent denunciations of those who sought material pleasure.

She loved that little car as much as Mother didn't. After she'd bought it the clergyman, Westmoreland, and his wife came by often to drive Mother to social and church gatherings and, after his wife died, the clergyman alone.

When I told Madelyn about Hilda and the car she said, "I'll bet it's the first time she ever felt really independent."

I looked at her, puzzled and a little irritated. This had been meant only as an anecdote, a sepia line drawing to start the sketch of the house where I'd grown up, a story to amuse. It didn't occur to me then that I might eventually add the darker shadings, the smudges of black charcoal that would fully represent it. Even Brian, with whom I'd lived for three years, didn't know that much about me. He'd been satisfied with outlines and had never pressed for details, and I hadn't volunteered them.

But with this story about Hilda, Madelyn, whom I'd known for only a few months, had stopped and changed direction, gathering humanness from the caricature where I hadn't intended to convey it. I felt unsettled by her comments, by her way of reacting generally to the things I said. It was as though she were walking into my suite without knocking first (something she, in fact, would never do) and was trying to make herself at home with my memories. She prodded, poked and commented until they must have been as familiar as her own.

"I'll bet that after all those years at your house, visiting her relatives on holidays and with church on Sundays, the car was like getting wings."

I wasn't certain she was right. Hilda didn't seem to need wings. "All she ever did with it was family errands. When she went to church, she walked. When she went to visit her relatives in Orillia, she walked to the train station. It wasn't her car."

"Yes, it was. Did anyone else ever drive it?"

Madelyn: until she met Sonny, everything she heard and saw was given form and meaning by her feminism. It seemed to her that all women born before about 1945, with a few notable exceptions, women who sometimes made it into history books and folklore but never into the families of people she knew, were not only victims, but were also unaware of their status as underdogs. This caused them to do things—to get sick, to take on ridiculous projects, or, in Hilda's case, to fall in love with a car—because they were unable to express themselves through appropriate channels, channels that were open to men.

Of course, her background as I gradually learned it explained her attitude, but my experience had not been the same. The men I'd known were weaker than the women, unable to do much more than pretend to assert themselves while their worlds were being fashioned by powerful female hands.

It has to do, I think, with control, and who's got more of it. In my experience, the women have always won hands down. But Madelyn's upbringing was different.

"You should see the way my mother drives, Diana. You'd never believe it was that quiet, family-centred woman you saw here last week. She drives like a maniac, like those teenagers who seem to be aiming for lift-off on the freeway. Some day she's going to hit a tree or a building, or another car." Madelyn sighed and ran her hand through her auburn hair. She was growing out a permanent then, and her hair was almost straight near the scalp but quite curly at the ends. It was a strange hairdo when looked at as a hairdo but on Madelyn it looked good. "And I don't think she'd care, one way or the other, if she did."

She looked up. "Well, she would if it were another car. That, she would regret. She likes other people a whole lot more than she likes herself."

I meet Hilda at the back door, me holding the screen door wide for her. She was tiny and aging when I left here and she seems no tinier nor more aged now. She must be seventy. She looks over her two full bags of groceries at me, her small grey eyes wide with pleasure and amazement.

"Praised be the Lord," she says.

I smile and nod, taking one of the bags from her. I'm grateful for it because it makes a hug impossible and a hug would have been unnatural, embarrassing.

She's still staring at me in disbelief as I put the bag on the table and begin to take things out of it, frozen chicken pieces, hamburger, cans of peas and salmon.

"I wondered who that car out front . . . ." She shakes her head of small grey curls as I take the other brown bag of groceries from her arms. It's as heavy as the first—I don't think I could have carried both of them at once.

"It's not mine," I say. "I rented it in Toronto, at the airport . . . ."

"You look fine." She is satisfied at last with her examination of me. "A little older, but that's to be expected. You look just fine."

I thank her, awkward at her warmth, her unconditional acceptance of me after all these years, the silence which encompassed her as well. The boxes of embroidered handkerchiefs I considered and passed over in Zellers at Christmas time, the bottles of cologne at her birthday, I wish I had them now. I thought it would be no kindness to mail gifts or even cards to her at this address: Mother would have known who'd sent them. Maybe Hilda understood that, and perhaps she expected nothing anyway. But standing now in her kitchen I feel a terrible remorse.

I ask her about her family and she chatters happily about her nieces and nephews, all of whom with one exception (a musician who she hasn't mentioned since he bought his first guitar), have created suitably Christian adult lives for themselves out of childhoods she once despaired of: they've gone to universities and married and had a dozen children each so far as I can tell. Within minutes I can no longer keep them all straight. One nephew has become a preacher, which makes her very happy.

"A proper preacher," she says, meaning one unlike Timothy Westmoreland. She does not approve of him, primarily because he takes a glass of sherry from time to time. Hilda's is a basic, restrictive religion and one which she seems never to have doubted for one minute in her entire life.

As she talks, she darts from cupboard to cupboard to fridge, putting things away onto perfectly ordered shelves. I smile at her back, at the thin body inside the smooth grey dress she invented as a kind of uniform, the skinny knobbled legs in support stockings and the small black oxfords. The apron around her waist provides the only colour, faded reds and blues. I remember when it was new.

Suddenly she turns, stricken, and wipes her hands on her apron. "Here I am putting groceries away and talking like a fool, and you're not even settled."

"It's fine. Really, I'm fine." I swallow the last of the coffee in my cup.

"Now, there's no need to make the bed up," she's saying to herself, "because I changed those sheets last week. But you'll be wanting towels and a washcloth. And something to eat. Is your suitcase in your room?"

"No," I say too sharply, then try to soften it with explanation. "I don't know how long I'm going to be here: my suitcase can stay in the

trunk of the car for now. And I'm not hungry. Please, Hilda, just go
ahead with what you're doing."

She looks uncertain, torn between what she thinks she ought to
do and what she's being told. Part of her kindness is that she won't ask
the questions that she wants to ask. I'm safer with her, my thoughts
more inviolable, than I am with anyone.

"Well, if you're sure . . ."

When I nod, she continues, ". . . then I'll get the last bag from the
car."

"I'll do it." I stand but she shakes her head.

"No need. There's little enough to do around here as it is these
days, especially since that Seabring woman came." She raises her eyes
in the direction of the upper storey.

"Who?"

"The nurse. Lenore Seabring."

As Hilda talks, she carries my cup to the sink, rinses it, wipes the
already spotless table clean and then the counters. I used to wonder how
she ever slowed enough to sleep.

"Mr. Guthrie, your brother, took it in his head that his mother
needed a professional . . . ."

"Hilda, when did you start calling my brother 'Mr. Guthrie'?"

She glances over at me. "When he asked me to call him that, if
other people were around, several years ago. Just seemed easier to do it
all the time."

She got his message. Mitchell is such a snob.

"He decided your mother needed a nurse, though Lord knows
I've nursed plenty of people in my time, including your grandmother.
He got Seabring's name from someone last time she was in the hospital.
Mrs. Guthrie wanted to come home, to stay home, but he wouldn't hear
of it if there wasn't a qualified nurse around. This Seabring woman
hasn't done a thing I couldn't have so far as I can tell, except maybe an
injection from time to time. But Whittick could have stopped by for
that. I'll bet she's costing your brother an arm and a leg—for nothing."
She folds the cloth over the faucet and heads for the back door. "I don't
like to see money go to waste, is all.

"I'll be right back."

Seabring could be Miss Florence Nightingale and Hilda would
find her superfluous and inept. But it's also typical of Mitchell to spend
money when he doesn't need to, to give the appearance of looking after
his mother in a superior way. Appearances are everything to him.

It's impossible to tell that she's just been in here and unpacked two bags of groceries. She'd be as horrified by Madelyn's kitchen as I was the first time I saw it—papers and books spread everywhere and a sinkful of unwashed dishes.

Madelyn's was the final stop at the end of a long Sunday afternoon during which I'd rejected six suites as too expensive, too dark and basement-like, too far from the bus, or too closely connected in some way to the people who occupied their upper floors.

I'd been on my own for six months, after the relationship with Brian, wobbly throughout, had been mortally wounded by his getting mononucleosis. The suite I'd fled to after his recovery, near the record store, was proving an unsatisfactory situation not only for me but also for the landlady, Mrs. Ferbey. She had strong suspicions about the relationship between my plants and the little black bugs which had lately infested her flour, and I couldn't stand the smell of her cooking which must, all of it, have been done in several inches of fat. I could smell her meals on my clothes when I was at work. I was determined to give her notice that very afternoon, but by the time I'd stepped inside Madelyn's door I'd decided I'd have to try again on my next day off.

I could have afforded a genuine apartment, but I didn't like apartments: they all looked the same to me. They made me feel like I was living in one compartment of one of the cartons that made up the skyline of Edmonton. I'd lived in a carton with Brian.

Architects seem to have become more creative than they were when I was looking at suites back then, five years ago. Maybe now I'll find something that's to my liking, something that isn't in a basement.

When I approached the small grey stucco bungalow near the university, an old house by Edmonton's standards and surrounded by tall thick blue spruce trees, I found a red-haired woman a few years older than I, leaning out her front door with one arm stretched before her to hold the screen door open. She was shouting at a group of children to get off her goddamned lawn before she came down and knocked their heads together.

"I can't get any work done with your bloody racket!"

The children grinned and moved their game of leapfrog about two feet to the left.

"Damned kids," she said to me as I started uncertainly up the sidewalk. "I guess you're the one about the suite? Diana Guthrie?"

She smiled, extended one hand, and introduced herself. "Thank God you're not another university student. I've had more of those than I can take." She paused. "You're not, are you?"

I shook my head.

"Didn't think so. You look too old for that. They're always having existential crises or some damned thing in my living room, looking for mothering when they get their sex lives screwed up and food when they run out of money." She shook her head. "Last one flunked every single midterm she wrote and one she didn't bother to get up for. Blamed it on 'the system'."

She studied me for a moment, then stood back to admit me to her house. "Excuse me. Please come in."

Her hair was short and wild with the permanent she claimed was her worst mistake of the year "so far". Her green cords were baggy, as was the scarlet sweater which was much too large for her despite her height, and was pushed up nearly to the elbows. She'd lost a lot of weight during her separation and divorce, she told me later, which pleased her tremendously, but she hadn't got around to shopping for many new clothes. She avoids shopping when she can.

"I keep pretty much to myself," I said, wondering why I bothered. I was now standing inside the door and after one look around the room I was already forming the phrases I would use to thank her for her trouble, to explain why the location wasn't exactly right.

There were metal bookcases against each wall, with the few bits of other furniture arranged in front of them, and every shelf was untidily jammed with books and looseleaf binders and stacks of magazines. The overflow was piled on the floor and spread across the coffee table and even the couch was strewn with papers and books, save for the one worn area of tweed upholstery where she'd probably been sitting when the children had disturbed her.

"I suppose you're worried about the kids, the noise," she said, studying my face again. Up close, hers was bare of makeup, freckled and grey-eyed, and she looked younger than she had when I'd seen her from the street. She was pretty, her face clean and totally separate from the dishevelment that seemed to have taken over the rest of her life. "No need to be. Those kids aren't mine. I'm a schoolteacher, and I live alone. You can't get much quieter than that."

She laughed and started across the room. "Come on. I'll show you the suite."

Her kitchen was as untidy and dark as the living room. Her kitchen table is empty of papers only in July and August and on that day there were several stacks of essays, half a foot in height each one of them.

She opened the door to the basement, revealing a completely

separate entranceway, the first positive sign I'd seen. The basement
suite was bright and airy, larger than I'd expected after the clutter of the
upper floor. The walls had been freshly painted, white, in all three
rooms and the rug in the living room and the bedroom was pale grey.
The furniture was light as well, pale browns and greys, and there wasn't
much of it. The whole effect was one of cheer and cleanliness. I
checked it thoroughly, twice.

Madelyn was apologizing for it. "It's kind of bare in here right
now, but I'm sure it'll look better when it gets some stuff in it. I didn't
want to do it white, particularly, but the paint was on sale. Carpeting,
too. A pattern would have been much nicer."

"I like it."

"You do?"

I nodded.

"Wonderful. Come up and have a cup of coffee while I find the
receipt book. I'll need a half month's rent for the damage deposit." Her
voice had a pleasant, lilting tone to it when she was happy and I found
myself drawn to her, curious as to how a woman could live alone, and in
a mess like that, and still seem so contented and self-assured. I'd lived
alone as well, more than once, but I'd always thought of it as a hiatus
between two relationships, a make-do situation.

I followed her up the stairs, and she told me she was planning to
replace the washing machine as soon as she could afford it. It was noisy
and old and right outside my suite, but she only used it once a week, less
often if she could get away with it. "I hate doing laundry," she said as
we reached her kitchen again. "Hate housework of any kind. But I
guess you've noticed that. Pour yourself a coffee, if you want one."

She turned the gas flame down under a furiously perking coffee
pot and absently slid an open magazine away from the vicinity of the
burner. "I think there's still a clean cup in the cupboard somewhere."

"Don't you want some references from me?"

She shook her head. "I'll take my chances." And smiled.

When she came back several minutes later, waving the receipt
book triumphantly ahead of her, I was staring at the counter. In the
midst of class registers, half a loaf of bread and crumbs from an enormous cookie jar, there was the toaster: and on top of it, an open copy of
The Joy of Sex.

I've puzzled over why I moved in there. It was obvious from
that first day that Madelyn wasn't going to be just a landlady to me. I
liked her, even though I was a little startled by her, right from the beginning, and I understood immediately why the students who'd lived in the

suite had taken their problems up the stairs to her.

At a time in my life when I was looking for isolation, for a time without attachments of any kind, I deliberately set things up so that isolation was impossible. I came to depend on her, and her on me, I think, even though I knew that friendships and relationships didn't last. I knew that at some point I'd have to learn to depend on no one but myself, and then I delayed that reality a little while by moving into Madelyn's basement.

She was a crutch for me and I was one for her, but now she's found another prop, more suitable to her needs because he's male. This time I'm determined to learn to live alone.

"What does Mother look like, Hilda?"

If she's surprised to learn that I haven't been up, she doesn't give a sign of it.

"Not too bad, considering what she's been through. She's a strong woman, Mrs. Guthrie is. She'd come back from the hospital after one of those treatments, sick as could be, and her hair was thinning quite a bit, and nothing would do but she'd sit down in the living room and have a cup of tea like she'd just come back from the . . . ."

"Hilda . . . ." I suck in my breath and let it slowly out again. We're standing side by side at the counter, preparing plates of cottage cheese, tomato aspic, salad and toast for Mother and Miss Seabring. And for Mitchell, of course. Mother's plate, Hilda's told me, will come back down on its tray untouched. "What I want to know is how she looks compared to the last time I was here."

What I want to know is what I'm going to see, to prepare myself for that.

She thinks about this for a moment, perhaps pushing her mind back to the day I left so she can provide the comparison I've asked for. Can she see the woman I remember? She was tall as I am, her waist and arms thickening by that time so that her figure would have been described as matronly. It was as though her unyielding nature had at last been made manifest in the flesh. Her clear blue eyes, that day, were as they'd always been, sharp and direct, angry without a trace of sorrow at my leaving.

"If you're going," she said, "that's fine. But don't bother to come back."

It's those eyes I want to know about.

"Well, she's thinner, of course. She's very thin." She's speaking gently, softly, preparing me now that she understands what I've asked. "Her hair is white-grey, most of it, and like I said, it's thinner than it ever used to be."

I can barely hear her for the pounding in my ears; I don't want to hear her. I stare at the tomato in my hand, the knife.

"She bruises, from the medication . . . ."

The door from the dining room swings open, silencing her, and Mitchell is here. He doesn't look at me.

"Miss Seabring's ready for her lunch." He nods in the direction of the dining room. "I'll take Mother's tray up. You can put mine in the fridge."

Now he looks at me coldly. "I hope you will take my advice, Diana, now that you've had some time to think about it."

I don't answer that. I don't think that what he gave me before was advice, anyway. It sounded more like an order. His mouth is a taut line of displeasure and he takes the tray from Hilda with a little jerk as though she'd been trying to keep it from him. He won't say what he thinks in front of her, which is not to say that he hasn't made his feelings perfectly clear. To Hilda as well as to me.

Hilda, uncomfortable, says when he has gone, "You really ought to eat something."

"Eat something" and "pray" are her alternate solutions to everything. That she's chosen the former this time gives me a more accurate sense of Mother's condition than a medical report could have done.

Mitchell crouches at Mother's door like Cerberus. I'm not afraid of Mitchell.

Chapter Four

An almost autumnal chill descended on Donellon during the night which followed Grandmother's fall. When I wakened the next morning, the cold damp air which had seeped through the crack at the base of my bedroom window had chilled me so completely that I could not distinguish my dread from physical cold. I pulled the bedclothes tight between my legs and curled toward the room and waited, still and taut, remembering without wanting to Grandmother's body jerk as that pale cheek caught the corner of the table, the mass of adult flesh a stun of sound against the floor. I squeezed my eyes tight shut against it and pressed my ears but again and again it came.

So I let my eyes skim the familiar room for anchors and at the place where my white shoes should have been in the shoebag on the inside of my closet door, I remembered that something had happened not only to Grandmother but to Mother as well, that night before, something that seemed unconnected but not totally separate, either.

In the front hall on my way upstairs, dragged by one arm faster than my legs could follow, we'd passed Father who was standing inside the open front door, huge fleshy moths dipping around him unnoticed.

When he saw me, he closed his eyes and sighed and leaned against the doorjamb.

"Shut the door, Wallace," Mother said sharply. "The bugs are getting in."

His eyes flashed open, surprised, but he did as he'd been asked.

She gave a tug at my arm and I followed her up the stairs, wishing she'd turn me over to him instead of handling this herself. Mother believed in physical discipline, Father in reasoning and in extracting promises. They didn't argue over who would try my case each time, but divided up the work on the basis of whose form of punishment was more appropriate to the misdemeanor I'd committed. This one deserved my mother, as I'd known it would.

She wheeled me around when we reached my chintz and yellow bedroom and took my arm as though to pull me across her swollen lap. Then her face, pale already from avoiding summer, tightened and paled still further. I thought this was a further deepening of her anger, a fuller awareness of what I'd done, but she seemed surprised by it. There were furrows in her brow, discomfort and a moment of confusion, and she stood very still, holding me still as well, cocking her head as though she were listening to something far away.

"Get undressed," she said, releasing me suddenly. "Get in bed."

I stood perplexed, afraid to move, and saw a film of perspiration form over her upper lip.

"Get into bed!"

I started pulling at buttons and sleeves, at straps and socks, fumbling and ineffective in my haste and my desire to appease her. She walked even and erect from the bedroom, pausing at the door to say, "I didn't need this, you know, on top of everything else. You'd just better behave yourself for once."

She turned out the light and left me confused, half dressed and trembling, my need to flinch unconsummated.

For days the pall of fog and chill hung over the house, and I was instructed by Hilda to stay inside.

"Because it's warmer, you silly goose," she said. "It's got nothing to do with being bad. Lord knows, no one's got time to think of things like that right now. It's warmer, is all, and dry in here, and we don't want colds on top of everything else that's going on. Just pray that everything turns out all right, Diana. That will keep you busy enough."

With other members of the family and with guests, Hilda maintained a silence that she probably thought of as respectful, not speaking unless spoken to, but to me it seemed a kind of distracted shyness, a weakness that aggravated me. With me, she talked a lot, in that quick way she has of doing everything, and I couldn't understand why she didn't tell others what was on her mind as well.

"Is she dead?" I asked her in a whisper that first morning.

"Who dead?"

"My grandmother."

She laughed shortly, mopping the polished wood floors around the carpet. "What has got into your head today? Of course she isn't dead. She's upstairs in your parents' room and she'll be right as rain in no time. Now you get out of my way and let me at that corner."

She volunteered at lunchtime, after she'd taken a tray up to Grandmother and brought it, plate empty, back down again, that my mother had gone off to the hospital to get the baby, early. The words were intended to explain but the ominous undertone to that word she'd added almost as an afterthought increased my apprehension and I sat near the French doors in the living room and watched the fog move through the trees and coat the lawn with dew.

Father came in just after noon on the second day of the fog, the first time I'd seen him since the moths, came racing in with the front door banging shut behind him into the kitchen with a cigar cupped in one hand unlit.

"A boy," he grinned at both of us. And then, "Dammit, Hilda! Pardon me, but dammit, it's a boy!"

He gave me a hug where I sat astonished at the table, gave Hilda one as well which seemed to unsettle her completely, then went rushing out again and up the stairs to tell Grandmother Wishart.

Hilda studied something inside her head until she'd composed herself and then her expression softened. "I guess that means there's a little brother for you, Diana Guthrie. A little baby brother. Praised be the Lord."

"I don't want to see her," I said as I followed my father up the stairs later that afternoon, him prodding the small of my back as I slowed again. "What's she doing in your room, anyway?"

"It's a bigger bed and firmer, more comfortable while she's recuperating. It's only until your mother gets home. Then she'll go back to the guest room. It's the least we can do, I suppose," he said, and added in a whisper. "Your mother's idea."

He gently poked my back again as I paused when we reached the upper floor.

I turned around to look at him.

"It's my fault, that she fell."

He shrugged. "Accidents happen. And this was an accident. But that doesn't take away from the fact that you were being extremely rude, to all of us, when it happened. You must learn to control your tongue."

Neither his words, nor even his eyes, behind those thick lenses, were as reassuring as I'd hoped they'd be.

"Where do you sleep?"

"On the couch. In the sunroom."

On the main floor, underneath those stairs we'd just come up, there was a room that was misshapen by the stairwell and had windows on two walls. It was large and bright, and very hot on sunny summer days. Father had moved his desk into it after Hilda moved into his den. Now he slept there as well.

"Nothing's where it was."

He laughed softly and stroked the back of my hair. "Never mind. Everything will be back to normal before you know it."

I stood inside their bedroom door, rubbing my clammy hands against my skirt. I had no idea why Grandmother had asked to see me, the person who'd caused her injuries, but there'd been no getting out of it. "Honour thy mother," Father had said when I'd begged to be excused. "'Grandmother', in this case."

The large spindled four-poster with the soft green counterpane seemed unfamiliar in the dusk of closed curtains in the middle of the day, in the smell of balms and rubs and a cloying, sweet-pine odour intended to mask the others.

Grandmother lay perfectly still and pasty grey except for a flush of dark purple mottled gold against her cheek, her hair pulled back into a thin rope which lay along her flannel nightgowned shoulder. Surely Hilda had been wrong: this woman must be dead.

Father prodded me forward, poked my shoulder gently and nodded encouragement when I looked up at him. I went to stand at last beside the bed, my nose closed at the back and breathing through my mouth against the smells.

She opened her eyes, slowly, fixing them on me clear and blue as a reflection, then reached out her right hand and clutched my wrist. I turned my head to plead with Father for assistance but he was studying the cold tip of his cigar. I stood, pulled close against the bed, and waited.

She spoke to him in a voice much weaker than the claw. "When will Edith be home?"

"In a few days, Mother. It was a long and difficult labour. She needs some time to rest."

"She's far too old to be bearing children, Wallace," she said, glaring at him as though he were the cause. "Women who are almost forty should not have to bear children."

He straightened immediately as though he meant to respond in the same tone of voice but he glanced at me, and instead said quietly, "She's not almost forty, Mother. She's only thirty-five." It was the first and only time that an adult mentioned another adult's age in front of me, in that house.

"It's very selfish of you to insist on a son."

I stared at Father, waiting for him to say something that would explain this accusation, but again he let the moment pass.

"It's a good thing you have Hilda," she went on. "I won't be any help to her. I hope you're not planning to light that thing."

He looked startled, as though he didn't understand her question, and then remembered his cigar. "No, of course not. And no one expects you to . . . ."

Why had she summoned both of us, when it was him she wanted to talk to? I tugged a little to pull my arm away but she held me tight, ready to draw me into this.

"You mark my words. It was the shock that did it. My terrible fall, the girl's running off that way. We're fortunate the baby lived." She moved a little in the bed but her grip remained firm. "The baby came early from the fright."

"Look, I didn't bring her up here . . . . We'll let you rest now, Mother," he said, turning abruptly toward the door. "Come along, Diana."

Unexpectedly, she tightened her grip on my wrist, squeezing with incredible strength for one so thin and pale, her nails digging at my flesh. I thought my knees would buckle from the pain but I didn't make a sound. As suddenly it was over and she released me, leaning back against the pillows and closing her eyes.

"I hope you're satisfied with the damage you've done," she said. "You're a very bad child."

I blinked and rubbed my wrist. Her hand had relaxed into impotence on the bedspread and I hurried from the room to join my father in the hall.

"She hurt me," I whispered, holding up the wrist.

"Shh," he cautioned, closing the door silently, but he'd looked toward the room with such rage that I felt vindicated. Almost as an afterthought, he bent and kissed my wrist.

Mitchell was christened three weeks later at Westmoreland's inaugural service in Donellon. It was the first Sunday after I'd started school and met the marvellous Jenny Haultain of the long gold hair, dark eyes and even darker lashes, a girl who even then had infinite composure and confidence. I'd told neither Mother nor even Father about her, sensing that they might not like her as much as I did.

All of our lives, Father's, Mother's, mine, were separating themselves from one another, as they'd begun to do the day that Grandmother arrived.

I ran a finger up and down the nap of the deep blue curtains as Hilda darted from china cabinet to dining room table with cups and saucers and little gold-rimmed plates. She knew about Jenny. I'd talked of little else as she'd given me cake and milk in the kitchen after the school bus dropped me off at home. She was pleased, she said, that I had someone my own age.

She was not, however, as impressed as I was that Jenny had worn a brand new dress, not just new to me but never worn before, every day so far. "You concentrate on the books," she'd said, "and never mind that nonsense."

Father was arranging glasses and liquor bottles on the sideboard, moving almost as quickly as Hilda was for the guests were expected at any moment, but unlike her he was whistling and his anticipation of the party had infected me.

The object of the festivities was in his crib, in the guest room with the cot where my mother slept. Grandmother was still recuperating in the master bedroom and Father still slept in the sunroom. Mitchell had disrupted most of the eleven o'clock service with howling, to my embarrassment and Mother's too.

"What an introduction for poor Reverend Westmoreland," she'd said in the car on the way home, stroking the bald head of my now-sleeping brother. They'd suggested I hold him twice since they'd brought him home from the hospital, and both times he'd started to scream. I'd refused after that. My feelings toward my infant brother were alternately irritation and lack of interest.

"If he can't handle a baby, he's in the wrong business," Father said.

"It isn't a business, Wallace."

He turned a corner and I squeezed the soft back of their bench seat to steady myself, perched on the edge of the back one to hear them.

"'Calling', then," he said, not quite sarcastically. "He shouldn't have answered the call."

"He handled it fine. I just wish he hadn't had to."

"Answered," Father went on, not paying attention to what she'd said. "Hell, it goes even higher than that. He should never have been given it. 'Suffer the little children.' The call should never have gone out at all to a man who turns purple when the baby he's christening makes a little noise."

"He handled it, and Mitchell didn't make a 'little noise'. He made an uproar. You're driving far too quickly, Wallace. You're going to kill us all."

Now, Mother came rushing down the stairs and into the dining room, her eyes blazing and her hands at her sides in fists.

"She wants to come down. All week she's been insisting that she wouldn't, that she wasn't up to it, and now she's changed her mind."

He continued to arrange crystal glasses which glittered in the sunlight as he moved them. "I think that's a good sign. It's a sign of improving health."

"That's not the point." She sounded close to tears. "I'll have to comb her hair and help her get dressed, and they're going to be here any minute." She pressed her lips together. "And you'll have to carry her. She can't possibly handle the stairs."

He took one last bottle out of the sideboard and set it on the tray. "If she wants to come down, let her."

"You aren't listening. It's not her, it's me who's going to have to do all the work. That wretched mark on her face still shows a little, and it'll have to be covered. She'll never agree to make-up."

"It's her face, after all." He sighed as I pressed my face into the thick dusty smell of the curtain. "Look, Edith, you've got to allow her independence or she'll never get better. She'll be here forever. You've got to encourage this."

His voice was slow and he looked tired when I dared to peer around at him. During the new clergyman's sermon, when Mother had been outside walking with the baby, I'd thought I felt him sleeping in the pew beside me and I'd sat nervously until the "Let Us Pray," praying that he wouldn't snore.

He poured a thimbleful of scotch from one of the bottles into a glass in front of him but instead of raising it to his lips as I'd expected, he turned with it to her. For the first time since the baby had come she was wearing a dress which cinched at the waist with a belt. It was pale yellow and she looked slim and pretty, partly because of the high spots of anger in her cheeks.

"You've been like this since she came," he said, coaxing. "Tense. And the baby's only adding to it. When you're upset, we all are, Edith. It'll be better, when she's strong enough to go home. We've got to encourage that."

"She wouldn't be up there if it weren't for us." Mother glanced at me and I looked away, out the window. "But you're ready to blame it on her, as usual. I have an obligation to her, Wallace. She's my mother."

"And what am I?" He held out the glass. "Take a sip of this. Take one minute to relax. If you're not down here when they arrive, they'll wait."

She looked at the glass and I didn't know whether she would take it or knock it from his hand.

Hilda, who'd absented herself the moment the conversation took a personal turn, swung through into the silence from the kitchen, took one look at the glass between them, and swung back out again, muttering about something in the oven.

"The oven?" Father said. "It's ninety-five degrees out there. That woman deserves a raise. Or severance pay." He held out the glass warmly, sociably, but with another glance at me Mother moved away from him and from the glass he held.

Her voice was collected, cool. "It's fine, Wallace. I don't need that. I'll help her to get ready and then I'll attend to Mitchell. Diana, comb your hair before the guests arrive."

She was part way up the stairs when the doorbell rang and she kept right on going.

The house seemed full immediately. The men stood in the centre of the living room with glasses in their hands, intent on conversation and their faces growing redder as they sipped. The women sat on the periphery with teacups delicately held, chatting to one another and apparently unaffected by the heat. The french doors were open wide to the back lawn, but no one moved outside.

Last to arrive were the new clergyman and his wife. Westmoreland was slimmer than he became later, his hazel eyes always full of a mixture of devotion and concern. He was tall and thick through the shoulders, almost good looking but not enough to offend anyone. His parishioners, the only exception I knew of being my father, had nothing but praise for the New Man after his first service, though they seemed less impressed with his spouse.

She was an enormous woman, dressed in black, who sat heavily between two other women on the chesterfield, arranged the yards of fabric in her skirt around her, and panted from all the effort. Her round face was streaked where the perspiration had dribbled through the mask of rouge and powder.

She greeted the women on either side of her and then looked around the room until her small eyes settled on me.

"Come here, you lovely little girl," she said as though I were edible.

I stayed where I was.

"Come here," she said again, more insistently. "I'm not going to hurt you."

Several of the women were watching me now so I did as I'd been told. I was disappointed that no other children were present. Dr. Haultain and his wife had arrived but there was no sign of Jenny. Christenings seemed to be adult events.

The fat woman smelled like flowers in the evening, thick and heavy, sweet. She put her arms around my waist.

Mother came into the room with the baby, sleeping now and angelic in his trails of bright white eyelet lace. The men nodded politely and Dr. Haultain clapped Father on the shoulder before they resumed their conversation, but the women kept their eyes on the baby until Mother handed him to his new godmother, Mrs. Robinson, from where he was passed at intervals around the room for inspection and approval the way his gifts would be passed later in the afternoon. They were all careful not to breathe on him.

"He's a good baby," Mother said to Mrs. Robinson before she went out of the room again. "I've been fortunate, at least, to have two babies who ate and slept without complaint. Although Diana," she nodded at me, "is getting a little pickier about her food as she gets older."

Mother seemed calmer now, pleased to be showing off her infant son to such a large audience. I willed her not to mention the brussels sprouts. She loved to relate my smallest accomplishments and my most insignificant misdemeanours to her friends, and my presence never made any difference that I could tell. It was as though I went deaf when her women friends arrived.

There was commiseration from one or two of the other women who then began to compare aloud their own children's infancies. Several of the anecdotes I'd already heard so those adults listening must have known them thoroughly. But that didn't seem to impair the conversation. They loved it, thrived on it. Their eyes lit at the recollection of how many hours each baby had slept on the first night home from the hospital, of how many months of colic each mother had endured, and some of their pleasure seemed to come from their abilities to recollect dates and durations so precisely.

"Come here to me," said Mrs. Westmoreland who had contributed nothing to the conversation of the women. Her voice was a gurgle, as jiggling fat as the rest of her.

Father followed Mother from the room, closing the doors behind him to seal off the view to the hall.

Mrs. Westmoreland drew me onto her lap with one thick arm, breathing hard again from the exertion.

"The Lord has not yet seen fit to reward us with a child," she said, clutching me to her massive bosoms, "but I know a great deal about children. More than some mothers do, I'll guarantee. You're jealous of the baby, aren't you? You wish someone would pay attention to you as well."

"No," I said. "I don't."

"Of course you do. You've been forgotten in all the excitement over the new arrival. I'll bet you'd like to be a little baby too, like little Mitchell over there." She began to rock me from side to side.

I saw the eyes of the women on either side of us meet. I looked down at the woman's freckled hands. The flesh of her fingers bulged around her rings and her nails were long bright drops of red. Beneath the veil of perfume she smelled acrid and unpleasant, and she was altogether too mealy soft, the way my mother's belly had been when she came back from the hospital.

I squirmed but she held me tighter, clutching me with one hand and feeling in her purse with the other for her handkerchief.

"It's certainly warm in here," she said and suddenly sneezed, spraying the back of my neck with moisture. I shuddered, wriggled, but could not get loose.

"Allergies," she said amiably and her husband, who had not appeared to have been listening, nevertheless went immediately and closed the french doors.

"Might as well draw the curtains, too," she said. "Keep the heat outside."

He did so and then, glancing at her with no more concern than he did any of his parishioners, he went back to join the men.

The hall doors opened and there was a sudden hush. There stood Grandmother, leaning heavily on the two canes Father had procured in anticipation of her eventual rising from her bed. She was shaky but she rebuffed his offer of assistance with a sudden irritated gesture of the elbow. She seemed thinner, smaller and much older than she had the last time I had seen her standing (and falling, in my memory, against the table. Would that vision never be gone?). Her navy dress hung loose and long and her right ankle was thickly bandaged beneath her stocking. The attempt to persuade her to camouflage the last traces of the bruise on her face had obviously failed: it stood proudly on her cheek, a faded yellow mark of testimony to the pain she had endured.

Slowly, stoically, her face grim, she limped toward my mother's armchair which had been vacated by a younger woman the moment Grandmother appeared. Conversations rose and fell around her as the guests greeted her one by one, the matriarch, then tried not to look her way and failed and tried again.

I waited for the eyes to turn to me, the cause of all this devastation.

The woman on my left leaned forward to whisper, "What in the name of . . . ." but she was ignored by the other women on the couch. They were watching Dr. Haultain who, tall and slender and younger than his hair, silver in the diminished light, had stepped from the knot of men to stand respectfully at my grandmother's feet.

"Pardon me, Mrs. Wishart," he said quietly, "but in my opinion you shouldn't be walking on that leg."

She peered up at him, her blue eyes sharp and clear. "Haultain, isn't it?" she said loudly. "I told Edith that Whittick didn't know what he was talking about. Exercise, he said. Pshaw! I agree with you completely."

There was an embarrassed pause as those within earshot located Dr. Whittick. Shorter than his colleague, broader and sandy-haired although he was probably fifteen years older, he was happily chewing date squares in the dining room and sipping coffee as he chatted with Westmoreland.

"I'm not questioning his professional judgement . . . ."

"Well, I am," said Grandmother. "Edith, I want Haultain from this moment on."

Mother flushed. "We can talk about it afterward." She looked at Haultain, imploring. "I'm not trying to . . . . You understand that Dr. Whittick has been our doctor for years."

"Not any more, he isn't," said Grandmother, determined, as Haultain glanced sympathetically in her direction. Neither of them looked flustered but they, and Whittick and Westmoreland who still weren't listening, were the only ones who didn't.

"Of course," he said. "We can talk about it later."

"I swear," said the woman on my right in a low voice, leaning forward to speak to the woman on my left, "there's going to be a battle yet. He's stealing patients from right under Hank Whittick's nose. I wouldn't let Haultain come near me."

"Hank's kind enough, and quite capable in his way," said the woman on my left, her voice equally low, "but he's from the old school. Haultain seems more . . . efficient, somehow. I doubt Hank even notices anyway. What happened to Mrs. Wishart?"

The fat woman behind me shifted hard from one buttock to the other to get more comfortable, shifting me as well.

"She fell," Mrs. Westmoreland whispered.

"How?"

I wriggled from her lap and backed away before that whispering mass of overheated flesh could say another word, could reveal the secrets she'd learned, from what sources I could not guess. I sidled through the press of drinking men, through the dining room and into Hilda's hot and empty kitchen, out through the kitchen door into the sun. The lawn was deserted, the people that Father had painstakingly cut it for shut close and steaming inside the house.

I found Noel in the water, his clothes in a careless heap on a rock beside his binoculars near the shore.

"Again?" he called from the middle of the pond, his brown shoulders bare and tanned as he treaded water to call to me. "You going to run away every week?"

"Be quiet," I said sheepishly, trying to conceal my pleasure that he was there.

He disappeared beneath the surface and came up splashing a little closer to where I stood in the sun. That splash was magnificent and I wanted to make the cool sound with my own body. I took off my socks and shoes and stepped into the blue-green water, the mud squishing between my toes.

"You coming in?"

"I have no bathing suit."

"So what? Who needs a suit?"

I looked up at him suddenly and back at the pile of his clothes on the ground beside me. "You don't?"

He buckled and dove, buttocks sparkling naked white in the sun for an instant before his face appeared again.

"I might hide your clothes. Then what would you do?"

"Don't act like a stupid girl. Just get out of here if you want to do that, okay?"

"Is it deep out there?"

One arm straight up he sank below the surface until only his fingertips were showing.

"I don't know how to swim," I said quietly as he swam toward me with clean even strokes until the water was shallow enough for him to stand.

I watched him curiously as he came dripping cool toward me. He seemed at ease with his nakedness and even with my looking at him, at the angles of his body, at the oddly different way that he was built. He was made like my new brother.

He was almost completely tanned, unlike me who had white places to show where I'd been covered all summer long. His body looked clean and cool and fresh and without thinking I put my hand out and touched his cool shoulder as he passed me. I wished my body could be cool like that. I still itched with sticky heat beneath my dress and underclothing and my feet, refreshed by mud, only increased my desire to be completely wet.

Noel sat on top of his clothes, quite still, his feet together and toed down toward the water, his arms loosely clasped around his knees, soaking sun.

"Your parents let you walk around like that?"

He shrugged. "No point in wearing clothes if you're going swimming."

"Yeah, but you could wear a bathing suit."

"Why? Nobody ever comes along. It's my dad's pond."

"I came along."

"Nobody important."

I made a face and he laughed.

I looked down at the smooth bare curve of his back.

"Your mother," I said after a moment. "Does she come swimming too, like that?" I thought of my own mother seeing me here with Noel, with him undressed, and glanced nervously back at the trees.

"She's dead." He looked out at the pond. "You want to swim or don't you?"

I was silent for a moment. I'd known that he lived alone with his father and had still assumed a mother. I didn't know why I'd done that.

"How?"

"It's not that hard."

"No. How did she die?"

"Tractor tipped."

"When?" I asked, fully curious, sitting down on the grass beside him. "Did you see it?"

"Yeah. I did." He looked at me fiercely. "I don't want to talk about that, okay? You coming in or not?"

I looked at the water, frightened at possibilities of death.

"I've got this friend? Her dad's a doctor."

Jenny wouldn't be afraid to go in there with him.

"Haultain. I know. I've seen you on the bus."

Not even naked, she wouldn't be afraid.

"She brought a pin and we poked our fingers," I said, "and then we pressed our fingers together. You ever done that?"

"It's dumb to make yourself bleed."

"No, it isn't. It was her sister who showed her how, and she's nearly ten. We're blood sisters now."

"It's dumb."

I pulled my dress up over my head and dropped my slip and pants beside it on the grass. My pile of clothing was unintentionally neater than Noel's was and I kicked a sock away from the other garments lying whitely on the grass.

I walked splashing into the water and he was right behind me. As the depth increased he told me to let my legs go and he put one hand flat under my belly to hold me. I put my head up, flailing, sinking, terrified at the water in my mouth and he shouted at me to take it easy, to relax, relax, relax. His hand was steady on my stomach and at last I did and he helped me to roll and float, his hand now firm in the small of my back, and I watched the clear blue of the sky. I was conscious of his dark eyes on my body as mine had earlier been on his.

"It's not over your head here," he said. "You figure it out," and let me go, stroking away to the centre of the pond. I stood and tried alone and in a little while I was swimming, not well but enough to keep me at the surface. Once, I lowered my feet and could not touch bottom and I yelled. He came and drew me closer to the edge. We splashed laughing with the water sparkling drops around us until it felt as though my legs and arms were lead.

Exhausted, we fell panting onto the grass beside each other, glad now of the heat.

When at last our breaths had slowed, Noel asked me what they'd done, the last time I ran away.

"Nothing."

"Nothing?"

"The baby came that day."

He stared at the sky, trying to put those pieces of information together, and then he began to laugh again and we giggled, rolling on the grass, until my stomach hurt from laughter.

There were perhaps a dozen people still gathered in the living room when I came back to the house, my hair still damp but not enough that Mother would ever notice. It was short and the sun had dried its surface quickly. My dress was smooth enough and my shoes still clean and I walked slowly into the living room, fairly certain that I was safe this time.

Mother was sitting in a chair which she'd pulled up close to the Reverend Westmoreland, her head inclined toward him. He was speaking quietly, almost to himself, his hands resting on his knees. His wife was beside him on the couch, perspiring, ignored.

When he finished speaking, Mother leaned back and nodded, her eyes sparkling now with enthusiasm. She looked beautiful that afternoon. "That's what I've been trying to tell him but he just won't listen. 'Honour thy mother' is a commandment, not just some silly flight of fancy the way he seems to think."

Her eyes happened on me then. "What has happened to your hair? Honestly," she said to the clergyman, "the girl's the dizzy limit." To me: "Aside from school, you will not leave this house for two weeks, do you hear me? And church, of course. Aside from school and church."

I nodded, relieved, thankful for the remaining guests whose presence had prevented more concrete punishment.

As I passed through to the hall, I noticed that Mother's armchair was no longer occupied by Grandmother. Upstairs, the bedroom door was closed and the guest room door ajar, the bed still empty.

I went into the bathroom and stood on tiptoe to grin at my sun-pink face in the mirror over the sink, and then I combed my hair as mother had instructed. When I came out again, Dr. Haultain was closing my parents' bedroom door behind him, starting for the stairs.

"Is my father in there?"

"No, dear. He's driving the Carroll sisters home."

"I wish Jenny had come with you."

He looked at me puzzled for a moment, then said, "Oh. I suppose you're classmates."

I nodded, a little puzzled myself. Surely she'd told him about me? But then, I hadn't told my father about her, either. We really were blood sisters, I thought, and felt a wonderful sense of belonging. Noel and Jenny had given me that sense, as I stood without them in the upstairs hall talking with Dr. Haultain. They were able to make me feel strong, even when they weren't there.

"She has the chicken pox. She won't be going anywhere for a day or two." He said it so seriously, so formally, that I wished I'd get them too.

When the school bus stopped at Noel's lane the next day, I patted the seat beside me as he slouched up the steps, his black, man-sized lunch pail in one hand.

"You can sit beside me," I said loudly. "Jenny's got the chicken pox."

He barely glanced at me but grumbled as he headed toward the back, "I don't sit with girls."

Saturday Afternoon

Chapter Five

The nurse, who is about sixty and tall and heavy, is sitting in the chair I've always considered mine, across the table from the window. When she sees me she quickly replaces her tea saucer, the underside of which she's been studying at arm's length the way some people read a folded *Globe and Mail* with breakfast, and forks a quavering wedge of tomato aspic into her mouth. Her charcoal hair is pinned in coils and piled high all over her head and some of the loops are working loose, creating a coiffure which is grotesquely reminiscent of the pompadours of Louis the Fourteenth. Her arms are thick and muscular and when she reaches for the butter dish, I see that the underarm seam of her white uniform is coming apart.

She glances at me and then suspiciously at the other placemats as though she's wondering where I'm going to sit.

"Ms Seabring?" I say, standing near the table. "I'm Diana."

She looks up again, fork midair laden with cottage cheese. "Pleased to meet you. 'Though it's *Miss* Seabring. None of these new-fangled euphemisms for me." She puts the cottage cheese into her mouth and chews. "Diana who?"

I stare at her, disoriented for a moment. I feel as though I've dialled a wrong number. "Guthrie. Diana Guthrie."

She still looks puzzled as she takes a bite from Hilda's sweet, pale brown bread, then brightens a little and says around it, "Oh, the daughter!"

"Right. The daughter."

"Please don't take offence. I saw your picture in the room. I just forgot the name is all, or maybe never heard it. Sit down, sit down. Hilda will bring you something to eat, I'm sure, 'though it's nothing to crow about, the food. I need my strength, you know, for the job I've got, lifting and turning the patient, changing the bed, all like that. But I bet I've lost ten pounds since I started here. Sometimes I have to go into town just to get a solid meal. Now, other places that I've worked . . . ."

"I'll eat later." I have this feeling that if I don't interrupt her, she'll go on talking forever, one idea connecting to another until her whole life has been unwound like a soiled bandage.

" . . . they've at least provided decent meals." She shrugs as I walk toward the living room.

"You just get here?" she asks, stopping me at the doorway with her question.

I nod, leaning against the doorjamb. I've been here at least two hours now.

"She's presentable, if you want to go up." Her eyebrows are thick and charcoal like her hair, her face flat and square and business-like.

"I'll go up later. Mitchell's with her now."

It never occurred to me that Mother would be anything but presentable. Are there times now, when she's not?

"She's probably sleeping anyway. I've just given her a shot."

"I'll wait until she's alone."

She snorts. "I don't know when you'll find her alone." She's wiping her plate clean with the last of her bread and she works at it until the dish is shining as though Hilda had just put it on the table. My stomach tightens as she puts the bread in her mouth. "Your brother's up there now and after lunch it will be the minister and then the doctor, and after supper those women come, all five of them at once. Lord knows it wears me out."

"Does Haultain come, or only Whittick?"

"One doctor's enough, I should guess. 'Though sometimes I wonder with Whittick. Must be close to eighty. Not that it makes a whole lot of difference but he doesn't seem to hear too well." She looks around the table for something else to eat but there's only the plate of butter. Or margarine, more likely.

There used to be "decent" food in this house, as Miss Seabring would call it, desserts with every lunch and dinner until just after Noel died when Mitchell, at the age of twelve and grossly overweight by then, suddenly started refusing anything but fruits and vegetables, lean meats and cheese and eggs. He'd found two books at the library, one on diet and the other on body building, and he followed them both like bibles, renewing them so often that Mother finally ordered him copies of his own.

The household accommodated him, of course. Even bread and rolls disappeared for a while, until Dr. Whittick at last managed to convince Mitchell that his body needed carbohydrates.

Mitchell gradually became an expert on vitamins and minerals, proteins and carbohydrates, calorie intake and energy output.

His superior knowledge in that area, and his improving shape, gave him a confidence that soon spilled over into the rest of his life, and his classmates at last began to accept and even to befriend him.

His friendships were never durable or of long duration. Mitchell insisted on being the ultimate authority in disputes over rules. He didn't like to share, and he would not quit playing anything—marbles, table tennis, checkers, baseball—until he or his team had won. "Best out of three," he'd shout after losing a game. "Best out of five," a little later. "Out of seven," "nine," "eleven." He practised everything he tried compulsively, until he really was better at games of skill and endurance than anyone he knew, but in the process he wore his friends out, one after another, and they went away. Others replaced them. He grew thinner and stronger, and the loss of friends didn't seem to bother him, as long as he could find new opponents against whom he could test his abilities.

The change in diet seemed appropriate to my mourning—it was the only sign that life had altered for anyone but me. The atmosphere of unreality that pervaded that year, my final year of high school, was intensified by the familiarity of the surroundings in which it took place. I went to school, to church, as usual, as was expected. Beak Zimmerman invited me to one school dance after another and seemed genuinely surprised when I refused to go. Even my graduation with honours after grade thirteen, proof that I must have done something with that year, seemed to suggest that life, even my life, had gone on in spite of Noel's death. The stoic meals that were on the table each evening were the only evidence that supported my emotions, my sense that nothing was the way it was, nor would it ever be again.

After much discussion and argument with Father, Mother had gone along with Grandmother's change of allegiance, insisting that Dr. Haultain attend to her as well and switching our medical business to his office, mine and Mitchell's. Father just as firmly stayed with Whittick, denouncing Haultain as aggressive and overrated and questioning his ethics on a regular basis. He saw Haultain at least in part as responsible for Grandmother's lingering in our house year after year and suggested that as long as she was ailing, Haultain had a regular source of income. The disagreement over doctors was just one tendon in the strain between them and it included me as well because Jenny was my friend. And yet, within just a few months after Father moved away and Grandmother went home, Mother went back to Whittick.

Madelyn would say: with those two overpowering influences on her life, her mother and her husband, at last removed, Mother was free to make a decision of her own. I don't agree with that. I think that all of her actions were motivated by perverseness. Haultain assumed that he'd "won us" from Whittick, that we were "his". Mother showed him that no one had control like that, not over her.

She was also busy proving to the whole community that even if Father had abandoned her (this was her interpretation—in fact, she drove him out. As she did me, eventually) she could still function quite nicely, thank you. She could make decisions on her own—which she did, with an obvious regularity. She'd designed for herself the costume of a martyr and was carefully fitting herself into it, one desolate limb after another.

Mitchell may have been too young then to notice, but he must know her well enough by now to see the pattern. His support of her seems a deliberate obtuseness.

Hilda comes in and offers tea to the nurse in the coldest and most polite voice I've ever heard her use, even for Westmoreland, and Seabring returns the animosity in kind.

"I don't think so, Hilda. I'm not fond of your brand of tea. Or perhaps it's what you do with it." She stands massively and turns to me. "I'm going for my walk. You take care that you don't tire the patient if you go up before I'm back."

Hilda and I stand at opposite ends of the dining room while she makes her exit. When I hear the front door close, I wrinkle my nose at Hilda.

"Charming." I shake my head. "I'll have some of your tea, if it's made."

She compresses a smile. "It is, but it's almost cold and very strong. I made it quite a while ago."

She's poured it over ice and added lemon and sugar and I'm standing in the hall, running my fingers over the places where the elevator used to be. There are no traces of it at all.

The house is quiet, muted sounds coming occasionally from the kitchen where Hilda is doing dishes. Afterwards, she's told me, she's going downstairs to her room to rest, hastening to add that it's all right with Mother if she does that.

Did she tell me that so I wouldn't think she was shirking her duties, or did she say it because she feels, as I do, the silent directives from the upper floor, commands that need no utterance fingering down like spiderwebs that cling and trap? I haven't lit a cigarette since I came in here: Mother doesn't approve of smoking. If she suddenly disappeared from her bed, whisked away in a magician's blink, I would know it immediately from the feeling in the house.

When Grandmother was up there, it felt a lot like this, as though the top storey had been pushed down and sandwiched us between, forcing us to whisper when she was napping, to maintain a quiet decorum even when she wasn't. I can see Mother's eyes, flicking a look at the ceiling, at Grandmother, before she commanded us to keep the noise down. She would be tense herself, hissing: "Stop running, right this minute!"

I rebelled, with looks and gestures and outright disobedience, but Mitchell knew nothing different. Grandmother had been up there all his life. All he wanted was Mother's approval and he'd lumber after her from room to room after she'd spoken sharply, showing her how quiet he could be. That only increased her tension, her irritation, until she'd order both of us outside to play. She didn't like my defiance, but that at least she could deal with. Mitchell's cowtowing drove her crazy.

And now with her up there the compression serves to confirm every kernel of my memory. Madelyn kept asking about my father, about my grandfather, about Donellon, suggesting that none of it was Mother's fault at all, that she was a victim of circumstance and deserved my pity. Sometimes she only raised her eyebrows to suggest that I must be exaggerating, or to show that my ability to understand was totally deficient.

But now I'm certain of it all again, certain that if light travels in the way I've read it does, that I could whip through space until I'd caught up with that burgeoning, hurtling rockpile of past experiences. And if I poked around enough I'd find the ones I've carried with me, each curve and roughened edge the same, intact, exact.

I must not have conveyed it adequately to Madelyn. Or perhaps her own experiences have made her incapable of understanding. She is unable to think of women as oppressors. It is, or was until Sonny came along, very simple for her: women were either liberated or not liberated, depending on how they scored on some checklist she carried around in her head. She felt sorry for my mother, and nothing I said could alter that. She wanted me to go home and smooth things over: for my sake, she said, as well as for Mother's.

She looked for parallels in her marriage, to illustrate what she was trying to say.

"I didn't have to whisper or tiptoe, or anything like that, of course, but I always felt that I had to act according to some predetermined set of expectations, Ben's as well as my own: we were products of the same way of thinking, he and I. I started to change soon after I got married, and I'm sorry I didn't see it coming before, and spare us both. He couldn't change, or didn't want to. He got married again, to a woman who's quite happy to do all of the things I didn't want to do: to cook, to clean, to sew, to entertain for him, to stay home and raise some babies. Not that I'm saying there's anything wrong with that: as long as one does it out of choice and not because it's expected.

"There was, and still is in a lot of people, some ideal of what a 'wife' should be and do. I had that misconception myself. I did it to myself as much as he did, set myself an obstacle course and then decided I didn't want to leap through the hoops." She looked up from the papers she was marking. "And that's what I think you did, too. You had some ideal 'mother' in your head and you wouldn't allow her to deal with the problems that arose with any ineptitude at all. You don't live there any more. Why don't you let it go? Accept that she didn't know what she was doing, and go back and get it done with. Accept some of the blame yourself."

"You may have hated being married, but you didn't hate Ben. This is a little different."

"Maybe you just think you hate her. After all these years, you'd probably find out you have more in common with her than you think, more in common than the colour of your eyes." She smiled cautiously.

I didn't like the strong resemblance I bore to my mother, to my grandmother, to the Leavenworths, and Madelyn knew that. But I'd given her the ammunition to tease me. I'd made light of it, concealing my exasperation, saying that Grandmother's determination was so strong that her blue eyes had passed through two successive generations of dark-eyed men and had come to me exactly the same colour as they'd started out. Madelyn saw that not as an illustration of Grandmother's strength of will, but as an example of my own obsessive interpretation of everything that had ever happened in Donellon.

"Because we're both women?" I made a grimace, to show her I wasn't angry. But I was. She drew all of the memories out of me and then made pronouncements on them. This was none of her business.

She tugged at the cap of her pen, pulled it off, replaced it. "That's part of it. But I also don't think it was all her doing. If you went back, you'd see that, too. You were only eighteen when you left. Children never see things clearly."

I reached my foot out towards one of the sections of newspaper which were scattered on the kitchen floor near her chair, then pulled it around with my foot so that I could read the headlines.

She was marking spelling tests, her hand skimming down the

page, check, check, until she reached the bottom and paused to write a comment.

We were spending a lot of time together, Madelyn and I. It was better to go out for dinner together, when we were too tired or too bored with cooking to cook, than it was to sit in a restaurant alone with a book open on the table to keep away intruders. Both of us were tired of intruders, and wanted some time to ourselves.

It was better to go to a movie together than to go to a movie alone, better to have company watching television than to watch television alone. I found her easy to be with, undemanding most of the time, and I was willing to put up with her occasional experiments in amateur psychoanalysis, which happened most often when I was careless enough to mention something that reminded me, or her, of my family. I was trying to train myself to avoid the subject, but I kept falling into it without thinking because I was so comfortable with her. Noel was the only person I'd ever confided in as completely as I did in her.

"It's a shame," she said suddenly, capping her pen again and putting it down on top of the stack of papers, "because I miss him. Well, not him particularly. It's been too long for that—almost five years now—and he's gone such a different route. No. Not him at all. But I do miss having a man around. That marriage wasn't right, but that wasn't the only problem. It was the whole concept of 'marriage' that I couldn't live with. I'm not sure I'll ever be able to live with it. It's a word that's got too much history, too much tradition, and it doesn't fit with what I want for myself."

"They're never what they seem to be." I thought of Brian, of all of the men I'd known since Noel, of their masquerade of strength, of their streaks of weakness that they concealed for as long as they could, but which were always there. Their public selves, their private selves, the impossibility of knowing what they would be until you had been with them long enough that retreat was difficult, and painful.

"I think all men are schizophrenic." I laughed.

She considered me, but with an expression that told me she hadn't really listened, and shook her head. "It's the giving up of independence that bothers me. I like the fact that this house is mine and that I paid it off myself. I like knowing exactly what I have in the bank—it used to drive me crazy when he'd write a cheque and forget to tell me about it. I didn't like his being able to interfere with the order in my life."

"Order?" I looked around her kitchen. "In your life?"

She laughed, and went to get two beers from the fridge.

"It's got to do with strength," I said, taking a bottle from her and twisting off the top. There was no expecting a glass when we were in her kitchen and I put the bottle to my lips and swallowed a mouthful of beer. "You can call it interference, dependence, whatever you want to call it. But women are stronger than men, and in order to make relationships survive, they have to hide that. That's the problem." I picked at a corner of the label on the beer bottle.

She smiled. "You've just defended your mother. She didn't hide her strength and your father left. Did you know you were saying that?"

"I'm not saying that." I shook my head. "It doesn't apply. My mother was on a power trip that had nothing to do with reality. She just used it for itself—to destroy other people. Strength, used properly, is healthy."

"Oh, shit. I give up on you." She sat down opposite me and took a swallow of beer. "Whatever the problems are, they're too big for me to solve. But I could still use a hug sometimes, one that had no strings attached to it, one that wasn't some kind of preliminary, explorative gesture. Ben sometimes did that: just came over and hugged me for no reason. I miss that."

She turned to another page of foolscap, lined its margin with X's, and wrote a long comment at the bottom. Then she leaned back and pointed at the newspaper, afterwards clasping her slim long hands behind her head. Her hair was a brighter shade of red at that point, and as straight as mine. She changes hairstyles every six months or so— often changing the shade of it along with the style. When I complimented the colour of her hair shortly after I'd met her, she said, "Clairol, Number 5E, if I recall correctly. Available at your local drugstore. Conditions while it colours. Great stuff."

She says that's one of the things she likes about being on her own: not having to match her hair or her dress to what someone expects of her. At least that's what she used to say before Sonny came along.

"They caught that kid," she said.

"What kid?"

"The one who killed his mother with the kitchen scissors."

"Good for them. But he isn't a kid. He's almost thirty."

"He's got to be insane."

Not necessarily.

Almost as though against my will, I'd been following the story in the papers and on t.v. I thought about it a lot, wondering how it had happened, what had pushed him to it. That "kid", as Madelyn called him, had sliced into some of my dreams, the way you do an apple, impaled the sections on the points of his sharp scissors, and offered them to me.

"Insane or not, I hope they put him away for life."

"So do I," I said, and pulled the label off. It was ragged, but intact.

There's a knock on the door and Westmoreland's in before I've had time to decide whether I'm going to answer it or wait for Hilda. He places his felt hat on the vestibule table, his eyes on me and his face flushed with the heat. I must look more surprised at seeing him than he does at seeing me.

"Diana!" he breathes on me, grasping both my hands and squeezing them. He's heavier than he was when I saw him last, and that combined with his height makes his presence almost overwhelming. I don't feel petite next to very many people.

"I knew you'd come. I said to myself, 'Any child of Edith's will not ignore her at a time like this.' " He shakes my wrists, exultant. "You've come back to heal the rifts. I hoped you would."

Unlike Hilda, Westmoreland rarely uses the word "pray" except on Sundays or at least within appropriate ecclesiastical settings. The rest of the time he uses "hope" as though it were a synonym. He's wearing his usual impeccable black suit and narrow white collar, so hard and sharp that it must hurt against those fleshy jowls. How can he bear it in this heat?

"How did she react? Was she up to talking? This is so good. So good." He beams warmly down at me.

"I haven't been up to see her." I've made my voice as flat as possible.

He sobers immediately. After a moment's thought he says, "Then, you'll come up with me. I can certainly see that it might be difficult after all this time . . . ." He nods, studying me. "It would be very difficult, for both of you."

I shake my head and pull away. "No. I'm not ready yet, to go up there. I need a little time." I look around me. "I just got here, Reverend Westmoreland." I sound panicky. I take a breath, deeply. "She told me not to come back. She's the one who should be healing rifts. Not me."

He shakes his head. "You're her daughter, that's for certain. You sound exactly like her." His voice is amused and tender, as though what I'd said amounted to little more than a pat of butter in his path. Not margarine, for him. "All right. I'll just go up and look in on her, and then we can have a talk."

I hear his footsteps on the floorboards above me, a door open and close and open and close and then Mitchell is coming down the stairs, slowly, deliberately. He's wearing a blue t-shirt now. He must keep a wardrobe in his room upstairs.

I turn to take my glass back to the kitchen.

"Come outside, Diana," he says. "I want to talk to you a minute."

I stop in the doorway to the dining room.

"Please?" he adds, sarcastically.

I put my glass on the hall table beside the phone, beside Westmoreland's hat, and follow him out. He sits on the top step of the verandah and rests his head in his hands. In the south, a bank of cloud is building, but it's still very hot in the sun and there's no sign of a breeze.

"What is it?" I sit on the step beside him but far enough away that there's no danger of contact.

He moves his head to look at me, as though to size me up for the speech he's about to make, then looks down at his hands which he clasps between his knees. He speaks deliberately.

"Seeing you now would be disruptive to Mother. She is very, very sick. I don't seem to be able to get that fact through your head. She's not the same person you remember." He clears his throat. "She's fought this illness with every ounce of energy she had, and you've been the farthest thing from her mind. You've got to put her needs ahead of yours, for once." He looks away, out at the drive. "For her sake. Go away."

"You want me to go. Westmoreland wants me to stay. I feel like a pushme-pullyou."

"I don't give a damn how you feel. It's her I'm thinking about." He rubs his face with his hands. "Westmoreland lives in another world. He thinks he has some professional duty to dispense advice, to interfere. He thinks God's telling him how he ought to manipulate everybody. But his tinkerings don't come from any higher power than himself. He doesn't know what he's talking about."

"He's known her a long time."

"So what? This is none of his business. He isn't family." His voice is taut. "He had no right to tell Mother you were here. That should have been up to me."

"You could have done it. You've been up there. Someone would have told her, sooner or later. The nurse, or Hilda. Hilda must go up from time to time."

He looks up, away from me toward the garage. "He walks around Donellon as though he owns it. He's got all these little goodwill missions that are meant to set him off to advantage. I really think he sees it as a coup that you've come back here. A coup for him. He's never once paused to consider what might be best for her."

"They've been friends for years."

He sighs, exasperated. "She asked him not to call you. Is that friendship, going against her wishes?"

He glances at me and the almost-sad brown eyes are so like Father's that I look away.

"So Westmoreland's got you in his pocket, too, eh?" Mitchell says. "You're going to go up there, because he wants you to? What I say doesn't matter?"

"I didn't say that, Mitchell. I didn't say I was going up."

"I'm her son. I've stuck with her, paid her bills for her, looked after the maintenance around here, and missed a hell of a lot of work since she got sick. Westmoreland comes and visits, offers spiritual guidance, screws things up and goes away again. I've done the real work."

"Mitchell, what I do will be up to me. It won't have anything to do with him or you."

"I should throw him off the property. You, too."

I spread my hands in front of me, stretching. "Why don't you, then?"

He doesn't respond to my challenge aloud, but it's made him angrier. He didn't say he'd throw us out because he means to do it, only because he'd like to do it. Both of us know that his orders have no effect around here.

"You are so damned selfish, Diana. You always have been. You stayed away out of selfishness, and now you're back because of it. You're toying with her emotions, and I think that's cruel. Where are you going?"

"To get my purse, to get my cigarettes."

He shakes his head. "You're an idiot. It's a stupid, filthy habit."

"Mitchell, stop it. We can't talk about anything if you're going to act like a little kid."

I wonder what it would be like to be a woman in love with Mitchell. He's a perfectionist—about his dress, his car, his house, and probably his relationships. He's never wrong. It would be very difficult to be in love with him, impossible to live with him.

I can avoid arguing with him, or can indulge in it if I please, because his approval is not something I seek. But a woman who sought his approval would never get it. No one is perfect but his mother, although I'm sure that she doesn't give two hoots about what he thinks of her. She's always taken him for granted. He's always been here.

He's an attractive looking package, but any woman who fell for Mitchell Guthrie would have insurmountable competition: a mother whose love is mainly his invention, an invention that meets all of his needs.

When I come back out I sit down and light a cigarette, blowing smoke away from his direction, before I say to him, "I'd have thought you'd have been glad of Westmoreland's support. It must have been a long haul. It would have been hard to carry it all alone."

"What support? Telling her you were here just now? I'd almost persuaded her to take a forkful of lunch and he came charging in with barely a knock: 'Edith,' he says," and Mitchell imitates Westmoreland perfectly, "'Wonderful news! Diana's just come in!' So much for food. And then he says, 'Mitchell, would you excuse us for a minute,' as though I were an orderly."

"You could have refused to leave."

"I could have refused to leave. There you go." He stands up, dusting off the back of his shorts—needlessly, I'm sure. Hilda must keep the porch as clean as she does the rest of the house. "You have no idea how sick she is!" He begins to walk away from the house, toward his car, then pauses, turns. "You want me to start a battle in the bedroom of a dying woman, is that the idea?" He comes back and stops in front of me, takes a deep breath and then says, with mock-clarity and reason, as though he were speaking to an idiot, "We are trying to keep things calm up there. Which is why I don't want you to go up. As I believe I've explained to you once or twice already."

I wonder whether he's angrier that Westmoreland told him I was here or that the clergyman supplanted him at Mother's bedside. Maybe the two are so inextricably connected that he wouldn't know the difference, even if he let his mind address it. Which he wouldn't.

"How did she react, when he told her I was here?"

"I left just then. I didn't notice." He reaches into his pocket for his car keys. "I'm not going to be a messenger. I would have done it once. I offered to do it for years, but not any more."

"I didn't mean to . . . ."

"To what?"

I don't know how I wanted to end that sentence. To make things between him and me difficult? To interfere between him and his mother? I shrug.

"I'm going for a drive or something. Until Westmoreland leaves." He nods at the clergyman's neat grey compact. "Oh God, here comes Seabring. If I'm needed, I'll be at the Fern. I'm going to get some lunch." He meets my eyes. "Don't do anything stupid. Precipitous. Think about what I've said."

I look up at the house, and back at him. "You don't need to go out for lunch, you know. Hilda's made you some. It's in the fridge."

He shakes his head. "I've been looking at Mother's plate too long. I'm going to get something else."

Something greasy and substantial?

He drives past the disapproving glance of Seabring who approaches me without a word and disappears into the house, and I watch Mitchell's car disappear into the trees where the driveway curves off toward the highway.

Chapter Six

Why isn't Mitchell afraid when he's sitting beside her bed, when she might stop breathing at any moment? Is it possible to love someone that much, that her death wouldn't frighten you? Or is it just some strength of his, the same one doctors and nurses, and clergyman, must possess? A steeling of the self? If that is true, then I'm impressed with him for having a strength that I most certainly don't have. Where did it come from? From her? From Father?

It is easy to trace the physical lineage in this family, to decide from whom came this eye colour or that bone structure, but the emotions and reactions are less easily pinned down. I've spent a lot of my life trying not to be my mother or my grandmother, despite the physical similarity that I can do nothing about and which fills me with distaste, revulsion even, when I catch an expression in the mirror which is theirs. I don't want to be like them, hard and unforgiving, incapable of bending to anyone. But it's harder to remember Father, to tell if what I'm doing is like him or not.

He reacted not with petulance, like Mitchell, nor with rebelliousness, like me, but with more devious and intelligent means, by drawing into himself and then devising some project to occupy him. He could give the appearance of being here, of working in our midst, without really being here at all.

After her fall, Grandmother had suffered one ailment after another. First there was the influenza which I'd brought home from school in the autumn, in lieu of chicken pox, and then a severe chest cold just after Christmas, both of which had been exacerbated by her lack of mobility.

The ankle had never healed the way it should have. Haultain said it ought to have been X-rayed and set properly at the time. Father said it was her mental attitude: she just didn't want to go home. Mother suggested that if that were the case, we ought to sell her house in Toronto and invite her to live with us, and then she would get better. Father wouldn't hear of it.

In the spring, her hips began to bother her, and Haultain suggested that she might be permanently wheelchair-bound. "She's not a young woman," he said. "She's had those joints immobile for far too long."

"But you're the one who told her to stay off her feet," my father said, very angry then.

"It was the right treatment at the time," said Haultain, cool and professional, unmoved by my father's anger. "Things have happened since that we never could have predicted."

"Not you, maybe," said my father. "You didn't know her."

"Wallace, you are selfish and unreasonable," Mother said after Dr. Haultain left. "You're not the one who has to attend to the house in Toronto. You're at work all day. What does it matter to you? She's my mother, and she needs my care."

"This is my house," he said firmly. "I didn't marry her. She . . . Her being here makes me feel . . . helpless. That's the word. I feel I have no control over my own life, over our lives, any more."

When there was no more talk, I moved from my eavesdropping position at the top of the stairs and tiptoed to my bedroom, thinking that they were always angry with one another. My father, particularly, seemed quietly aggravated all the time. And so I was pleased and relieved when he started his first big project.

During the long summer evenings and on Saturdays, he started working on the elevator. Over and over again he measured the height of the walls around the stairway to the second floor, the floors and ceilings, the angles everywhere of soft-looking wood, dark bannister molding, then went to his den beneath the stairs to make drawings and notes on little pieces of paper.

He ordered books with diagrams in them of pulleys, and pictures of motors and elevators, too, of course: elevators of every kind and type from every part of the world. For a while he became so fascinated with the subject of "elevator" in its generic sense that he abandoned his own project to study its history and evolution, drawing my attention to a cleverly designed lift and attempting to teach me to say the word in several languages.

Mother tried to discourage him, insisting that Grandmother would be up and about in no time.

"You've been saying that for ages, Edith, but she only comes down on Sundays when you insist. If she could get down without my having to carry her—you know how she hates that—she'd be on the road to recovery."

They were speaking quietly, almost in a whisper, for her room was at the top of the stairs.

"She's moved back to the guest room, at least. You're in your own bed. I don't see what you have to complain about."

He said nothing to that, but held the level against the angle of the oak trim which edged the stairway. Mother was still sleeping in Mitchell's room, although he was almost a year. She said he still woke up in the night, and so did Grandmother, and she didn't want to waken Father when she got up to attend to them. It seemed reasonable to me.

"I think it's a waste of time and money, but I suppose it's your money and your time."

"I suppose it is," he said, watching her ankles between the posts as she carried baby Mitchell up to have his bath. It seemed she was always carrying him then. I figured he was too fat to walk.

I thought of myself as Father's daughter, and Mitchell as Mother's son.

I was delighted with the project, deceived into thinking that we were working on it together, unaware that it was the beginning of his withdrawal. Maybe he didn't know that either. He seemed glad of the company and glad again to come home from work once he'd started on it. Instead of closing the door to his den, the sunroom, right after supper while he read the paper and the mail, he welcomed me in there and both of us would pore over the drawings he'd transferred now to large white sheets of paper, sketchy marks to indicate the stairs and the elevator's platform and little numbers with fractions all over the page, connected with ruler-straight lines.

When the planning was done and the actual construction began, fat Mitchell crawled around, chewing on measuring sticks and pencils until Mother finally came and took him off to bed. That was the time I looked forward to most, when we could really get to work. Our working time was short, so we made the most of it. There was no hammering after nine as Grandmother needed to rest. She'd acquired bed sores and, with the heat, she was having trouble sleeping.

"We have to be careful here," he'd say. "No errors anywhere. This is a very well constructed hallway and the bannisters cost me a lot of money. We've got to be able to get it out again without leaving a trace, as soon as she goes home. Planning for the future, that's what it's called."

I nodded solemnly and handed him the yardstick. I liked working close to the bigness, the strength of him, liked even the acrid smell of his sweat, a smell that no one else in the family ever made.

"Don't know why I didn't think of this months ago," he said, pausing in the midst of the tuneless whistle with which he accompanied himself during any physical labour. "The Lord helps those who help themselves."

He was determined to build it himself. He constantly corrected himself to include me, but it always came back to that. The design he'd finally settled on was his, adapted and extracted from other sources but duplicated nowhere. His den took on the look of a carpentry shop for he stored all of his materials and tools in there as they arrived from Toronto and New York and Montreal. We'd go down to the train station with the pickup he'd borrowed from Mr. Fletcher.

I saw a lot of Noel in those days, when I think of it, on the bus every day and when my father went to borrow something. But he was aloof and Jenny and I were particular about who we talked to. In fact, we rarely talked to anyone but one another: a whisper from one of us to another girl would send the other into piques of jealousy, and boys were out completely. We had terrific battles and were inseparable—like sisters, I supposed.

We'd collect the latest shipment from Toronto, Father and I, and he would be barely able to contain his excitement long enough to get the packages home and unloaded before he examined whatever piece of wood or bundle of metal rods had most recently arrived. One day it was the electrical system which would make the whole thing work, and that day we didn't get it home but opened the parcel right there on the station platform, sitting on the boards under the curious gaze of the stationmaster while Father explained to both of us how it was going to work.

It was to run up and down the stairs on a pulley system with a motor that would lower the platform to the landing, arc it around the two curving rails which looked like train tracks, then lower it again to the downstairs hall. A metal lip would hold the wheelchair on the platform until the switch which stopped the mechanism automatically dropped the flaps as well. I asked him, trying to suppress my amusement at the vision, what would happen if the flaps came down by mistake when she was halfway down the stairs. His reassurance that it couldn't possibly happen was a not-unexpected disappointment.

As the elevator gradually neared completion, Grandmother eyed it with increasing alarm on Sundays when he carried her down to the wheelchair, which he'd placed in the downstairs hallway before he went for her. She never spoke when she was in his arms but sat primly, icily, until they'd reached the lower hall. Then she started to talk.

"There'll be no room for a body to walk," she said as she examined the metal ties with an impatient flick of her blue eyes.

"Of course there will, Mother," he said. "That's the beauty of it.

It takes practically no room at all, considering what it does. I just carried you down beside it, didn't I?"

She didn't like to be reminded of that. I think it was her greatest shame to have to be carried down, but she had reacted with horror when Father offered once to move her bed into his den. In this house, which was so much like the Leavenworth house on the far side of the river, bedrooms belonged on the second floor, and that's all there was to that. There was no bath downstairs, which was her excuse at the time, but I think she was afraid that people might wander into her room and see those things she preferred to pretend did not exist. Her nightgown. Her teeth, in a glass, at night.

"Well, there's no need on my behalf, I'm sure," she said that Sunday. "I certainly hope you don't think I'm going to use it."

"Who else, Mother?" he asked so gently that I was sure no one but me could hear the exasperation. "You'll be much happier when you can join the family more often."

"I'm not risking my neck in that contraption. One 'accident' in a lifetime is enough for me. Decidedly enough."

"Come along," said Mother, mollifying, taking the handles of the wheelchair and turning it away from the stairs as she cast an "I told you so" look at Father. "Dinner's almost ready."

"Isn't that girl's skirt a little short?" she said, fixing her eyes now on my hem. Her face seemed a little more wrinkled, more paper-like each time she came down, and her eyes by contrast sharper because they were alive.

"Now, Mother. She's a growing girl."

"That's certainly no excuse for immodesty."

Mother sighed. "All right. I'll have Hilda turn it down this afternoon. Please, let's eat dinner before Mitchell wakes up from his nap."

I'd told Jenny about the elevator with great enthusiasm and insisted that she come over and have a look at it. To my mind, then, its magnificence compared with the Haultains' frequent visits to the exotic city of Toronto, and I couldn't wait to share my own luxury with her. No one else in Donellon had an elevator in her house: Jenny readily agreed to that, and was as excited about seeing it as I was about showing it to her.

The day that was set for her visit, I could barely contain myself during the afternoon's classes and I made as much mileage of the incident as I could. I even told Noel, in my petulant, excluding, little-girl voice, that Jenny was coming to see the elevator and that no one else was allowed to.

She got off the bus with me at my lane, and we ran all the way to the front door. I pulled it open with a flourish, insisting that she close her eyes, and then I drew her into the hall. She was wearing a pretty, lacy-blue dress and the skirt of it stood out around her, thanks to a beautiful crinoline which had a blue velvet ribbon drawn through its hem.

"Open your eyes."

She did.

"Where is it?"

"There." I pointed proudly to the wood and metal construction that bordered the stairway.

"That's not an elevator," she said, greatly disappointed. "Elevators are inside walls."

"It's a different kind," I said, faltering, aware of the mess on the stairway as I hadn't been while Father and I were working on it. "A new invention. It isn't working yet, but it will be soon."

"It's not an elevator. I know what elevators look like."

She didn't say it unkindly. She was as disappointed in it as I was. As I led her into the kitchen for cookies, wracking my brain for other excitements in the house that I could show her, and coming up with none, I knew that she had a certain power over me. Tomorrow she'd be asked to report at school on the wonders that she, exclusively, had been invited to see.

Her family was different from mine. The Haultains had no grandmother who'd been ailing in an upstairs bedroom for so long that it was hard to remember a time when she hadn't been there, who seemed to have recovered only enough that she was able to let us know how little she approved of all of us downstairs. Jenny didn't have a Tweedledum for a brother, banging pudgy fists against her bedroom door and wanting to come in.

I began to find my family eccentric and detestable. My father's dislike of Dr. Haultain seemed nothing more than lack of awareness on his part of how fathers ought to behave.

In late autumn, the elevator was completed. Father took me up on the platform where the chair would go, put my hand on the bannister to steady me, and moved the switch on the side of the newel post. The platform creaked and groaned and then, miraculously, up we went, noisily but more or less smoothly, to the landing. There the platform made a sudden jerk, shifted, jerked again and ground up the last five steps. There was no sign of Grandmother at the top although she often sat there at the doorway to her room, her expression shaded by the darkness of the hallway and the light behind her. When she was there, I could read her iron aura, startling me when I bounded up the stairs.

The pressure of Father's hand on my shoulder told me how pleased he was with what he'd made. At that moment I was amazed by him again, impressed with him. He'd made it, and it moved.

"Never built anything from scratch myself before," he said quietly. "I'm kind of pleased with myself, if I do say so myself. Let it be a lesson to you, Diana. You're never too old to try to do something new."

I nodded and smiled, proud of him. He was capable and strong: he could mend anything. He would mend everything.

At the top, he touched another switch and the flaps responded perfectly as the machine fell silent.

Without a word we turned and he started it up again and down we came, the two of us still as commanding officers, the smooth thick railing slipping beneath my hand.

Mother waited at the bottom, kneeling to hold Mitchell in her arms because the noise alarmed him. He'd grown too big for anyone to lift and had learned to walk, I think, as a form of survival: Mother could no longer carry him to the table.

Mother refused to try the elevator, despite Father's pleas, and so he took Mitchell up on it, ignoring his screams, and when they came back down Mitchell was standing triumphant beside Father, clutching his pant leg with one hand and shouting with pleasure. Mother went to find him a snack, and not as a reward.

Grandmother restricted herself to the piece of hallway between her bedroom door and the bathroom for several days after the elevator was finished, and on Sunday at dinnertime she said she wasn't coming down.

"Ever, Mother? You're never coming down again?"

"Wallace!"

"Don't be rude, Wallace," Grandmother said. "I'm not coming down on that thing, is what I'm trying to say."

"But you don't like my carrying you."

"I will not kill myself."

"Dinner is getting cold," Mother pleaded, looking at the stairwell as though she wished a hole would open and deposit all of us on the main level. "Roast chicken, Mother. Your favorite. It's getting cold." She seemed incapable of talking about anything but dinner.

"All right," he said, as Mother helped Grandmother to her feet, to lean most weakly against the railing while Father carried the wheel-chair to the hallway below. "I'll carry you this one last time," he said, lifting her as easily as if she were a bundle of sticks, and carrying her down in their usual unwelcome embrace to set her in the chair. "But I'm not carrying you up again."

Her back like a steel ramrod she unlocked the wheelchair and went through into the dining room and the two of us waited at the table while Mother and Father argued in the hallway as though we couldn't hear them.

"Do you know how long it took me to build that thing?"

"No one asked you to. In fact, I recall telling you not to bother, several times. She's an adult, after all. You don't tell her what to do."

"I have noticed that. Once or twice."

He relented when it became obvious that Mother was going to endeavour to carry her up herself, but he didn't like it. That was the first of the really long silences between them. They just stopped talking to one another, about anything.

For weeks Mitchell was the only one to use the elevator and every time we heard the familiar squeak and groan, Mother rushed out of whatever room she was in to take him off it.

Father moved all of his tools to the garage where he'd started to build a workbench and he bought a television set for the den: our first. The Haultains had had one for a year. They'd bought it in Toronto.

"I can't stand it any more," Mother said one night, one of the first things she'd said to Father in days. "Mitchell's going to pinch his fingers at the very least. Can't you take it out?"

"Absolutely not. It's there for a reason and it's going to be used for that reason, by God. You'll just have to discipline him better."

The silence resumed.

But after dinner one Sunday, when the four of us were watching Ed Sullivan, Mother methodically spooning strawberry shortcake into Mitchell's mouth so that she could hear the singer, we heard the machine start up. Mother automatically stood but when she realized Mitchell was at her knee, she sat down again, incredulous. We heard the elevator grind slowly down the stairs and stop, with a "flap" as the rim hit the hardwood floor.

"Have to put some carpet under that," Father said, his voice even.

She wheeled herself into the doorway and glared at him, triumphant but not, it seemed to me, at having conquered the fear of the eleva-tor.

"I noticed from my window that the gladiolus bed is full of weeds," she said. "They ought to be taken out before the snow."

She wheeled herself into the room, edged around and parked beside Mother's chair. The singer sang on, unnoticed, on the small black and white screen in the cabinet. She folded her hands in her lap and, speaking to Mother but still looking at Father, she said, "You'd better stop feeding that child so much. He's a most unpleasant sight."

Grandmother was down.

Chapter Seven

Mitchell came to Edmonton for the first time when he was twenty-one, nine years after I'd left Donellon. In his letter, he said that he was driving across the country before he began law school. This was his final opportunity to take so much time off, he said, and he wanted to see Canada. I was impressed with the maturity of his letter, with his ability to plan his life so well.

I was nervous about seeing him, this brother who'd been a boy when I last saw him, who was now a man. But I was also pleased. I thought that something might be established between us that could circumvent Mother, that perhaps some family connection was salvageable after all. A brother: I'd almost forgotten I had one.

I welcomed him hugely, taking two days off work to show him my city, which is at its finest when it's seen in June. I stocked the refrigerator with everything I thought he might possibly like or crave, not thinking he might still be thin, and I tallied his age in my head twice, double-checking, and then bought beer and wine.

He arrived on a Friday afternoon and our meeting, in the street in front of the apartment I shared with Brian, was awkward and unsiblinglike. I was impressed with his lean figure—I hadn't assumed that his crash diet would have any long term effect—and with the city-wise self-confidence which he'd acquired by going to university away from Mother, in Toronto. I was taken aback by his physical resemblance to our father: his eyes particularly, and his voice.

I took him to the small one-bedroom apartment on the third floor of the walkup. It was hot, but Mitchell refused a beer and asked if I had mineral water. I didn't, so we went with glasses of ice cubes and water to sit on the tiny balcony, and we talked in uncomfortable bits and pieces about my work, his schooling, until Brian came home from work.

Brian and I had been living together for almost two years by then, and had grown used to one another. He owned a store which sold windsurfing equipment in the summer and ski equipment in the winter, and I'd met him at a marketing seminar shortly after I became the manager of Rosen's Records.

Ours seemed to me a perfect arrangement. We were both so

busy with our respective stores that our need to relax was the greatest thing we had in common. Our favoured forms of relaxation were almost identical: we were both spectators. We liked going to movies, to hockey games, to plays. We liked the same musicians, the same filmmakers, and the same restaurants. I'd hoped we could continue like that, both of us allowing the other the freedom to work until we dropped, both of us coming home to be restored before we went back out to work again. Both of us loved our work and there was a high degree of contentment and happiness in that time we spent together. I assumed that our relationship might be refined with time, that it would avoid any drastic evolutions.

Mitchell and Brian hit it off immediately and I might as well have been somewhere else for all of the attention I was paid that evening by my dark-haired brother and my blond-headed mate. They talked hockey and argued football, and Brian afforded Mitchell all of the respect he'd get when he really became a lawyer. Mitchell loved that, and returned the compliment by asking Brian questions about business management which I could have answered as easily.

I didn't mind. I sat listening, stood listening while I made dinner, sat listening while we ate, stood listening while I did the dishes, and finally sat, listening, until after the sun at last went down at nearly eleven o'clock. I learned that my brother's mind worked in an extremely logical fashion, as though he imposed the order first and then set his ideas into it. What I didn't see was that the two of them were intent on liking one another for reasons that had to do with me.

When Brian went to work on Saturday, grumbling that I never took a day off work for him, I showed the city to Mitchell. I was glad that Brian couldn't be along. I was ready to talk to my brother.

We became easier with one another as we wandered through the university and through the parks that edge the river valley. I kept neglecting to point the things out to him that I'd intended to show him as our talk became more hurried and intense. I wanted to tell him everything about myself, my work, my life, and to prod him for details about people I hadn't seen in years, some I hadn't even thought of since I left. But throughout the conversation, I felt dissatisfied, as though we were skimming surfaces.

We barbecued steaks on Saturday night at Brian's insistence. Cooking beef over an open flame was his ultimate gesture of Western hospitality, and Mitchell accepted a beer from him and then another, and finally the three of us were happily, familiarly soused.

I learned more about my brother from watching him with Brian than I had from talking to him and later, as I was trying to let Brian know with firm gestures that making love while my brother inhabited the next room was not what I had in mind, I learned about Brian. He felt Mitchell would make him a perfectly good brother-in-law. He was pleased with my offering. I laughed and turned my back to him. I had no interest in children and I could see no point in marriage if no children were involved.

Mitchell had told me that Mother was fine, and we'd both avoided the subject further. It wasn't until I was walking him down to his car on Sunday, pointing the direction he should take to get onto the highway to Jasper, that he asked when I was planning to come home.

"I can send you the money," he said. "I've been here, and now it's your turn to visit us."

"Us? Have you been concealing a girl friend?" I teased, my arm around his shoulder.

"No." He laughed. "I had one, but I couldn't afford to keep her. I mean me and Mother."

I dismissed the suggestion with a shake of my head and a laugh—impossible—unaware even after he'd driven away that the whole purpose of the visit had been embedded in that thirty-second exchange.

I walked back up to the apartment feeling satisfied and even triumphant. I'd acquired a dimension I hadn't ever hoped for or even thought I wanted—a blood connection—and he'd updated memories for me which made me feel less severed from my childhood.

Jenny Haultain, he told me, is now Jenny Hargreaves. They live in Toronto where Geoff practises law with an ancient and respected firm, and aspires toward a seat in the Ontario legislature. Mitchell said, without the slightest trace of sarcasm, that she was a tremendous asset to his career, that her dinners were sometimes written up in magazines, along with photos of their expensively renovated home. Their two children attend a private school. Mitchell approves of everything about the Hargreaves and I think that if he ever decides to marry, he will look for a wife who's just like Jenny.

I wonder if he even knows about their third child, Jenny's and Geoff's, who'd be almost eighteen by now. He must know, but he's never mentioned it. How do Geoff and Jenny reconcile that memory with their fancy renovated home?

I have trouble disengaging the last vision I had of her, hair in plaits with a leather band around her forehead, sandaled, denim-clad, difficulty replacing that with Mitchell's version. But perhaps what has happened since shouldn't surprise me: children rarely turn into the adults they seem to be rehearsing for. Still, I'd expected something less usual from Jenny.

Even now my friendship with her seems one of critical importance in my life, although it lasted only six years or so, until she discovered boys. Discovered is probably not the best word for it— Jenny spoke of boys with a proprietary tone, as though she'd invented them.

Madelyn's told me that her two close childhood friendships went into similar hibernations when the three of them turned twelve, only one to emerge, in a different form completely, when they were finished high school. So I suppose that Jenny and I were not unique. But for several years, until she got pregnant and moved away, I was certain that our separation was only temporary, that anyone with whom I'd shared every secret I could think of and some that I'd made up, must come back to me eventually.

But what I considered friendship then was probably no more than envy on my part and need for audience on hers. She'd told everyone at school that my "elevator" was nothing more than a big mess on the stairway, and instead of being angry with her, I had been ashamed. Perhaps children are too self-centred to be capable of genuine friendship.

Jenny did more research into the subject of sex than a person would likely need in an entire lifetime, acquiring most of her knowledge from her father's textbooks before she'd even had her first period. This milestone she managed to attain at the age of eleven years, ten months, boasting of it to me as though the box of Kotex and the snake-toothed belt were the latest fashion items from Toronto.

She discovered later, of course, that knowledge is no substitute for a really high quality condom, one that won't spring leaks with a little bit of handling.

In the summer which followed our graduation, in chiffon dresses, from elementary school, she put as much of her new knowledge to empirical testing as she could without actually losing her virginity. She was saving that, she said in that new woman's voice that made me feel taller and lankier than I already was, and backward as Donellon, until she was sixteen. In the weeks before her parents took her to the cottage on Georgian Bay, she went steady with four boys, discarding them one after another until she started with Paul Racine who was tall and sharp-featured, the son of one of the workers in my father's factory. He was headed for grade eleven, again, if he decided to go back. She told me he might go to Toronto instead and look for work. Toronto and work: in the past year she seemed to have aged a dozen years while I'd merely put in twelve months.

My body stubbornly refused to initiate me into the bloody mysteries of womanhood (mysteries to me then despite Jenny's lengthy and irritatingly patient explanations of fallopian tubes and sheddings of the lining of the uterus) and had even failed so far to produce a breast. Despite these basic faults I did everything I could to catch up with her: we'd done everything together for so long and I would not be left alone to mould with my aberrant, or at least primitive, family just because my body refused to mature at the rate hers had. I missed our whispering confidences, missed her walking beside me, making me more acceptable by her attention.

Father was now reroofing the house in the September sunlight, his back to the sky and sweat on his skin as he climbed doggedly, silently, up and down the ladder. It was too high for me to help, he said, too dangerous. In the years since the elevator he'd put shutters on every window, built a workroom for himself off the garage and heated it, installed a ramp which was intended to get Grandmother's wheelchair down the front steps to church and ultimately, of course, out of the house completely, but which had never been used. ("I'm not plunging headlong into the gravel just to hear one of Westmoreland's sermons," she'd said when it was done. "Thank you very much.")

The house in Toronto had at last been sold and the furniture dispersed, a lot of it throughout our house, so there was no question any more of her moving back to Toronto. There was talk sometimes of her getting an apartment in Donellon, in the new seniors' building, but nothing ever seemed to come of it.

Mother and Grandmother, who were the only two adults who'd retained any interest in raising me (Father having abdicated all roles but those of breadwinner and carpenter), refused me makeup. I kept a tube of lipstick and a compact in my tartan schoolbag and headed for the girls' room as soon as I reached school. They refused me shorter skirts and so I rolled the waistband of my kilt under my sweater before I got on the bus.

These subterfuges seemed so insignificant that I almost hesitated to confide them to Jenny, when I compared them to her striding off to the Fern Cafe in full daylight, when she was supposed to be in the library, for a coke with Paul Racine. My strategies seemed pale and useless compared to her parking with Paul behind Lazenby's barn to prod with tongues and grope with whole hands, when she'd told her parents she was going to a young people's meeting at the church.

I didn't find the prospect of groping and prodding very appetizing, my emotions having kept pace with my body, but illusion was more important than genuine desire and I knew that what I needed was a boyfriend. I set out, cool-headed and deliberately, to acquire one.

Noel was in the eleventh grade with Paul and although we hadn't spoken often since we were small, I summoned up the necessary courage to smile hello one morning when he climbed up onto the bus. He swung into the seat beside me, which surprised me. I thought these things took longer.

"Finally made it to the big time, eh?" he said, mocking.

I shrugged, coolly, as Jenny would have done.

"Survived frosh week?"

"It wasn't so bad," I said.

I'd been ignored during the hazing of the week before. Jenny had been treed with a garden hose by Paul across the street from the school and he never even smiled as he soaked her until her nipples showed. Despite her shouts for help the thing had seemed intent, naked and personal, between them. She knew that none of us in the crowd across the street would have dared to take the garden hose from Paul or even ask him to stop, and I'm sure that's why she shouted.

"It's pretty stupid. Frosh week."

I glanced at him.

"Yeah. I guess it is."

He was a head taller than I was and his dark hair was longer than it had been when he was younger, still wavy and thick but clean and combed. He wore a pale yellow shirt with his blue jeans, unlike Paul who never wore any shirt that was not bled madras, and he carried a camera slung over one shoulder moving it so automatically to avoid its knocking into things that it might have been a sensate extension of his body. He would not impress Jenny much, but he would have to do for now.

"I saw the picture in the paper," I said, nodding at the camera.

Hilda had pointed it out to me during the summer, a photograph of a cat and a dog eyeing one another warily through a wire fence. Noel's name had appeared under it. "How'd you get them to do that? The cat and the dog, I mean."

He shrugged. "I didn't have anything to do with it—just took the picture. Editor likes that kind of crap when the news is slow, which it usually is around here. Crap. That's all it is." He stared out the front window of the bus, looking sullen, and I felt I'd offended him. The magazines insisted that the way to a man's heart was through his ego, and that one ought to ask questions and not babble on about oneself. Women's magazines have never served me well.

"Where's Haultain?" he asked me suddenly. "You usually sit with her."

"She's getting a ride with Paul, in his T-bird."

"It's not his. It belongs to his uncle." He glanced at me. "She's too young for Racine."

"No she's not," I said. "She can take care of herself."

He ran his fingers over the black camera case, looking down at it, as the bus slowed and then stopped to let Vern Lackington on. Vern looked curiously at me then asked Noel a question about a math assignment. As Noel turned to answer, his knee touched mine and I instinctively moved my leg away before I felt the shock of the touch. The feeling went right through me, brushing against my throat and making my heart pound before it lightly grazed me deep between my legs. I glanced down at Noel's knee, at the male knee which had just touched mine, and I understood what Jenny was talking about.

I tried to put my knee back against his, but the gesture seemed mechanical and deliberate: his was now too far away. My elbow touched his side instead and he apologised and shifted, fell silent once again.

We were crossing the bridge to town, climbing the long hill. My face was flushed, and the school was too close. I gave it one last try.

"You ever go to the pond?" I asked, my voice a little higher than I'd intended.

"Sometimes," he said, looking down at me. "Why?"

I shrugged. "Wouldn't mind seeing it again."

"You can go there any time you want—it's practically on your property."

"But it isn't on our property."

"Doesn't matter. You don't need permission."

I pressed my knees together and took a little breath. "I couldn't go there myself. Your father wouldn't like it."

"He wouldn't care."

I shook my head, not looking at him.

He sounded amused. "Well, I can always shoot some film."

I had trouble shaking Mitchell who followed me down the lane and insisted on knowing where I was going and why he couldn't come. In the past he'd been a source of embarrassment in public but a curious comfort when we were alone. He and Mother seemed to agree that food meant love and approval— both in her offering of it and in his consuming of it. He ate to please her and eventually, of course, to please himself, and she fed him in part I'm sure to atone for her displays of disgust at the obese monster she'd helped to create.

For years he'd been waiting at the end of the laneway when I got off the school bus every day, him immense and hideously short to be wearing the manclothing that fitted him through the waist and arms, his frightened boy-eyes pleading with me not to ignore or tease him as I would do if Jenny were with me. But when he and I were alone I found I could make his timidity go away a little if I read to him or walked beside him slowly through the woods, showing him mushrooms he must not eat, pointing out butterflies and moths and telling him the things I'd learned in school.

Sometimes when we sat on the lawn and I was sure no one was watching I'd put out my hand and stroke his thin brown hair or rub his back and I liked the way it lulled him, made him happy. In a strange way it made me happy too, to have him need me, love me, find me flawless. He learned everything I told him quickly, perfectly, to please me.

But that autumn he'd started school and he hated it, hated the taunts of other children, the poorly disguised loathing of his teacher, and he seemed to cling to me every minute I was home. Mother would not listen to his complaints of stomach aches but sent him irritably off to school each morning on the bus. Having girded him in invitations for rejection she sent him firmly off to be rejected.

I wanted him to be strong against her as I tried to be, to be ready always to return her chill with chill. I felt that if only he would become a little tougher, if he would let Mother, people, matter less, he would be better off. His need for her approval, an impossible need to fill, was beginning to make me want to look away. And so I told him to get lost as I walked quickly down the lane, a book under my arm for appearances, and despised the look I knew would be on his face if I turned back toward the child I'd abandoned in the drive.

I arrived at the pond before Noel did. It was a warm calm evening and the leaves, still thick upon the trees, were shot with reds and golds and yellows. The air was hazy with pale smoke and I breathed deeply of the familiar autumn smell of burning leaves. A fish broke the water into sluggish circles and it seemed that the world was moving so slowly that it must at some point stop.

I wished it would, stop now, that the grandmother who always talked of getting better but never did would be frozen properly erect into her wheelchair until the end of time, that the pandering lumbering Mitchell would never beg my affection again, that Mother would stop trying to alter our behaviours to please her mother, and that Father would stop being so damnably uninterested in it all. I wished that Jenny would vanish, too: "You mean that creep with the *camera*?" she'd said.

I wanted to stay alone forever in the chestnut shell of that auburn evening.

He came through the trees and waved before he turned again into the bush and emerged once more on my side of the pond. He wore a red flannel jacket like a hunter and two cameras were slung this time from his shoulder on a black nylon cord.

"How many cameras do you own?" I asked.

"This is it." He sat down on the long grasses about two feet away from me.

"Last time you had binoculars. You're always looking through something."

"Yeah. I guess I am. Cameras are better though—you can take something away with you."

He raised one to his eyes and focussed on the trees he'd just come through. I listened to his clickings, trying to think of something else to ask, but his answers had a firmness about them that seemed to discourage further comment. He looked comfortable and easy in this place, and I felt ill at ease by contrast. I had nothing to do, no reason to be here.

I opened the book in my lap, a hardcover collection of short stories by Poe that my father's sister, Alma, had sent me from Vancouver for my birthday. I always found gifts from this aunt I'd never met a disappointment: clearly marked "book" on the outside of the brown mailing wrapper, there was no sense of mystery to them. Surely Vancouver must have more magic in its stores than things I could find as easily on the library shelves at home. But after several months I'd begun to read the book and now I was going through it for a second time. I found the language difficult in places but the tales were terrifying and grotesque, compelling in spite of or perhaps because of their complicated wording.

"There's no way, really, to get it on film either," he said suddenly.

"Get what?" I pointed a finger half way down the page I'd been pretending to read.

He lowered the camera and looked out over the pond. "I might get something that will jog my memory, make me remember the smell, the quiet, but that's it. No one who wasn't here will be able to get it from the photographs I take. In a way, it's as useless as a pair of binoculars."

"Why bother then?"

"I keep hoping. I mean it's there, isn't it? I can see it." He looked over at me, shaking his head a little at his own foolishness. "But something's always missing after it's developed."

"Maybe it's because a picture's flat." I nodded at the pond, at the trees, at the sky blue-gold and vast.

"That's part, but it isn't all." He raised the camera again and I went back to the book.

After a while he said, as though there'd been no pause in the conversation, "I can get the ordinary stuff just fine. It's scenery like this, the stuff that's really nice to look at, that won't come out on film. Sometimes I don't think it even exists outside the mind of the person who's looking at it."

"My father says that beauty is in the eye of the beholder." I was attempting to concentrate on what he was saying, trying to follow precisely where his ideas were going. But most of my mind was busy being pleased that he was talking to me at such length, and wondering whether he'd shared these ideas with anyone else. I was thinking that he was handsome.

"The mind. Not the eye. That's the point." He glanced at me and then down at the bullrushes near the shore. "I took a picture of my father's hands. A close-up at the kitchen table. They were all rough and dirty, like usual." He smiled. "My dad thought I was out of my head. But that one came out exactly right. I bet that if I took a picture of a steaming pile of cowshit even in black and white, you'd be able to smell it. But this . . ." He gestured at the brilliant gold of sun on the tops of the trees, the light and the dark reflected in the water, and shook his head. He wrapped the case around the camera and snapped it shut.

"Maybe that's it. Maybe there's no point in trying at all. There just isn't enough to it." He was talking to himself. If I'd continued looking at my book instead of looking at him, it would have made no difference. "Nothing in Donellon seems to have enough to it."

I sighed and looked at my watch. I was getting nowhere.

He shrugged. But as I stood he said, "Would you do something for me first?"

"What?"

"Pose for me. I want to try something."

I considered him suspiciously. "What do you want me to do?"

He laughed. "I just want to take a picture of your face, but I want you to look scared. Okay?" He was putting one camera down on the grass, opening another, arranging, adjusting as he spoke. "Just sit down there, or stand there, it doesn't matter which, and pretend you're looking at something just out of the range of the camera that really terrifies you. A rattlesnake or something."

I shifted uneasily. "Come off it, Noel. I can't do that. I'm no actor."

He really was weird. Jenny was right.

He paused and looked up. "Sure you can do it. What's the worst thing you can think of."

"Mitchell. Eating." I laughed uncomfortably.

"Be serious."

"All right. I'll try."

I did try, but my face felt artificially posed, like a mask. It must have looked the way it felt for he said, "No."

I tried to imagine the house of Usher, but it was impossible to visualize a dank mausoleum on that golden evening. And it wouldn't have helped anyway: I knew that. I could never understand how actors could show emotions, even with their voices, and at school I'd stopped trying to get parts in plays like Jenny did. I preferred to paint sets.

"All right," he said as he snapped one picture after another. "Turn your face a little to the left. No the left, so the sun's on it. That's it. No. Concentrate. That's better. Yes, that's better." Click, wind, click, wind, click.

What was he doing? I knew from the feeling on my face that it wasn't what he'd asked for. Whenever he spoke he drew me even farther away from any hideous vision I was trying to conjure up. At last, he came over and took my head in his hand and turned it the way he wanted it and his touch was so unexpectedly gentle—I couldn't remember ever having been touched that gently—so soft, that I turned toward him in surprise as again the awareness of him went through me. I saw the place on his profile where his throat was hard, where it had been smooth when he was younger, and his presence, his maleness, enfolded me like the smoky bonfire smell of burning leaves, the smell that seemed the same colour as the evening. I looked away.

If I'd been an actor, I could have smiled at him, encouraging him to kiss me. Perhaps have leaned forward and started it myself.

I bent for my book.

"What's the matter?"

"I can't do it any more," I said, not looking at him. "I'm going."

He hesitated for a moment. "I guess I've got enough for now."
He turned back to his cameras, adding something about how the pictures
might have been better if the day had been grey, if he'd done it in black
and white.

As I walked away from him I was aware of my body and the way
I wanted it to look as I'd never been before. In my mind's eye, my skirt
was too long, my socks sliding down toward my shoes, my legs too thin.
I held myself straight, my book at my hip, and although I doubted that
his eyes were on me, it didn't really matter. I'd discovered in myself the
beginnings of my adulthood and my femaleness, and I was confused
enough by that.

My first period came soon after, and I went to tell Mother. She
did not seem to place any emphasis on the fact that she was female, and
her mannerisms would never have been considered "feminine". She was
deliberate and business-like, and her dress and make-up (powder where
her nose shone and a hint of redness on her lips when the occasion was
particularly festive) were governed by what was practical.

Femininity seems to me to be a talent and a skill, like acting, and
some of my friends have had it and some have not. It appears to be less
fashionable today than it was when I was growing up: that fluttering
deference that was intended, I suppose, to be a refinement of femaleness,
allowing it to be taken out in public. I was resentful when I saw others
so good at it, when I had never learned it. A more honest and vigorous
awareness of being a woman—and of being proud of that—seems to be
more highly valued today, among women at least, than is femininity.

And so I told Mother that I had my period, not as a compatriot,
but as a child who was supposed to advise her parent of any physical
aberrations. She responded with the kind of look she gave Mitchell
when he found it impossible to get the buttons to meet their holes on
some shirt she'd bought for him. She hurried off to her room, to get the
things she'd been saving for the occasion.

I was surprised that she'd been thinking about it enough to
prepare for it. When she came back she started to stammer something
about what went where. I took the box and the smaller package from
her, irritated at her confusion, and said in a voice intended to put great
spaces between us, "Please, Mother. I already know." I would never
take my physical problems to her again.

She stared at me, actually concentrating all of her attention on
me, her sharp blue eyes as cold as mine. "Well, you shouldn't," she
said, and paused, eyeing me suspiciously. "I suppose you know what it
means as well?"

"Yes." Bored and slightly supercilious. "The spongy lining of the uterus builds up to receive the fertilized egg . . ."

"Stop it." For a moment I thought she was going to slap my face. But she took a breath and went on. "What it means, Diana, is that you need to stay away from boys. Do you understand me?"

I assured her that I did, and she left the bathroom immediately, perhaps afraid that I'd continue with the technical details of why I should stay away from boys.

I went back to school on Monday, full of my news, and ready to reassume my position as kindred spirit to Jenny Haultain. But Paul had demanded his ring back late on Sunday night, and Jenny wasn't interested in any blood but his.

One cold afternoon about eight months after my arrival in Edmonton, I stood in snow that crunched when I moved on it, and contemplated the purchase of a soft yellow sweater with a turtleneck. It was being modelled at that moment by a headless mannequin in a storefront window on Whyte Avenue, about three doors down from the record shop where I'd found a part-time job.

I looked past it at the store itself: linoleum floors, white neon lights, racks and racks of clothing close together. Jenny would never have set foot in there. And the sweater, when I looked at it again, had a dirty mark at one cuff and a thread coming loose at the collar.

I shook my head at it, shivering, and turned into the four o'clock dusk of the city I hated more and more as the winter ground interminably on. Winters in Ontario were less brutal, it seemed to me then, despite their sudden, furious storms. They were shorter, and the snow was softer.

For the first time I was homesick: not for my home and family, that was certain, but for a countryside that was gentler than this. As I walked, trying to ignore the squeak of snow under my boots that sent cold fingers up my spine like hard chalk on a blackboard, I wished that I'd bought the sweater to add a layer of warmth beneath my coat and wondered how Jenny could still have such power over me after so many years, with so many miles between us. What had we had to cause such a bond in the first place?

But in a town the size of Donellon, she and I must inevitably have been companions: two girls in the same class at school, one the daughter of a doctor, the other of a fairly successful businessman—we really had no alternatives. Our later separation was caused by the fact that we were ill-matched in the first place, and my years of trying to impress her were futile, a waste. Our quasi-friendship was a product of the narrow little snobberies and class structures of the town: we were as influenced by them as the adults were.

I've been as stupid with Madelyn as I was with Jenny, now that I think of it. She wears no rings, no necklaces, no jewellery of any kind, and neither do I any more. She says rings and chains are symbols of the male's possession of the female, gifts given for centuries with linked and gleaming strings attached, and that she'll never see them as innocent little baubles. She says, "You see a fifty-year old woman in the grocery store with diamond earrings, heavy gold bracelets, expensive rings on her fingers, and you can bet your ass that she didn't earn the money that paid for them. When you earn it, you don't spend it on crap like that."

I've used those words myself.

Madelyn wears no make-up, nor do I. She says that if men must face the world bare-faced, pimpled, wrinkled, whatever, then so will she. I would say the same if someone asked me.

I think she's right. I think.

I've never stopped to consider whether I'm adopting principles that I have not invented to please her, or because I believe in them. I wore makeup once for Jenny and now I don't for Madelyn, as though by trying to be like them, I'll ensure a lasting friendship. Imitation is a form of compliment. It doesn't work.

And by a similar token, or the flip side of it, I've done so many things in a deliberate and consistent attempt to be as unlike Mother and Grandmother as I can possibly be, and yet they still haunt my bathroom mirrors.

I seem to be little more than a series of reactions to other people, to be made of fragments that don't belong to me.

Chapter Eight

Westmoreland finds me at the front of the house, pulling weeds from the gravel and adding them to the neat pile I've made on the grass beside me. The heavy wall of dark cloud is still rising in the south, even more forbidding because of its slowness, its apparent determination to meticulously blacken every inch of sky.

"Here you are!" he bellows as he appears at the side of the house and strides toward where I'm sitting on the lawn. "I thought you'd be out back where it's a little cooler."

Relaxing? Under her window? In the lawn swing?

He leans against the fender of his grey car, a little way from me, crossing his thick arms over his chest and his feet at the ankles, and smiles down at what I'm doing. "I'm surprised a weed would dare to grow anywhere in Hilda's territory."

I smile back, cautiously. I know he hasn't come to discuss the recalcitrance of dandelions and quackgrass.

His suit is immaculate and pressed, his black shoes recently polished and what's left of his grey hair is neatly trimmed. Widowers and other suddenly-single, older men I've met have often had a bewildered, slightly unkempt and underweight appearance which seems a cry for help, but there's none of that in him. His high red forehead is spangled with perspiration and his lips are moist and fleshy.

He watches me pull tiny weeds with my index finger and thumb for several moments before he says, "Diana, I'm concerned that you haven't been up to see her. You need to see her and you know it: that's what brought you here." He pauses. "I can go up with you, if it'll make it easier."

I shake my head. "When I'm ready, I can go alone."

"The time may not be as appropriate, later, as it is now. She's a very sick woman."

"If it's too late, it's too late. I can't go up there until I'm ready to." The small dandelion I've gently wrenched from the ground has come away without part of its white root. I've never, not in my entire life I don't think, pulled up an entire dandelion, and I toss this one on my pile with disgust.

"If you let this opportunity pass, you'll regret it until the end of your life." There's a little emphasis on the "your" to remind me of my mortality.

I sigh. "Reverend Westmoreland, I appreciate your concern, and your offer of assistance. But this is between us, between me and her. It's not anything you need to trouble yourself about."

"She's a member of my congregation. I've known your mother for years. I feel an obligation . . ." He stops and looks down at his folded arms. "I want to do whatever I can for her."

His voice is less even than it was and I look up at him curiously. He pulls a huge white handkerchief, white as his stiff collar, from his back pocket and wipes his forehead. "It's very warm here in the sun. Do you think we might walk in the shade a little, while we talk?"

"Of course." I stand and brush the grass from my hands and jeans. I like the feel of the sun, too hot on my face, but I won't argue about it.

"She wants to see you, you know."

I look up at him sharply. "Did she say that?"

He smiles. "Not in so many words. Of course she didn't. She's as stubborn as her daughter. But I can tell."

Again I study his face. There's a tenderness there and I wonder if it would be the same if it were Miss McAllister or Mrs. Kenyon dying in the upstairs room. No doubt it would. That is his job, his perfectly practised persona. Parsona.

We've reached the shade of the tree-lined drive and it's only marginally cooler, even that relief gone within a moment or two after we've entered the shadow. He is walking very slowly with his hands clasped behind his back and I keep obedient pace with him.

"A year or two ago," he says, "there was an incident in the parish, a terrible thing." He's taken out his sermon-voice. It's even, polished, paced. "A young boy, just seventeen years old and the only child of two very fine members of the community, took his father's car out one night and drove it off the end of Maynard Street." He pauses, slowing himself still more. "Perhaps Mitchell told you about it?"

I shake my head. This is the parable part of the sermon, I suppose. It's going to teach me that when a person dies, it's too late to tell her what you wanted to say when she was still alive.

"I don't have anything I want to say to her."

"Just listen for a moment, Diana.

"When he hit the river bank, the car burst into flames. This was an A student. Top of the class. Well-liked by students and teachers. He could have done anything that he wanted with his life. But instead, he decided to end it." He looks at me thoughtfully as though he's moving something around in his mouth with his tongue.

We aren't talking about Mother. We're talking about Noel.

"Over and over again his parents asked themselves what they could have done to prevent it. They tormented themselves with things that you and I might consider silly. They retraced the boy's whole life, berating themselves every time they'd dealt with him in a less than ideal way. It all came down to detail: 'If only I'd let him go camping with his friends'. 'If only I'd told him I was pleased with his marks'. 'If only I hadn't left the car keys on the hall table.' If only, if only, if only. His mother said at one point, 'If only I'd hadn't cooked liver that night. He hated liver.'

"We might consider that silly, you and I, because we know that they didn't cause him to kill himself. And none of those little, last-minute details mattered."

He looks at me for affirmation, but I don't react.

"The truth of the matter, and it took me some time to come to terms with it myself, is that there's nothing anyone could have done. Not one thing. He didn't reach out. He didn't ask for help. He never indicated to anyone that anything was the matter."

Westmoreland's stopped walking now, and so have I, and he's studying my face intently to draw my complete attention to what he's saying. "It seems to me, Diana, that some people are just bent on self-destruction and there's nothing anyone can do about it. Nothing." I can feel the heat of his breath on me. "No one causes another person to kill himself."

"It might have made a difference if the keys weren't there. Maybe he would have asked for help the next day, if he hadn't had the opportunity to kill himself that night. Maybe the situation was so oppressive that the liver was the last straw. Maybe it *was* the liver. How can you ever know?" I speak flatly, as though I'm not really concentrating on what he's saying.

He shakes his head firmly. "I'm beginning to believe that there are certain character types—maybe it's a chemical imbalance or something—character types with a drive to self-destruct . . ."

"We're talking about Noel."

He nods. "Yes."

"That's got nothing to do with this, Reverend Westmoreland. That's done with."

"Your problems with your mother are directly related to Noel's death."

I stare at him astonished—at his conclusion, but especially at his gall.

"They aren't. You didn't even know Noel Fletcher. How can you tell me that he had some chemical imbalance when you didn't even know him?"

"I can't. Not definitely. You're right." He pulls his handkerchief out again and wipes his face, then begins to wave it around while he talks so that he looks a little like Pavarotti. "It's how his death affected you that I want to talk about."

"It's done with. He's been dead for years. And it had nothing at all to do with my leaving. Except that the same thing that killed him drove me away as well. It's this stupid, oppressive, sick little town, people like my mother and her friends, and my brother, and everything they stand for—which is nothing. All that matters to them is one-upmanship, is being better than the next person: being richer, better-behaved, having the most successful children. People, what's inside them, relationships don't matter at all. There are no people in this town, just stupid shells of people." I walk a few steps forward, irritated with him for letting me go on, for not interrupting to argue with me. Does he think he's a goddamned psychoanalyst or something? Letting me 'talk it through'? I despise the stupid manipulative role he's playing. "Even the weather squeezes you."

I turn back to look at him. "He was going to leave, to get out, but she pushed him. *She* was the last straw for him. It wasn't anything new, though. It wasn't his death that made me feel about this place, about her, the way I did: it was there all along. All she wanted to do was to overpower everyone she knew. She asked for them to leave her. She pushed them away."

"Let's go back to Noel's death," he says gently.

I shake my head. "Let's not." I have already said too much. I have no idea how much he knows about that night. What will I say if he asks me, How was it, exactly, that your mother pushed Noel over that edge, Diana? I do not want to discuss, describe that night to him.

"It seemed to me at the time that you felt he'd done something courageous."

I claw through my memory, wondering how he could have come to that conclusion. Come up with nothing. Shake my head.

"Suicide is never courageous. Courage is facing the ordeals life has to offer."

This is the moral, then, of the parable he's constructed. I scoop a handful of gravel from the drive and begin to pitch small stones into the trees. Shit.

"Platitudes."

He steps beside me, one hand up as though to touch my arm, but then he lets it drop. "That may sound like a platitude to you, but I believe in it," he says. "Your mother has shown that kind of courage, you know."

And I have not. I ran away.

"You know," he goes on, "I've discovered something in my work that may not have occurred to you. When a person dies, in an accident or from a sudden illness, the relatives often blame God. 'Why did He do that to me?' they ask. 'What have I done to offend Him? I hate Him.' And then, of course, they feel guilty for having such emotions.

"But in suicides, the emphasis shifts a little. Instead of God, the relatives and friends blame themselves, blame other people, and blame the victim. If 'victim' is the right word: the survivors are the true victims in a suicide. The blame and rage and guilt are just as real, and just as futile and misplaced. Your mother was trying to protect you. She didn't kill Noel."

"I don't believe I mentioned him. You did. Noel's got nothing to do with this."

He obviously knows something about that night. Now I recall that Whittick knew, as well. Mother called him. Perhaps everyone in the whole of Donellon knew. Knows. Maybe it's become part of the history of the town. Like Jenny's pregnancy. Inscribed in time.

I want to get away from him.

"I think my coming here was a mistake." I'm digging in my shoulder bag for my keys.

"Look." He sounds firmer, almost angry. "I've just been up there with her. You have not. She's a strong woman, always has been, and I admire her very much. She's suffered terribly, and is suffering now, more than she lets on to anyone, certainly more than you'll allow yourself to contemplate, Diana. If you went up there you would see." He snorts deeply, like a bull, angry. "I wouldn't dare to suggest that perhaps that's what you're afraid of. You helped make her life difficult and now you're making her dying difficult as well. You have it in you to ease it a little, to seal something up that was adding to her pain. Stop thinking only of yourself. You owe it to her, to go up there and let her pass away with peace between you."

Would it be so difficult to go up and do as he's asked, to smooth it over? I imagine myself doing that, one step after another, and shake my head.

I am afraid. He's right about that. What I feel is fear. It's immobilized me, but I don't know what it is that I'm afraid of.

I pick up another stone and throw it hard. It hits a tree trunk and ricochets straight back before it falls into the underbrush. "If I go up there, it won't be out of pity."

"I'm sure it won't." He sighs, sounding tired.

I look back at him. "Do you know that Noel feels you haven't any right to be here?"

"Noel?"

I flush. "Mitchell. I mean Mitchell, of course. He thinks you're intruding on a family matter."

"I'm sorry to hear it. I'll talk to him."

"But you aren't going to do anything about it?"

"I think it's up to your mother who she wants to see at this point." His voice is very calm.

He doesn't bother to try to keep up to me as I walk quickly back toward the house. By the time I've reached the cars, the mask of cloud has hidden the sun. It feels no cooler.

As I'm about to back out he comes to stand beside the driver's door, looking contrite. As I shift into reverse, the car stalls, and I sit with my hands on the keys in the ignition, waiting to hear what he'll say.

"I hope I haven't driven you off. You know I never intended to do that."

"Mitchell wants me to leave. You want me to stay. Both of you tell me you're acting in her best interests."

"What do you want?"

"A drink of scotch. That's all. I'm too damned tired to drive all the way back to Toronto, so you needn't worry. I'm just going to the vendor's. There's nothing but bloody sherry in the house."

The car doesn't start again immediately and he pauses on the porch, waiting to offer me assistance. His sense of pastoral duty, his professional talent to turn the other cheek, knows no limit whatsoever. But the engine turns over, and I'm out.

I drive slowly down the hill toward the bridge, groping in my bag on the passenger seat for my lighter because the one on the dashboard has not popped out again.

I'm missing Madelyn.

I was very comfortable with her, accustomed to telling her everything that happened to me, and to listening to her talk about the things that had happened to her. I made anecdotes out of incidents at work, revising them in my mind until I had the wording that would amuse her. I told her the things that hurt me, some of the fears I had. I knew her so well—I knew how she'd react to whatever I was seeing, thinking, doing. It was as though she were with me all the time, watching what I watched and hearing what I heard.

I wish she were here, that Madelyn. She'd be irritated by my inability to go forward or to go back, to go up or to stay down. But she wouldn't push. And she would listen.

But that Madelyn does not exist, and I must remember that. Our friendship was convenience to her, a relationship to stop the gap until she met a man she could share herself with. I thought if one of us did that to us, it would be me. I was the one who actively sought relationships, discarding them quickly when they weren't right, when they didn't measure up to what Madelyn and I felt must be possible.

And then, as it turned out, Madelyn was the one who lacked the patience. And now when I need to talk to her, Sonny is there, and I must wait until the time is more convenient. And when it is, I don't feel like talking.

I want this to be over. I want to return to Edmonton where I will begin again to learn to live alone, as I set out to do all those years ago when I left on the train for Vancouver. It's been a long time since I had no one at all to talk to, but I feel strangely emotionless about it. I can't even work up a proper anger with Madelyn at the moment. I feel numb.

I've got to get this done with here, somehow. As long as I postpone this, avoid them, Mother, Westmoreland, Mitchell, I'm as thick in it as I ever was, bound to them as firmly as I was to Madelyn when we were close. Being truly isolated, complete unto myself, would mean that I would not react against them, either, as I am doing now.

In order to touch the strength I know is in me to do the rest of it alone, I have to get through this. It's stupid to depend on other people.

The sky is completely overcast now and from the bridge the river looks steel grey, turbulent and dangerous, but there's still no breeze on the branches of the trees. The only air on my face comes through the open window from the motion of the car.

Over there is the foot of Maynard Street where that kid in that car came hurtling through—to roll, and roll, and burst into hot flame that lit the night. From inside, the headlights made a jumble of the trees before the brighter light consumed him.

From a glass jar filled with buttons of every shape and colour and size which she'd placed on the table next to my new aloe vera plant, Madelyn was extracting those buttons which were small and white and had four holes, in an attempt to match the ones still secured to the silk shirt in her lap.

"Is it a joke?" she asked.

I turned the television on, the volume down, so we wouldn't miss the news, and came back to sit at the table across from her.

"Is what a joke?"

"You buy a plant every time you stop seeing someone. They stand around here like memorials or something."

I smiled. "You're crazy. You could find a unifying theme in a pile of dirty laundry."

"Why not? But look around you, Diana. That African violet over there was David Fishman. The dracaena was Bob Kimball. And here is Stuart Kennelly: an aloe vera plant." She held a button, which definitely didn't match, against the shirt.

"And the spider plant was the day Rosen made me manager. Buying plants cheers me up, that's all. Some people buy clothes, I buy plants."

In the bathroom were two that I'd brought from the last apartment, and on top of the refrigerator, the prayer plant that Madelyn had given me for Christmas, "to save the souls of the others."

She pointed at the aloe vera on the table. "Nonetheless, this little monument suggests to me that we've seen the last of Stuart. Am I right?"

I shrugged. "I'm not really interested in him. I knew that before I went out with him."

"I liked him."

"Then you go out with him."

"It sounded to me like you liked him, too."

"As a friend. Nothing more."

"Then why did you go out with him?"

"What is this? An inquisition? I haven't noticed you folding sheets with anybody lately."

Madelyn hadn't been anywhere with a man for about two years. They asked, from time to time, but she refused. She couldn't see any point in wasting time, she said.

"At least I know why I haven't. I've been scared. After going through one divorce, I'm not anxious for a repeat performance. I'll probably get over it eventually. I hope. But you keep starting them and then stopping them."

"It's never right."

She shook her head and slowly emptied the button bottle onto the table.

"Then, why?"

"He got tickets to Nana Mouskouri. I told you that."

"You are a conniving female."

"No, I'm not. I intended to pay for mine. He was the conniving one. He came into the shop last week and said he wanted to see the concert, and he didn't want to go alone. Seemed reasonable to me. I've known Stuart for years, and I thought he understood that I wasn't interested in anything more than a friendship."

"But you are."

"Not with him. He's interesting—very bright, but he'd make a lousy mate. He's totally disorganized. He must make a bundle teaching at the university, but he can't hang onto it. He's always writing bad cheques. That's how I met him, when he came in to make good a cheque for some records he'd bought. He's been on his own for about six months, and he's looking for a manager. Anyway, I said I'd go, but I was paying for my own ticket."

"And?"

"It wasn't until I took my wallet out half way to the auditorium that I realized he wasn't going to let me pay him back. It went downhill from there."

She glanced at me as she began to pull buttons back into the button jar. "Being a bad manager doesn't mean he'd be a bad company. If he likes you and you don't want to look after him, he can learn to look after himself. You haven't given him a chance."

"Thanks, Mother," I said. "I like, liked, him as a friend, but as soon as it threatened to go onto another level, I wasn't interested. He's not trainable. I'm not surprised his wife left him. It must have been a full time job looking after him." I paused, studying her. "What are you talking about, anyway? You left a marriage that had exactly those same problems."

"Among others. But what's right for me isn't necessarily what's right for you." She shrugged.

"I don't need anyone to need me, either. Love and dependence are two entirely different things."

The news was over and I'd never got around to turning the volume up. There hadn't been anything on about Proulx, I didn't think, so it didn't matter.

"They're assessing Proulx before he goes to court," I said as I turned the t.v. off and went to plug in the kettle for tea.

"Assessing who?"

"Proulx. That guy who killed his mother."

She sighed. "They'll find him not guilty by reason of insanity and he'll be out, scot-free, rehabilitated, within a year or two. They'll figure any son-of-a-bitch who'd kill his mother has got to be insane, by definition. The whole system makes me sick."

"You don't think he's crazy?"

"Anyone who kills anyone is crazy, but that doesn't mean he should get off."

I was morbidly curious, drawn to every facet of this murder. I'd been wondering about the funeral. Who would go to a funeral that had been made necessary by such circumstances? How could a family ceremony, as a funeral certainly was, take place when one member of the family had killed another? It had been private, according to the papers, and no mention made in the obituaries. Would they have let Proulx out, if he'd wanted to attend? No, that was ridiculous. And yet, he was innocent until proven guilty. Refusing him permission would have been pre-judgement, wouldn't it?

He was forty-five years old and had never had as much as a speeding ticket in his life. Neighbours, the people who'd lived near the house he and his mother shared, were shocked. As neighbours always are. They said things about the lovely garden they'd had, but what I wanted to know from them was what she'd done to make him do it.

Madelyn said, "I don't agree with capital punishment, but there has to be some kind of retribution. They can't let a man get away with killing a helpless old woman, with a pair of kitchen scissors." She pulled the bottle closer and stirred the contents with her index finger, peering at the newly exposed buttons on the surface. She was working idly now, absently, having abandoned the search for an appropriate button. Someday she'd probably take the shirt to the Goodwill Store. "It's got to do with strength. The law has to provide some compensation, protection, for the weaker ones at least—older people, children. People who by their physical structures are the potential victims."

"Just physically weaker? Psychologically doesn't count?"

She looked up. "I don't know. Both, I guess. But physically, particularly."

"Maybe he was the victim. Maybe she wore away at him day after day, drip, drip, drip, until he couldn't take it any more."

"He could have left."

"Maybe he wasn't even strong enough to do that."

"Diana," she said, "don't be thickheaded. Nobody asks to get killed. That's what I mean about protection, or deterrence maybe. No matter what she did or didn't do, she was bound to lose in the end because her son was a forty-five-year-old male who weighed about sixty pounds more than she did. No contest."

And, I wondered, if they'd both been female, about the same height and weight? Then would the psychological strength of one have had more bearing on the case?

Everything has to do with strength. Women are more resilient than men, more self-reliant. They've had to be for centuries. I sometimes think that women who cast off their fears, and their appearances of it, will never find a mate. The strength is in them not to need, not to depend, for people have been depending on them for centuries, forever. It's a strength that isn't found too often outside women, although women have gone a long way toward maintaining the illusion that it is.

But it was that strength, misused, that made my mother what she was. And Grandmother as well. Theirs was clad in iron, and there was no room for warmth in it.

I thought I could love Brian as I'd loved no one since Noel. He was strong and independent, a companion. Neither of us leaned. For a long time I thought we'd found what I believed that both of us had been looking for: a situation in which we could pursue our separate careers, without competition, without strings. We were monogamous, and we trusted that in one another, which left us free to spend evenings working at the office, to go to lunch with business associates, to travel when we had to, without fearing jealous rages at home on our return.

Just after Mitchell had been to visit, Brian began to talk about wanting a family. I was reluctant, for I'm not fond of children, but I didn't want to lose him. And so I listened: to his promise that we would share responsibilities, to his assertion that having a child would not interfere with my job for more than a month or two, to his conviction that eventually my biological clock would go off too, and to his statistical proof, gained from extensive reading in the area, that if we delayed, the risks of abnormalities in the infant would increase.

We could afford a nanny, he said. And a house. There would be nothing to it.

We argued about it, off and on, all one winter and all one summer. I'd almost accepted his thesis that I had strong, if latent, maternal instincts, when he got sick. Over the next few months, I discovered that I had no maternal instincts at all.

He'd never had so much as a cold in all the time I'd known him, and very little illness in his life before. At first, we thought it was exhaustion, too many years of working too many hours. But he went to a doctor who sent him for tests, and we learned that he had mononucleosis. Immediately he got sicker.

For weeks he did nothing but nibble without interest at food he was no longer interested in preparing, and sleep. He slept fitfully at night, disturbing my sleep, and napped all day on the couch in front of the television set. He worried, constantly but unenthusiastically, about his business, so I ran back and forth between the record shop and The Wind and The Snow. When I got home he was angry that I'd been out so long.

He was depressed, and I tried to draw him out of it with conversation until it came to me that when he wasn't up and active, we had nothing much to talk about. We'd avoided physical contact since he got sick, partly because he was too ill for passion, but also because I didn't want to catch the disease from him. He suspected that I was seeing someone else, accused me of consorting with a different friend, acquaintance, associate almost every day.

He didn't want to hear what I'd done at work, what I'd seen on the way home, how much tomatoes cost per pound. It seemed to me that there wasn't much of anything to our relationship at all. I quit trying to revive him and became silent, and he reacted to that with the same mixture of anger and self-pity as he did to everything I did. He was petulant at my ability to get up and go to work. He was frightened at being sick, and at my health, and he wanted me to stay home and fill his time, to take his fear away. He became weepy in his frustration at himself.

The time came when I couldn't stand to look at him, to see the weakness in him. I found that I despised him and his need for me. I didn't want my resources to be the ones he needed to tap. I wanted him to be my equal. I'd seen the soft underbelly of him, which had been there all along, and I would never not see it again. If there were children, I would be the caretaker, for all of them.

I stayed until he was recovered, but even after he was better, I heard the traces of his need in everything he said. Just before I left, he said to me, "Blue is a cold colour. Eyes shouldn't come in blue."

I felt alternately guilty and lonely after I'd packed and left him. Sometimes I felt both at once. But I couldn't change the way I'd felt, the way I continued to feel, about him. Once the crack had opened up and I'd seen in, I couldn't forget that it was there.

I never told him what the problem was. I couldn't have. He

would have been astonished, hurt. "But I was sick," he would have said. "I'm better now. I never get sick." And then, considering, he would have added, "How can you be such a fucking selfish bitch?"

Madelyn made me see that there was no possible future in that relationship, that nothing between Brian and me could have succeeded. We were wrong for one another.

I thought it was my problem, but she placed it in a larger context: women, children, men, traditional roles. Fortunate, she said, that I'd got out of there before we married, before any children came. She made me see myself as having acted more wisely than I'd given myself credit for. She made me feel free instead of cold.

But now, two years later, Madelyn folded the silk shirt neatly and put it down on the floor beside her. "Maybe we just haven't put enough into our relationships," she said. "Maybe the problem is that we aren't willing to work on them."

"Madelyn, what are you talking about? You've said yourself, a hundred times, that we don't need to put up with all the things that women did before, and that men are having trouble adjusting to that. 'We're out of sync,' you said. 'Maybe the next generation will be better.' "

"I don't know."

"You're just horny."

"Maybe I am. Maybe that's enough reason to put an effort into something. Not just sex but love and hugs and companionship. I mean, you and I are good friends, and if one of us got sick for months or suddenly became incapable of handling our finances, or something, it wouldn't matter to what we have. Would it?"

"Because it wouldn't change anything about us. Because neither of us would expect that the other one would 'fix it', 'take care of it', 'make it go away'. We'd just get through it together. Women are stronger."

"So what? They can't live alone. It isn't natural. It doesn't feel natural to me."

"Living alone is better than living with compromises."

"Nothing's perfect."

"Oh, Madelyn. How much imperfection are you willing to live with? That's the question. You want a cup of tea?"

She shook her head. "You know what I think? I think we think the men are the ones who are all fouled up, but I think that we don't have it sorted out properly yet, either. The more I think about it, the more confused I get. I don't want to be alone, Diana, not forever. But now my standards are so high that no one can fit into them. I don't want to lower my standards, and I don't want to be alone. The women's movement has created a kind of ideal situation in our minds which no one can live up to, not even us. I think we've gone overboard on the opposite side of the boat, but we're still floundering around in the ocean."

"It's our ocean, for a change."

"Small comfort, when you're drowning."

"You want things back the way they used to be?"

"Of course not. But there has to be a middle ground. But if there's a middle ground, then it's the women who have to give. Again. I just don't know. I'm tired of being a god-damned groundbreaker, a carrier of the banner, and yet if I put it down, just for a minute, and say to a man, 'I don't care what you believe in, I just want a hug,' then I'm a heretic, a traitor."

"Out there, there's someone who's exactly right. You just have to wait until he comes along."

She laughed. "That's what my mother said when I was about fifteen. I don't know if it's true. Especially if we're wandering around with the assumption that men are guilty and never give them the chance to prove that they're not."

The longer I lived with Madelyn, the more I sounded like her, and the less she was beginning to sound like herself. She'd taught me so much about why I was the way I was. We both knew it wasn't easy, but it was the way it had to be.

I assumed it was a slump, something she'd get over.

It wasn't.

Chapter Nine

The telegram from Father arrived on a Wednesday evening near the end of October when Mother was down three in a six spades contract, doubled. She'd just remarked to Mrs. Gardiner across from her, the person she held responsible for their reaching that impossible contract in the first place, that only a miracle could prevent their losing the last two tricks as well, when Hilda came in with the envelope.

Four of the women were at a card table which Hilda had set up in the middle of the living room rug, and from the dining room where I was half-heartedly working on a jigsaw puzzle I could see only Mother at one end of the bridge table, and Miss McAllister and Mrs. Robinson who were sitting out that rubber on the chesterfield.

I'd ignored the temptation to accompany Hilda to the door when the bell went, despite the fact that a ringing doorbell on a Wednesday night was extraordinary, just as I'd repressed the urge several times earlier to get up and stretch my legs or to ask for a brownie from the plate on the sideboard opposite me. By suppressing every sign of enthusiasm I'd hoped to communicate my contempt for the women, but so far my behaviour had apparently served only to make them forget that I was there.

Before she'd been stranded in that six spades contract, Mother had been listing yet again the difficulties of accommodating an invalided mother ("She has her own ways of doing things, and they're not mine") and two intractable children, the younger of whom was always whining and hungry and the elder never satisfied no matter how many new freedoms she was allowed ("She's only thirteen, after all").

Mother was in her early forties. She'd put on some weight since Mitchell was born, but her weight was solid and hard, and she'd grown not softer, but more massive. If her upper arms had any flab to them, her dark-coloured, sleeved dresses did not reveal it. If her stomach and hips were fleshy, corsets and girdles concealed that too. Her legs were firm and strong, her best feature, slenderer than the rest of her, but they too were always covered, in silk stockings that glistened and made a slickering noise when she crossed her legs: which she did at the ankles, and never at the knees.

Ladies didn't cross their legs at the knees. Ladies didn't spread their skirts around them before they sat down. Ladies never raised their hands above their shoulders in public. They did not, therefore, apply their lipstick at the dinner table. They never went downtown without gloves, or to church without a hat.

My mother was a lady, by her own definition of it. This was not a concession to being female for the opposite of "lady" was not "gentleman," but "tramp." She was never unkempt. When she appeared in the hall, first thing in the morning, her greying hair was already pulled back into a roll at the back of her head and she was clad from neck to ankle in a full-length dressing gown. She didn't go downstairs until she was fully dressed, and since I'd turned twelve I was expected to dress before breakfast, too.

Her countenance was usually serious, perpetually ready to assume an expression of disapproval, and she found plenty to disapprove of in those she had to live with. When she smiled, she always kept something back. It was as though there was a perfectly ordered world inside her head which provided her with the gauge she needed to judge the world outside. That inner world was hers, and she wouldn't come completely out of it. We could not have her, her expression seemed to say. We would not possess her.

I didn't want to, anyway. I thought her old-fashioned. I thought her manner of dressing outmoded and her endless sets of rules foolish. I complied with them in front of her, mockery in my manner as I offered my seat to an adult or spread my table napkin in my lap before I raised my fork, and I flaunted them when I was away from her. I wouldn't let her have me, either.

Mother talked to her women friends in a low voice that she used with no one else. It gave the illusion that she was confiding in them, telling them all of the things that she could say to no one else. But she was not. She never mentioned the silences that grew like brick and mortar between her and Father. They rarely exchanged a word.

I think that spouses were a measure of one's worth to that group, even to Miss McAllister who attributed her lack of one to the war. Other members of one's family were fair targets for complaint and condemnation, but husbands were not mentioned except in passing. ("While Harold was out getting the car . . .") And yet the support and sympathy Mother received from her friends about the rest of us was used as additional cement to seal and thicken the wall between her and Father: because the women understood, she was convinced of his unreasonableness.

Mother and Father rarely argued. Theirs was an extraordinarily polite estrangement. I felt pressed by their silences. The air in the house was cotton batting when both of them were in it, and I tiptoed through it, silent too, finding it hard to breathe.

Mother was in good spirits that evening and the women's chatter irritated me. I despised them. I wanted to go out, and had asked to do so at the dinner table but Mother'd said, "It's a school night," as though I'd been bereft of brains to consider making such a request.

"So what?" I'd said, in exactly the same tone of voice. "I just want to go for a walk."

"Watch your tongue," said Grandmother opposite.

She'd had surgery on her ankle during the summer and was becoming more mobile. She was stronger, physically, than she'd been in years, and was able, when she was rested, to walk with increasing steadiness with two canes. Father had taken out the elevator.

Mitchell watched the three of us curiously, shovelling food into his mouth.

"I'll handle this, Mother," my mother said. "You stay in, Diana, on week nights. You know the rules."

"I have no homework."

"I don't care. A rule is a rule. Take the plates to the kitchen."

"That's Hilda's job." I only dared use that tone when Father wasn't home. I was not particularly afraid of him either, but he didn't argue back. He responded with a lowering of the eyebrows which suggested that something terrible might happen if I didn't stop immediately.

"Not tonight, it's not." Mother's voice was rising and becoming more brittle, and her eyes were going back and forth from me to Grandmother.

"Edith, you take too much from the girl."

"I'll handle it, Mother."

"I'll take the dishes out," said Mitchell cheerfully, his mouth empty for once.

"Shut up, Mitchell," I said, standing with two plates.

Mother glanced at him as though she wished he'd take my advice. She said, "Don't be rude to your brother, Diana."

Mitchell smiled victoriously.

Our dinner conversations were like that when Father wasn't home, filled with verbal battles that were left off only to be resumed the next time we sat down together. No one ever won them, of course, but Mitchell always thought he had, which aggravated me even further.

When the women had arrived for bridge, Grandmother had gone

upstairs. ("Never had much use for ladies' groups," she'd said.) Mitchell had gone up, too, at quarter to eight. I had another hour, but I'm sure I would have been happier if I had no time left at all, if I'd been forced for some reason by Mother to leave the dining room. I was trapped.

I fitted another piece of grey-white into the sky and looked with disgust at the hundreds of other pieces spread around the table. I'd chosen the puzzle from the stack of them in the basement storage cupboard, selected it particularly because I knew it was very difficult. I remembered my parents working on it together years before and complaining about how difficult it was. I didn't recall that they'd ever completed it.

But by choosing it, I'd snared myself. I was sick of it with only the border done and the other pieces turned right way up, but I couldn't leave it now when they'd all notice if I moved. She would say: "Thought it might be a little much for you. Be sure you put it away before you go upstairs."

Women Playing Bridge While Girl Does Jigsaw Puzzle. I was stapled into the genteel tableau and every voice inside me was shouting to scramble out. I didn't look up when Hilda said, "Mrs. Guthrie, this has just come for you." It seemed to me that only an act of God could prevent my spending the rest of my life, head down, fitting one piece of sky into another.

"Dear Lord," Mother breathed, dropping her two remaining cards onto the green baize cover of the card table as I raised my head. "It's a telegram."

The two women on the chesterfield came immediately to the table, their backs to me cutting off my view of Mother.

"You'll have to open it," said Mrs. Kenyon at Mother's elbow.

"I can't. Not for a moment, anyway." There was an unusual note in her voice—fear, I think—which frightened me.

"Well," said Mrs. Robinson gently, "it isn't Wallace or it would have been the police here. I'm sure he's still at the office."

"Perhaps we should call him," said Mrs. Kenyon.

"And not the children, or your mother," added Miss McAllister almost cheerfully. She'd antagonized the four of them earlier by making a grand slam on the first hand of the evening, and she'd been trying to make amends ever since.

"Who then?" asked Mrs. Williams after a small silence.

"Perhaps it isn't bad news, after all," said Miss McAllister.

"Do you want me to . . ." Mrs. Kenyon leaned forward toward

Mother, toward the telegram, her hand out.

There was the weight of the cotton batting again on my chest, heavy on my arms, my legs.

"No, Margaret. I'll do it. If you'll excuse me, please . . ." Her voice still wasn't very strong. "I think I'll go up. I'd prefer to look at it upstairs."

"Of course," someone said gently.

"I'll come with you," said Mrs. Kenyon, firm. "You others wait down here. I'm sure everything is just fine. It's probably addressed wrong, intended for someone else."

I heard them climb the stairs.

Hilda came through to the dining room, twisting her hands together, and went back into the kitchen. I wondered how she could move at all. I waited, staring at a piece of puzzle and at the place where it belonged. Back and forth, my eyes moved between the space and the piece of grey I knew would fill it.

Then Mrs. Kenyon spoke again, back downstairs.

"It was Wallace, after all."

I looked fast toward the living room but could see none of them now from where I sat.

"What was it?"

"No, Enid. He's all right. Alive. But he isn't coming home."

Into the silence I thought I would lower my forehead toward the pieces of puzzle, but I couldn't move.

"Ever?"

Silence that must have been assent, because someone said, "It's another woman."

"He says not," said Mrs. Kenyon flatly. "He says a lot of things, none of which is any business of ours."

"Where is he?"

"He sent it from Toronto. Lord knows where he might be by now."

They all began to talk at once.

"How could he . . ."

"It makes no sense. There must be someone else."

"Edith is a saint."

"She certainly doesn't deserve this."

"She never said a word against him, the poor soul . . ."

" . . . no worse a wife than any of us."

There was a long silence, then.

And into it, Mrs. Kenyon said, "Perhaps you're right. About the other woman. He wouldn't admit it, of course. The . . . I'm going to go up and tell her. She might feel better."

"Some little snippet half his age."

"The money. She'd be after money."

"That telegram. It must have cost . . ."

" . . . and with her mother, and the children . . ."

"The children. Dear Lord. Diana's at the table." Miss McAllister appeared at the door of the dining room and said in a very different voice, "Diana. You're still here. You just go up to your room and do your homework now. You must go up there. Everything will be all right."

When I went up, I said to myself that I wouldn't come out of my room again until Father came back home. I lay face down in the darkness and pulled the pillow over my head, afraid that I'd hear the sounds of my mother crying but I don't think she did, and stared at the sheet against my face. After a long time, I heard the car start and when everything in the house was quiet I went back down to the dining room and swept the pieces of puzzle back into the box, even the border that I'd finished, and put the cover on it. I looked for a moment at the picture on the front, remembering my parents' heads almost touching, but not quite, as they worked together on it many years before.

I wondered why people bothered with jigsaw puzzles anyway, when it was clear from the pictures on the front exactly how they'd turn out. What challenge was there in that?

Nothing like it had ever happened in Donellon, at least not to anyone polite. No one at school spoke of it to me, nor did they speak to me of anything, and so I felt avoided and at the same time intensely studied. Mother's friends backed away to give her time to recover. She accomplished this in her room, primarily, and Grandmother didn't come out of her room very often either.

Mitchell and Hilda and I seemed to be alone in the house. When Mitchell asked where Father was, I told him to shut up. He shrugged, as though he'd expected nothing more than that from me, and as though he hadn't really cared that much to know. It was Mother he missed, and he never asked about her.

Hilda seemed quieter and busier than usual.

The school nurse, Mrs. Harper, a tall thin woman with orange hair, called me into her office three weeks after Father left and asked me to sit down. When I had, on a chair beside the cot where sick students got to rest until their parents came to pick them up, she asked if there was anything I wanted to talk about. She looked nervous. I said that I was fine. She asked if I'd had any headaches or other unusual symptoms. I pointed out that I hadn't missed any school all year. She said that was good and sent me back to class.

One Sunday morning very early, when it was barely light outside, I awoke with the sense that I'd been awakened by someone in the hall outside my room. I opened my bedroom door just enough to see Grandmother standing, fully dressed, in the doorway to her room, the room which used to be for guests. She was still unsteady on her canes but she seemed less aged out of her wheelchair, more powerful all the time. She was glaring at someone who was standing in the bathroom doorway, out of my line of vision.

It was Mother. I couldn't see her face, but I heard the surprise in her voice.

"Mother!" she said. "What on earth are you doing up at this hour?" She started across the hall and I saw that she was wearing her blue plaid dressing gown. "Let me help you back into your room."

"Oh no, you don't," Grandmother replied. "I've been awake all night and now there are a few things I'm going to say to you."

She gave a warning flick with her cane at the hem of Mother's dressing gown and Mother backed away.

"I don't know what you think you're doing, Edith Wishart," Grandmother continued, "but you've made a terrible mistake. It isn't proper, and it will be the ruination of your children."

"Mother . . ."

"Just be quiet and listen to me. You may think this is all very modern and good, but it is not. It most definitely is not." She shook her head, her sharp blue eyes sparking, her expression livid. "If you don't change your mind this instant and insist that he come back home, you'll rue the day you sent him out for the rest of your miserable life. You make some effort, do you hear me? Wash your face and comb your hair and tell him to come back." She adjusted her weight on her feet, her eyes cautioning Mother not to speak during the pause: she wasn't finished. "Your father and I had some trying times, let me tell you. Don't you think we didn't. But we didn't quit. We stuck it out to the bitter end, do you hear me, Edith? Leavenworths stick it through. Wallace may not be perfect, but you married him. You made your bed: you lie in it. Now, go out and bring him back."

"I don't know where he is."

Grandmother drew herself to her full height. "In the meantime, Edith, I refuse to look as though I'm condoning this immorality by staying here for all of Donellon to watch and comment. I'm moving to the hotel until I find more suitable accommodation. And," she brandished her stick again at Mother's hem, "I won't set foot again in this house until your husband has returned."

She turned, her shoulders straight, and walked slowly, painfully, back into her room. She closed her door.

Mother saw me peering through the crack as she turned toward her own room but she didn't seem to care that I'd overheard. She paused and closed her eyes for a moment, putting one hand out toward the wall to steady her. She took a deep breath and opened them again, and her face was composed and her eyes cool blue and strong.

"I don't know where he is," she repeated, not to me but to the air. Or God. "I don't care where he is. I don't even care where he is."

That morning, later, after Hilda had taken Grandmother and her suitcase to the Donellon Hotel, Mother and Mitchell and I attended church for the first time in almost a month. The three of us sat alone in the front pew, in full view of rest of the congregation. Mother had led us to that seat, her head back and her shoulders straight, and now she was singing the hymns and repeating the prayers loudly and evenly.

It was during that Sunday morning service that my brief and guilty moments of anger with Father disappeared and my rage with Mother took hold. She had driven him out. She had reduced the family to three. She'd shamed me before these people and I hated her.

In the intersection at the four-way stop at the top of the hill on the Leavenworth side of the river, the Toyota stalls and refuses to start again. After several minutes during which I alternately attempt to get it started and to let it sit in case it's flooded, a middle-aged couple pulls a cream and wood-grained station wagon in behind me and he climbs out of the driver's side. I'd like to tell him that I can handle this without assistance but I can see from his set expression that he's determined to take over and probably prepared to argue if I resist his offer.

He introduces himself as Donald MacDonald, " 'Mac' for short," and asks me to get out of the car. Before he does anything else, he must satisfy himself that the problem is not an incompetent driver, that the car really will not start and that the turning of its key indeed produces nothing now but an ominous little click. He gets out and goes around to the front and I stand by the open hood with my arms crossed and my teeth clenched. Would he have done this if I'd been male? Tried to start it, taken over without consultation? Of course not.

His amusement at my suggestion that he might have booster

cables in his car further infuriates me, and I'm angry with myself for having asked him. I forgot where I was. Here, booster cables are the tools of a mechanic. In Edmonton, they're nearly as standard as spare tires. When it's thirty-five below, it can be a four-hour wait for a tow truck, and self-sufficiency is only common sense.

I slam down the hood without explaining my question to him, once he's had a thorough, inconclusive look around inside. People who are in quandaries as I am now should always be left alone. They should not be burdened with the necessity to be polite on top of everything else.

"We could push it out of the roadway," I say and he nods.

"Bigger problem than I can help you with," he says. "Might be expensive before you're through."

I want to make certain that the car's in neutral before we try to move it, but Mac for Short is there before me, almost rude as he pushes me out of the way and assumes that he will take the driver's door and steering wheel while I push from the back. I think he thinks he's being gallant.

When his wife gets out of their car to ask if she can help, only half-way out of the car and in a tone that suggests that she doesn't really mean it, he instructs her to stay right where she is and mutters something to me about her back.

We at last manage to move the car against a curb and out of the way of traffic, not that there have been more than three or four cars past in the last ten minutes. Then he says they'll drive me to the service station. I refuse his offer, thanking him for all they've done already, but he's insistent, determined to play the role of saviour for as long as he is able.

They appear to be in their early sixties and I wonder if they have so much time on their hands that they must drive around looking for good deeds to perform. I feel immediately contrite for such cynicism, but his brand of kindness is irritating because it whittles away the self-respect of the beneficiary.

I climb into the back seat of their station wagon, hemmed in by kindnesses, and listen as she prattles sympathies and tells me how fortunate I am to have escaped before the downpour. I would welcome rain.

One block later, just as she's asked me where I'm from, he pulls to a stop in front of Zimmerman's Texaco and I get out quickly, murmuring thanks. I watch them drive away.

As soon as I'm rid of them I know that my irritation with their generosity was disproportionate, and before I go into the service station

I make an effort to relax my shoulders and my forehead. It doesn't do much good. If only the shower in the house weren't across the hall from Mother's room. If only it would rain.

"Excuse me."

I approach the broad back of a navy coverall worn by a man who is noisily poking around in the change compartment of an open chocolate bar and gum machine. It's not Mr. Zimmerman, who I'd assumed would be there as he always was when Father brought in his car, nor is it one of his employees. Before he turns around, I know that it is Beak.

He stands slowly and turns a full and curious face toward me. His blond hair's receded considerably and his pate is pink. He's about the same size that he was in high school but then more of it was muscle. He recognizes me as well and his expression softens, his brown eyes beginning the smile.

I briefly return his smile and then turn toward the big glass window, looking out at the street I've just come down.

"I rented a car in Toronto. It's broken down, there at the corner, at Maple Street."

Behind me his high, soft voice says, "What kind of car is it?" He's taken his cue from me, but my heart's still racing and I know my face is red.

"Toyota. When you turn the key, nothing happens."

I can feel his eyes on my back. "I'll see what I can do, but I have to warn you that I don't have a whole lot of parts for Toyotas. Most people around here drive American cars. But if I can't get it started, I'll put it in one of the bays and have a look."

"Thanks."

I hear him poke a button to release the drawer of the till and then rummage around in there for keys. I walk over to the counter, depositing the Toyota's keys between us. I keep my eyes on them.

"You want to come?"

I shake my head. "I'll wait here."

"There's coffee if you want it. I'll be back in a jiffy."

Part way out the door he stops to say quietly, "It's good to see you, Diana."

I nod and watch him walk out to the red and white tow truck.

I wonder if the cushion he gave me one Christmas is still inside the toy box in my room. It had an iridescent picture of Niagara Falls painted on some shiny bright blue fabric and there were gold tassels at each corner. Jenny tore the present from its tissue paper wrapping on the way home from school the last day before Christmas holidays and waved it laughing around her head, yelling, "Look what Diana got from Beak!" until I grabbed it, laughing too, but not with any of her delight, and shoved it back in my school bag.

If Beak were a cushion, that is the cushion he would be.

Jenny set me up with him because Beak's parents had a rumpus room in their basement and didn't get home until after six. Jenny and Geoff were running out of places in which they could display their devotion to one another.

"He's a football player," she said to increase my gratitude. She didn't need to do that: I was as grateful as I could get. I had a date, at last. Sort of.

When he returns, the front of the Toyota hooked to the back of the tow truck, I've poured myself a coffee from the Easy Brew in the corner and am sitting on a white wooden chair, sipping. The station is much cleaner and better organized than it used to be.

He backs the car into one of the bays, disconnects it, and parks the tow truck before coming back into the shop. He punches the cash register open to drop the keys inside.

"Those damned rental companies make me mad," he says, slamming the car door closed again. "There's damage to the front end of that car. They should never have let it on the road."

I exhale cigarette smoke. "It wasn't damaged when I got it."

"Oh." He pauses, probably glancing at me. "Oh," he says again, and then, "The electrical system's haywire, for sure. It could well be more than that."

He sounds like he knows what he's talking about but he was failing both math and industrial arts when I knew him in high school.

"Will your father be back soon?"

"He's retired." He straightens from writing up the work order to look at me. "This is my place now."

His uniform is clean and pressed and his heavy saddle-gold work boots, with laces undone, look new.

He's gone back to his writing and his lips, when I look at them in profile, are unusual, demarcated from the rest of his pale skin not only by their deep, almost purple, colour but also by their shape. I cannot now imagine how I kissed him.

"Did you hit anything important?" he asks lightly without looking up.

"No. Just the ditch."

He carries the work order over on a metal clipboard for me to sign, proferring a white plastic pen with the words, "Donellon Texaco, B. Zimmerman, Prop." printed in black on the lower barrel. He seems too near, the fabric of his coverall almost touching my blue-jeaned knee, and I sign quickly and hand the clipboard back to him, relieved when he moves away.

"This might take a while."

"It's all right. I'm not in a rush."

He takes a deep breath. "But I heard that your mom . . . I could drive you home."

Mom. What a strange word to use for her.

"Let's just wait and see what the diagnosis is, okay? Maybe it'll turn out to be something you can fix in half an hour."

"Well. If you're sure," he says uncertainly. "It wouldn't be any trouble."

"I'm sure. Please, Beak, don't worry about me. Just see what you can do about the car."

Convinced at last, he carries the clipboard through the door into the bay area of the station and I go for another coffee.

There was something tentative, shy and gentle, about the way Beak touched me, slowly, ready to draw away at any moment if I said so, that appealed to me as much as did the newness of it all. He slipped his hand along the bare flat of my stomach and up again, under my sweater, sliding around to find the clasp of my bra at the back. He couldn't undo it and Mother's prudishness was in me as though I'd had a conscience of my own, so I couldn't help him, could not communicate by complicity that I was enjoying this too.

But he came back doggedly to try again at the front and eventually we wriggled to the carpet and he managed to push the tight new undergarment up and out of the way. I recall the startling pleasure that he brought me, his hands touching as though to learn along the roundness of my breasts, and fingering my nipples.

The more he touched the more I wanted him to touch but I didn't dare move my hands from where they were clasped around his neck. I didn't have the nerve to touch him in return, nor was I sure I wanted to. His maleness frightened and excited me, the unfamiliarity of it, the increasing hardness of him where he was pressing against my leg. He tantalized and repelled me all at once. Our kissing grew perfunctory as our attentions wandered around my breasts, him touching now not only with fingers but with his lips as well. My eyes were closed and I'm sure his were. We couldn't have borne to look at one another then.

If only it hadn't been Beak. The body was fine, a football player's body, and the way he moved against me was wonderful and less frightening every moment as I was drawn into the pleasure of my body, and if only Beak's brain and mouth had not been attached to the boy beside me . . .

But they were. His hand rubbed up against the inside of my knee, almost as though by accident, and I moved a little so that it might accidently go higher. Mother was gone from me and I'd forgotten about Jenny across the room on the couch, where she was groaning under the weight of Geoff Hargreaves.

And then he said, "I love you, Diana. We'll get married as soon as I finish school." He said it in a whisper, but he might as well have shouted.

His conscience assuaged, he went back to rubbing at my breasts with all of the exuberance he'd shown before. But suddenly my nipples hurt and my breasts felt exposed, my bare stomach cold. His words had sent my thoughts onto a hundred different tangents some of which ended in visions of my mother but other, more painful ones, of my father. I felt ashamed.

"It's getting dark," I said, and kept him there for a moment to shield me while I squirmed to get my bra down and straightened my skirt.

"It's almost dinner time," I said. When I looked at my watch, it was. "She's going to kill me."

To Jenny, under the squirming back of Geoff, I said, "We have to go. Right now."

Geoff stopped moving and she looked up at me from under him, totally disarrayed but, I found when she stood up, clothed where it mattered, and said, "You're such a fucking drag."

When I came in the door late that afternoon, Mother was reading in the living room and she called me down from the stairs, up which I'd been trying to disappear. I came into the living room and stood sullenly just inside the door. The only light in the room came from a floor lamp which cast white on her book and yellow around it, around her.

"You're late." She wasn't pleased.

"Sorry."

"You aren't sorry at all. You are never sorry. Even your voice sounds unsorry." She put down the book and stood. "I can't permit this, Diana."

I said nothing.

She walked toward me and I felt a little nervous. It had been years since she'd hit me but I could never be certain that she wouldn't.

When she was close enough to slap she stopped and stared at me. "What have you got on your neck?" she said, underlining every single word and making large spaces in between them.

Her voice dropped. "Go to your room," she said.

I didn't know the answer to her question myself until I'd had a chance to look in the bathroom mirror, several hours later. In the meantime, I'd been lying on my bed while Mother paced up to my closed door and away again. I assumed she was rehearsing the lecture she'd deliver and determining my punishment.

In the end, when she finally opened my door, there was no lecture. She kept looking at my neck, agitated and disgusted, pacing, repeating over and over again, "You shall not go out for two months, do you hear me?" "You will stay at home for two months, Diana." "You will come home directly after school." "I cannot permit you to go out."

I didn't take my eyes from her, and at last she said, "No one had better ever see that . . . thing. And I'd better never see another one," and then she left my room.

On my right breast, there was another mark just like the one on my neck, and after a while both marks went away.

After the two months had passed, I had no interest in renewing my position as liaison between Beak Zimmerman's rumpus room and the still-passionate relationship of Jenny and Geoff. This displeased Jenny, and later she would claim that if it weren't for my refusal to double-date, she never would have become pregnant. I forced them to be alone, she intimated, and to uncover the parts of her she would not have uncovered in my presence.

Beak finally stopped begging me to come over after school, but not before I'd cached in my toybox, on top of the souvenir of Niagara Falls, one lacy pink heart-shaped box of candy and a basket of chocolate Easter eggs in a bed of yellow, plastic straw.

Beak Zimmerman. He was proud of his last name because it was the same as Bob Dylan's was before he had it changed. I'd never heard of Dylan, so he played the flat-voiced poetry for me: "See That My Grave Is Kept Clean" was some of the background for our passion.

I'm not certain why he's called "Beak." Jenny said that Geoff said that he'd received the nickname from the guys who'd seen him in the shower after gym. I laughed but felt there must be an enormous gap in my understanding of physiology because I had no idea what she was talking about. I still don't.

He's going to have to order a part from Harding. He can't possibly repair it before Monday. He is slowly apologetic, kind, and there's nothing for me to do but accept his offer to drive me home. The frustration in my throat is like a fist and I follow him silently out to the truck. He's opened the passenger door for me and he waits until I've climbed up inside and then he slams it shut.

"It isn't much," he says, patting the dashboard once the engine's started, "but she's all mine."

Most people who say things like that have the good grace to sound as though they're delivering the lines in quotation marks. Not Beak. He says it as though he'd invented every word of it.

I open my door and put my foot down on the step.

"Where . . . ?"

"My suitcase. It's in the trunk."

"I'll get it. You stay put. You don't even know where I left the keys."

When he gets back, he deposits the case on the floor beside my feet. His short fingernails are black.

"I appreciate your driving me."

"No trouble at all," he says, reaching one hand to grasp the passenger seat as he twists to back out of his parking spot. "I know you didn't come home to visit, but it's good to see you anyways." He turns the truck into the street, hand over hand around the steering wheel. "What've you been up to since you left?"

"Not much."

"You're living in Calgary, right?"

"Edmonton."

"Working?"

I sigh. What I don't want is questions, questions that will make me have to think. More than anything else right now, what I don't want to do is think. I want my mind to be as still and thick and grey as that huge slab of cloud which is over us. Over Donellon. How far will it go? Will it cover Ontario? Will it spread across the prairies toward Alberta? Will it cover Canada? The world?

It covers me, and that's all I can be certain of without a television set to make the rest of the world my size. For all I know, the cloud may stop immediately beyond the reach of my vision. It covers Beak and me.

"Pardon?"

"Where do you work?"

Ladies never inquire as to a person's age. Nor do they ask a person's occupation, lest it be construed as a subtle attempt to discover that person's income level. A lady never pries.

"In a record store."

"Been there long?"

I nod. "Off and on since I moved there. Except when I was at the U of A."

"I bet you run the place. The store."

He's delighted when I nod again. "I knew it. Always knew that you'd go to university, get a really good job like that some day. I just knew it. It wasn't only your marks, but the way you acted was different, too. Smarter than just about anyone else. Rest of us never got off our back ends and did much of anything but you did, moved to a new part of the country, started right from scratch. Not that I ever could have done it anyways, not me. Right out of high school I was married . . ." He talks on and on as he drives more slowly than he needs to back to the house, telling me, it seems, every single thing that's happened to him since I saw him last. I try to focus on his words, staring out the passenger window.

But my efforts to concentrate don't work. Once he drops me off I'm going to be stuck in there. Now I can't leave, without a car, even if I want to. And I'm going back to the house before I would have, had I had the choice. Somewhere along the way I've lost control.

I keep my head turned away from him but I know from the way he suddenly clears his throat and stops talking that he knows I'm crying. It's so stupid. I cry when I'm feeling sorry for myself. I don't cry very often.

As soon as he stops the truck in the driveway, he leans across me and pops open the glove compartment, revealing a box of kleenex.

"Thanks," I whisper after a few minutes, during which neither of us has spoken and I have done my best not to make any noise as I regained control of myself.

Now I swallow and turn to him, attempting a smile. "Sorry about that. I don't usually fall apart in tow trucks."

"Or anyplace else, I bet. You Guthries always were pretty good at keeping stuff to yourselves." His smile is intended to comfort.

"Not all of us. My mother and brother, yes." I keep my phrases short, trying to keep pace with my halting breath. "But my father and I . . ." I shake my head. "Not the same."

He stares out the front window at the house. "That year after Noel died, you never let it show. Not once."

"That was the worst year . . ." I inhale. "It must have shown."

"No. It didn't. I didn't know your brother then, not till he pumped gas for my dad one summer after you left. But you're right about him. He got his thumb caught in a jack one time? I'll never forget it. Turned pale as a sheet and there was all this blood spurting out but he didn't make a peep."

He shakes his head, remembering. "Now me, I'm not like that at all. Whatever I'm feeling's written all over my face, and my kids are as bad as me. Other kids beat you up for stuff like that."

I remember that I thought he was going to cry when he brought me the basket of easter eggs and I refused it. I took it, so he wouldn't.

He laughs. "I had to become a football player to get anywhere at all. But I hated every minute of it. Push-ups. Laps. It was God awful. It's nice to grow up."

My breath is still a little uneven but the tears have stopped. I glance over at his face, so foolishly contented. How could anyone be contented with being him?

"I guess I'll go in now." I close my hand around the suitcase handle. "Please. Don't bother. I can get out myself."

"I'll call you when the car's ready. Might be Tuesday, though, with the long weekend."

I'm standing on the gravel. "Thanks, Beak. You've gone to a lot of trouble."

He looks down at his hands on the steering wheel. "I lost an aunt. Last summer. She was sick for quite a while. I know what you're going through." He glances at me. "If there's anything I can do, and I don't just mean about the car, let me know."

I nod and start to close the door.

"Diana . . ." His face grows pink. "You were pretty special to me. I'll never forget what we had together once. I'd do just about anything I could for you."

What did we have together? What in the name of God does he remember? As the truck disappears down the laneway I wonder if it's possible that he's carried me around with him through all these years the way I've carried Noel. He's so syrupy kind, so saccharine concerned, that he's made me feel again the way he did the day he gave me that awful pillow. If I needed someone, and I don't, the last person I'd call would be him.

I look down at my suitcase, remembering its contents: the black things at the bottom, the change or two of clothing on top of the plastic bag. I didn't intend to stay long, maybe not even as long as I have.

Rain grazes my arm. I wish the blackness of that sky would find an opening and pour out its moisture on the suffocation of this heat, this place, but there are no more drops and even the one that touched my arm no longer cools but has become a part of my envelope of sweat. Squeezed inadequate from such a sky that tiny drop was no more than one dry heave.

"I know what you're going through," Beak said to me. But he only knows what I should be going through. Trapped between the black-grey clouds and the dry earth with that house of dying in front of me, to be entered yet again, I need a deluge where there is only threat of one.

Chapter Ten

Before he left Father also built a woodshed, a well-constructed lean-to with a green shingled roof, against the north wall of the garage. It's empty now of logs, its floor a mulch of woodchips, and I rest my back against a beam filtering slivers through my fingers and onto my legs which are splayed in front of me. The house stands to my right, huge against the charcoal sky and when I close my eyes, I can still see it. Mother's still inside: mind, soul and all. If she were dead, Hilda's would not be the only car in the driveway.

I want her dead. Or more precisely, I want her gone. I don't want to think about her up there any more. I don't want to find out whether I'm going to confront her or whether instead I'm going to compose myself as she taught me so well to do, and let her tiptoe away from life, away from me, unchallenged.

Mother and Westmoreland and countless Sunday school teachers all told me that punishment for iniquities in this life will come when we reached the next. Can I assume that when she crosses into death she will suddenly be made aware of her injustices, of her inhumanities? Or even more important, that she will pay for them? How can I assume that, when she, when those people whom I do not respect, invented the god I was given, or at least defined him.

But what I'm doing now, and what I've done all day, says not that I am trying to come to a decision about how I'll face her, but that I haven't got the guts to face her, period.

I want all of it taken from me, but even her death won't do it. It would have, had it happened before I arrived this morning, but now I've let the opportunity pass and pass and pass and if I find her dead, I will have chosen to find her dead. I'm involved now in her dying no matter how desperately I may wish not to be.

I squeeze my eyes, but the pain has started. My ability to control myself, my feelings, began to escape when I saw Beak and I can't get the stopper in again. I can't get away from it. Everything I think of comes back sooner or later to that woman upstairs in the bed. Her death has become the focus of my life.

When she had the ramp taken out, and it came out as easily as the elevator had—the way Father had planned it so that not a trace was left that it had ever been there—I thought it was everything of his that she was trying to get rid of. But the woodshed's still here and so are the shutters he put up. (I open my eyes to confirm this but there aren't any windows visible from here.)

The same week as the ramp went, she packed up his clothes in cardboard boxes and sent them to the Salvation Army, she donated his desk and his easy chair along with several other still-usable items to Hilda's church, and she got Hilda to trade in his car.

Mother threw Father out after he had left. I wonder if there's anything left in my room.

I went to find him after I'd finished grade thirteen. His only other relative, his sister Alva, lived in Vancouver and he'd sometimes talked of taking us all to visit her, to see the mountains and the ocean. I was certain he was there.

It had been five years by then, since he'd left, and I hadn't heard a word from him in all that time. I didn't begrudge him silence. Year after year I'd increasingly empathized with his need to escape from her, and from Donellon. I felt more strongly all the time that I was his ally and that he was mine. In my sense of isolation after Noel died, I needed him, the other person who'd been forced into exile by her lack of empathy, by her harshness. He was the only person in the world who might possibly understand. I very much hoped I'd find him.

Mother stood with her hands on her hips in my doorway and coolly watched me pack the suitcase. "The two of you belong together," she said.

"What makes you think I'm going to see him?"

"I didn't say you'd see him. I said you belonged together. You won't find him."

"I'll find him."

"Never."

"I suppose you know where he is."

She nodded, her expression still ice cold. "He's remarried. He doesn't want to see you."

I turned on her.

"You're full of crap," I said. "If you know where he is, why wouldn't you tell us? Why haven't you told us? You're making it up."

She said nothing.

"You're making all of this up. I'll find him. And it doesn't really matter if I don't. The most important thing is getting out of here."

I snapped the lid shut on my suitcase.

"If you go," she said, "don't bother to come back."

She turned and went across the hall into her room, closing the door with a tiny, impersonal click.

"Don't worry," I said quietly toward the hall. "I won't."

On the four day train trip across Canada, I had more time than I needed for reading, for crossword puzzles, for studying the train schedule, for watching the changing scenery and weather, and for thinking. In the tiny roomette, which I left only at mealtimes, I decided that I could accept a woman in my father's life, could accept his having another wife, because I understood what had driven him to it. He would be surprised, of course, at my easy acceptance of this new woman (I visualized her as blonde, brown-eyed, slender and, for some reason, talented at the piano) but he would be delighted and relieved by how well we got along. She would be a friend, closer to my own age than mother was. None of us would ever be in contact with anyone in Donellon again.

Aunt Alva was kind and sympathetic, accommodating me readily in the guest room of her North Vancouver apartment so that I felt when I was shown into it that if I decided to stay forever it would be no inconvenience to her.

She had no idea where he was, she said. She lied to me adeptly, easily.

"I wish I could help you. I really do. But I haven't heard from him in years."

I explained that I had to speak to him. I told her I felt about my mother the same way he did, and needed to tell him that. Still she wouldn't budge. She defended my mother—she went that far: defended the indefensible, a woman she barely knew, saying that Wallace should not have deserted her, no matter what. She spoke reasonably, unemotionally, and I knew she couldn't mean it. She was protecting him.

I took the bus downtown day after day and walked, seeing his back in restaurants and queues for movie theatres and hurrying to get closer, only to discover that it wasn't him. The size of the city unnerved me, but I had Aunt Alva's library phone number and still had some money of my own. The buses she'd instructed me to take took me where I wanted to go, and back to her apartment again. I told her I was sight-seeing, and indeed I did walk through Stanley Park and Chinatown and down by English Bay. She wished she could come with me, she said, but she had to go to work.

The city had been beautiful when I arrived, the mountains—

which had given me claustrophobia as the train met them at Jasper and then passed through them—had relented at last as we approached the blue and white, sunlit ocean. But within a few days the weather had turned grey with driving, relentless rain, and mist when there wasn't rain, and I knew that without Aunt Alva's help, I wasn't going to find him.

She wasn't about to help me. Instead, she asked me if I was thinking of looking for a job. She warned me that jobs were impossible to find in Vancouver.

In the day coach back I saw Mother's face triumphant three thousand miles in front of me. I almost got off at Jasper, but I didn't want to face the terrifying possibilities of those immense mountains jabbing sky every morning of my life, and so I waited until the train stopped at Edmonton. I cashed in my ticket and walked out into a city where I knew no one at all, where there was no chance of seeing Father in the backs of other men, no memories of Noel. If Beak thinks that's courageous, then I'll let him think it.

I walked ten blocks to the YWCA and two days later answered the "Help Wanted" sign in the window of Israel Rosen's record store.

It seemed entirely appropriate to be living in a basement room eight blocks from where I worked, in that flat and sapling-treed city with a sky so huge that there were no anchors in it. It seemed right to be eating meals from the landlady's discarded china, eating macaroni and cheese when I ran short before payday. It was appropriate that I should be buying scarves and mittens at the Goodwill Store and I felt bitter and stoic when they didn't warm me. That first winter was so consistently cold that even Edmontonians complained about it (I didn't realize then that Edmontonians complain about every winter), and when I developed bronchitis in late December and lay alone and feverish listening to carols on the transistor radio in my room, I thought that it would serve Mother right if I died there in that icy, empty city. The vision of her sitting self-righteous, abandoned by those she'd only tried to help, enraged me.

But refusing penicillin was a pretty ineffectual way of committing suicide, and I didn't want to kill myself anyway. My suicide, whether caused by nonintervention or by active courtship, would have been interpreted by her as regret on my part for having deserted her.

I wouldn't do her any favours.

As I began to recover, I grew increasingly angry with her control over me, with the way my mind returned and returned to her. I'd come all this way, and I would eliminate her from my life and from my thoughts.

I was working in a small dark shop on Whyte Avenue where customers were rare and the owner seemed as dispirited as I. Rosen was a name respected in Edmonton, but in furs and lumber and not in records, and it was one of Israel Rosen's many despairs that new customers were usually drawn by the name his brothers had made locally famous than by the fine collection of records that he stocked.

He was a short and balding man of about fifty-five who seemed bewildered by everything: his wife, his customers, his lack of customers, himself. His one passion was his classical music and he couldn't understand why the paying public did not clog his aisles. When people did come in, he left them alone, as he preferred to be left alone when making purchases. Most of them wandered out without buying anything at all.

He didn't really need an assistant except to cover for him when he went home for lunch but perhaps he felt less lonely with someone else around. He was a kind man despite his taciturnity and he made my position a full-time one as soon as he realized I was trying to live entirely from my income. He left my salary where it was when I decided to go to university, and for five years I worked at the record shop part-time and was paid a full-time income. It wasn't until he made me manager of the store that I realized how ill he could afford what he had done for me. I'd expressed my gratitude earlier so many times that by the time I really meant it, it was too late to raise the subject again.

I was incommunicative like him, dusting and sorting and carrying out my other duties without initiating conversation. I worked there for seven years before I told him what had been obvious to me from the day I started: selling symphonies and operas in a location where most of the pedestrian traffic was university students was a little like trying to sell tofu to junk food addicts.

"But my records are wonderful—Stravinsky, Mozart, Dvorak—what else is there?"

"They are beautiful. Of course," I said. "But it's not good business, Mr. Rosen."

He put his hand out flat. "You got a better way, you try it."

I started stocking Elton John, Rod Stewart, and the Stones. I ordered Makem and Clancy, Joan Baez, and Cat Stevens. I developed a comprehensive jazz section. I don't like jazz so I had to seek advice from the customers, and they liked that.

Later there came The Village People, The Police, and Michael Jackson, and now it's Madonna and Julian Lennon. I'm beginning to outgrow the music that I carry in my store.

I designed window displays that would reflect the new direction that Rosen's Records had taken and it worked, of course, but beyond what I'd expected. Students, it appeared, would spend the last dollar in their pockets on an album that they liked, foregoing food and drink if necessary as long as there was still a roof to protect the stereo from the elements. Within two years, he'd made me manager and we'd hired other salespeople, one full- and one part-time.

Now Rosen comes in only once a week to the busy brightly lit store and his visits are as brief as he can make them. Cyndi Lauper blasting from four speakers is more than he can stand. We usually hold our meetings next door in the coffee shop.

Instead of retiring and taking his wife to Europe as he'd always said he would if he made enough money to do it, he's opened another classical music shop downtown and he runs it alone, locking the door when he goes home for lunch at two. Rosen's on Whyte pays the rent for Rosen's Arpeggios, but I've seen him with his brothers and his wife and I think he's satisfied.

And so, Beak Zimmerman, the future just sort of came about—I didn't really plan any of it at all.

I roll onto my stomach and rest my forehead on my hands on the grass. I'm hidden here—not invisible, but hidden. I can't be seen from the house and if Mitchell drives up he won't be able to see me either.

I was reading a book on the porch one humid morning in late July when the cord of wood arrived that my mother had ordered from Mr. Fletcher. Mitchell, who was almost nine by then and should have been playing ball with other boys, was driving his fire truck around behind me and telling me every few minutes to stop reading and come and play with him, when Fletcher's pickup truck came into the driveway and I saw that Noel was at the wheel.

Fletcher was clearing a lot to the north and selling off the lumber and Mother had seen the ad in the Donellon paper. Somehow she'd managed to persuade Fletcher to split and stack the wood for her for the same price he was offering it to everyone else unsplit. I'd known the wood was coming—had been sent out to supervise the unloading of it—but I hadn't expected Noel. He'd been seeing Sylvia Asher, tawny-skinned and sensuous-looking, during most of the previous year while I'd been fending off Beak, and I'd heard he was going to work in Grand Bend for the summer.

"Where'd you want this stuff?" he called. He looked hot and

tired and irritated.

"Woodshed. Over by the garage," I said, standing and smooth-ing my shorts. "Go inside, Mitchell."

"Why?" he said, then "No," without waiting for an answer, and he headed toward the woodshed to meet Noel, with me behind him.

Noel had crossed into another generation since the last time we'd been at the pond together. His jawline was angled and harder, shaven. The work he'd been doing had broadened his shoulders and his thighs and when he swung down from the truck, unlocked the tailgate and began to unload the wood into neat stacks beside the garage, sweat trick-ling from his dark and curly hair, he looked more man than boy.

I wished that Mitchell, who was babbling questions like, "So, what grade you going into, Noel?" and "So, how are things, Noel?" and shifting from one heavy leg to another, would go away. I knew that if I told him to he'd ask me "Why?" again, and I didn't want to answer that in front of Noel.

"Let me help you."

He nodded and I went to work beside him, silently, as he answered all of Mitchell's stupid questions patiently and thoroughly, continuing even when my arms and legs were screaming from the exer-tion, until the final piece of wood was stacked. Mitchell didn't lift a finger.

"I guess you got your driver's license, eh?" Mitchell said hap-pily, his face flushed in the sunlight. "You gonna get a hot-rod or some-thing like that to drive?"

"I don't think so, Mitchell," Noel answered, wiping his forehead with his arms. "They cost money and there's other things to spend money on besides cars."

"Like what?"

"Oh, lots of things."

"Want a lemonade?" I asked.

"You out of beer?"

He smiled to show that he was joking. "Lemonade's great," he said and walked over to the shade of the oak, wiping his forehead again with his arm. Mitchell was following him, preparing to settle on the grass beside him, when I grasped him by the shoulder of his T-shirt and dragged him away to the house with me.

"I want to talk to Noel some more."

"You come and help me."

When we got inside the house I promised him I'd give him my allowance for two weeks straight and play with him for an hour after

Noel had left if only he'd stay inside.

"Trucks?"

I nodded. "Trucks."

He shrugged and started up the stairs to where Mother was taking her afternoon rest as she always did after she'd visited Grandmother at her new apartment in town. Grandmother complained about everything connected with her new place but refused to move back in with us, despite Mother's efforts to persuade her to return. When she did visit the house occasionally for dinner, she acted as though the place didn't smell quite right. I dreaded her visits.

It took Hilda so long to squeeze the lemons that I became impatient and jumpy, afraid that Noel would leave before I got outside again, and I dashed back and forth between the tray with the pitcher on it and the window (from which I couldn't see the oak tree anyway) until Hilda finally said, "If I add a little extra water it'll be faster and he'll never know the difference."

She held the back door open for me and I carried the tray with the pitcher and its two glasses slowly and carefully around to the side of the house.

Noel was still stretched out on the grass, his hands beneath his head, and Mitchell was squatted beside him.

"I thought I told you . . ."

"Mother said I had to come down. She was trying to rest. I didn't want to, honest." He looked at me with sad brown eyes. "I would've rather had the money."

Noel looked amused and my fury at Mitchell was increased by my certainty that he knew exactly what he was doing.

"I heard you got a job in Grand Bend this summer."

Noel nodded. "Then my dad needed help when he sold the land so I couldn't take it." He accepted a glass of lemonade and drank it down.

"You want some more?"

"Thanks."

"I want some too."

I glared at Mitchell. "There isn't enough. Go ask Hilda to make you some."

He pointed at the pitcher. "There's lots in there. I'll just get a glass."

While he was gone I asked Noel questions about school and helping his father for the summer, until it occurred to me that my questions sounded exactly like Mitchell's, pandering, and that his answers came back in the same tone of voice, polite and thorough and uninterested.

When Mitchell came back I left the talking to the two of them and sat staring at my lemonade. A little black insect began to crawl around the rim and down into my drink. I crooked my index finger and lifted it out and then I poured the rest of my lemonade on the grass, all the time combing my mind for the one statement I could make or question I could ask that would display my maturity, my intelligence and wit, while at the same time pointing out Mitchell's lack of it and our vast difference in age.

"Well, I guess I better get back," Noel said when he'd finished the second glass. "Thanks again." He stood and smiled at us, the children, and turned toward the truck.

I hurried to catch up with him.

"How's the photography? You still doing that?"

He nodded. "I've got a dark room now. It's really the kitchen and it drives Dad nuts, but if I'm going to have to stay at home and work for him, he's going to have to put up with it." He looked at me. "I'm saving for a wide-angle lens."

"What kind of stuff do you take pictures of? Still trees and water?"

He shook his head and leaned against the fender of his truck. "All kinds of things but mostly in black and white because I can develop them myself. That's what I like the best is being able to carry through right from the beginning to the end."

"I'd like to see them."

"Would you." He smiled at me sardonically. "They're not very pretty."

"Doesn't matter. You must be pretty good after all this time."

He shrugged. "Nobody else likes them."

"I'd like to see them, too."

"Go away, Mitchell," I said.

Noel smiled at Mitchell. "I'll bring some over tonight, after I'm finished work. If you're sure." He glanced at me.

I nodded.

After he'd gone Mitchell said, "I want to be just like him when I grow up. Except that I'll have a hot-rod."

"You can't be like him, Mitchell." I went to collect the glasses from under the tree. "You're too fat and dumb."

"So are you."

"I'm not fat. Or dumb."

He watched me for a minute and then he asked, "Now will you play with me?"

"No way. I told you if you didn't come out ..." I considered for a moment. "If you don't tell Mother that he's coming over tonight and you go with her to the dinner at the church, I'll play with you."

He thought about that.

"One hour a day, all week," I said.

"What about the allowance?"

"That, too."

"It's a deal. I'll go get my trucks." He paused and looked back at me, scratching an ant bite on his fleshy leg. "You in love with him or something?"

"Don't be such an idiot. Of course I'm not in love with him."

As soon as Mother and Mitchell left for the church dinner, Hilda at the wheel of the little red car, I began to get ready for him. I remember that the dress was cream-coloured and lacy which surprises me for it seems so unlike me to have had a dress like that. Maybe it's the one I was confirmed in.

I sat in the white rocker on the porch and felt that, save for the length of my skirt, I must look like Scarlett O'Hara or someone, rocking on the verandah with a book open in my lap. I did not look at the book, in part because of the long bright rays of evening sun which shone directly in my face and hurt my eyes when I opened them. Eventually I heard the sound of a motor but it was only Hilda coming back and she said on her way around to the back door, "You look very nice, Diana." She didn't say anything about the illness I'd pled to escape the dinner at the church.

I sat, trying to peer at the driveway against the sun and listening for the sound of the motor. Perhaps he would walk. There. Movement in the trees. A squirrel.

If he came by truck instead and asked me to town for a coke, I wouldn't hesitate. Mother be damned—I'd face the consequences when I had to. I'd slide into the seat beside him and when we got to the Fern, I'd order coffee instead of coke and we could talk about his pictures, look at them spread out on the table in front of us, and maybe his hand would touch mine. I recalled his jawline perfectly.

The sun edged below the treetops and my face and arms felt cooler. I waited, afraid that Mother and Mitchell would get back before Noel arrived, increasingly afraid that he wouldn't come at all. I thought that maybe I should walk to the end of the lane and meet him there. But still I didn't move.

And then he came, and he was still driving the pickup, still in his work jeans. He walked up the steps of the verandah smiling and I stood to meet him, feeling his presence before he reached me as though it shimmered and sparked around him.

"You're all dressed up," he said. "You going out?"

I shook my head, my face burning, but I didn't take my eyes from him.

"Well, here you go then," he said, handing me a large brown envelope. "You can keep them if you want. They're extra prints."

"Thank you." I started to open the envelope, to draw a picture out so I could tell him how wonderful I thought it was but he was already half way down the steps again.

"You don't have to go."

"Still got another load to do tonight. My old man's a slave driver. I'll be seeing you, okay?"

I nodded and watched him go, slim back, hard thighs, strong long legs. He got into the truck and drove off down the driveway.

I thought of Sylvia Asher, beautiful, dark and bright, and I looked down at my frilly, childish dress. I hated her. I threw the book, still in my left hand, as hard as I could at the chair, knowing the gesture was as childish as I was, but unable to prevent it. I stopped myself before I tore the envelope to shreds and, tears running down my face, I went to collect the book. My rage had left no mark on it.

In the morning I really did feel sick, and Mother and Mitchell went off to church without me. Mother said she'd call Dr. Whittick as soon as she got back, although, she said skeptically, I didn't appear to have a fever. She sincerely hoped that I was not merely attempting to get out of going to church.

I sat in the garden swing outside and spread the photographs out on my lap to look at them again. They were strange, meaningless pictures when I first looked at them, but as I studied them more closely I began to see that they were photos of pieces of larger things—a bit of root from a tree stump, the handle of a pump, one paw from a kitten out-of-focus with the floorboards clear beneath it. They were strange, like puzzles, and I became intent on solving each one of them by studying them up close or holding them far away from my face until I'd figured all of them out but one. It looked like a patch of dried grass with a wire running through it, the wire thicker at one end than at the other.

If he'd come back, just once, I'd be more grown up and casual. I closed my eyes and swung back and forth in the sunshine, feeling strange and almost nauseous because I'd been so silly the night before. I felt as though I'd been caught doing some private thing that no one else should see. But when I compared how I felt to having the flu or even to having cramps from my period, I didn't feel sick at all. Because it was Sunday and I was not in church, I felt the way that certain of my classmates must have felt when they played hookey from school: free and trapped at the same time.

He startled me, half way across the lawn before I even noticed he was there.

"My dad would make me work today, too, but some of his customers don't like it."

He settled into the white wood slatted seat of the swing, across from me. "What do you think of them?"

I swallowed and made my eyes less wide. "I liked them." I wasn't sure that was true. I'd seen what he was doing, but not why he was doing it. I looked down at the photos in my lap and took a breath. "I think I figured all of them out but this one."

I held it out to him and my hand was shaking a little.

He looked down at it, at me. "Dead rat," he said. "Got it with warfarin. That's the tail of it."

"Why'd you take a picture of that?"

He looked at me sullenly for a moment. "Everybody asks me that. You don't like them."

"No." I shook my head. "I think they're really clever. I had trouble figuring some of them out. I think they're wonderful . . . puzzles." I looked at him, at Noel Fletcher, who was sitting in the swing in my back yard, to which he'd actually come voluntarily, and I did like the pictures, very much. "I think they're great. I'm just wondering how you pick what part of things you're going to take a picture of."

He leaned forward a little, holding out the photograph so I could look at it again. "I wanted to see something. I wanted to see if you could tell from the tail that the animal was dead. Does it look like a live tail or a dead tail? Is there any difference?"

I shrugged. "I know it's dead. You told me that. I can't tell."

"So it's not right, you see? I didn't do it right. You should know exactly what it is and then the question would mean something. Maybe I should have put the haunches in there, too." He scratched his head with his long fingers and studied the photo. "But that wouldn't work either. Not if the foot was in there because I think you could tell from the foot, from the way it curls. You could tell from that."

"Well, I think it's interesting anyway." I wished that the swing were smaller, that the seats were closer together.

He leaned forward and took another couple of photos from the pile on the envelope on my lap and began to explain what he'd been trying to do with them. It seemed from what he said that he was not trying to make puzzles at all, but was trying to think about learning something about the whole from one of its parts.

A lot of the things he'd photographed were dead or inanimate and he was looking for signs of animate in them. Playing tricks with himself, with the viewer. Concealing lifelessness.

I listened carefully, intent on him, and he talked for a long time until I heard a car on the front drive and stood up in alarm. I thought I'd have warning, that Hilda would leave to go back for them, but they'd been driven home by someone else.

"You've got to go."

"Why?"

"Out through the back there, through to the pond."

"I don't understand." He was getting up so slowly, far too slowly.

"My mother . . ."

But it was too late. She came charging through the open patio door, already angry. "What is this Mitchell tells me about your allowance?"

She stopped. She glared at me, the anger increasing until her eyes burned blue. "I thought you were sick. Of all the . . ." and glared back at him. "Get out of here, Noel Fletcher. And don't come back."

I went into the house. I didn't watch Noel leave. Just inside the patio doors I ran into Westmoreland, looking serious and concerned, and he grasped my shoulder briefly to say, "He's not good enough for you."

In the hallway I passed Mitchell, grinning, having discovered a new way to ingratiate himself to Mother, and if Westmoreland hadn't been there I would have pasted him in his fat lips.

Noel. Oh God, I can't bear to think of you when I'm in these places where we were once together. Lean and tall, shirt smelling sweet and freshly laundered, I bury my face into the hollow of your shoulder and turn until your lips can cover mine. Your finger runs across the ridge of my nose, my eyebrows, marking space for all time. Is there a place on one another that we didn't know, by sight, by touch? I could move my hands to show you how well I recollect, could mark the width of your shoulders and your hips. Could mark the height I reached to pull your head to mine.

I've never loved anyone as much as I loved you. My body is the gauge by which I measure yours forever.

There's a hand on my elbow and a cold washcloth is pressed into my hand.

Hilda's voice is gentle beside me as I cover my face in the coolness of the cloth, rub my eyes with it.

"I'll put your supper on a t.v. table in the den. I'm going to put your suitcase in there, too, instead of in your room. You might find the den more comfortable. It's warm upstairs, in this hot spell."

I look down at her hand on my arm, small and sturdy and assured in contrast to the darting rest of her. Those hands once set upon a task move certainly, folding linen tablenapkins into perfect squares or shucking peas one after another into a large glass bowl or holding a loaf of bread firmly as she slices it through and through and through. When I used to watch her work, when I was small, I'd feel my eyes grow heavy as though I myself were being stroked by those caring hands.

Now I feel her presence, gathering, straightening, smoothing.

"When you feel better, you come in. You've got to eat something."

I take a deep breath, pull one of Beak's kleenexes from my pocket to blow my nose, and nod.

Saturday Night

Chapter Eleven

Hilda's made a macaroni and cheese casserole because I used to like them and salad because Mitchell's in the house somewhere, but the sight of food, the smell of it—no. Not even to please her. I put my fork down and lean back on the soft gold couch, close my eyes against the sight of the plate on that t.v. table, against the walls of bookcases which are not as full as they used to be, against the tea tray that stands where Father's desk once was.

I wonder if he has another desk in his house in Massachusetts. I wonder if he builds things to get away from his new wife. I don't know whether I hope he does or not, but I'm certain he would understand the way I feel right now, the confusing meld of past and present, the scribble of emotions.

I keep my eyes closed to prevent their dashing from object to object around the room. Every item in this house has memories connected with it. Does she never buy anything new? No. She doesn't. Once decorated, the house was decorated for all time. It's not a symptom of laziness, for she thinks nothing of turning the house upside down for cleaning—she washes all the walls two times a year, in autumn and in spring, pitching in with Hilda, with relish, the sleeves on her housedress rolled up to the elbows as she scrubs for days until the whole house smells of Lysol. So it isn't laziness that's prevented her from recovering the furniture or replacing it. It's miserliness. She would call it "economy", and disapprove of anyone who didn't practise similar restraint.

The spider plant in my bedroom at home needs a larger pot. Its roots are bound tight, so tight that it can't breathe, can't draw the nourishment from its roots. I noticed it just after Sonny moved in with Madelyn, and I decided I would transplant it when I moved, so I haven't even started to look for a new pot. It sends white shoots almost every day in new directions, desperately trying to start new plants, to gasp air and food from hastily fashioned leaves because its roots are failing it. It makes long unhealthy shoots and tiny clumps of too-pale greenery.

If I were home, I'd transplant it now. It sounds like a calm and normal thing to be doing—to be adding soil and fertilizer and tapping out the root ball, and I wish that I were doing that right now. I wish that I had something to do, something calm and normal. I wish I'd brought my knitting.

No. Knitting in this room would make me think of Grandmother. Thinking of knitting in this room has made me think of Grandmother, who died one week before my finals at the end of grade thirteen. I put down my books to go to the funeral and before the reception afterward was finished I went back upstairs to study. A lot of people came to her funeral.

I feel I'm straddling the line that's between being sane and not. I've read that as long as you're aware of your own imbalance, you're still on the side of sane, but I'd argue with that right now. Lack of sleep is part of it, but there's a sensation of being two people at once which is also part of it. My mind leaps from Father to Madelyn to Sonny to Noel to Mother to Mitchell, who began to get thin the day after Noel died.

When I've been drunk—if there were real liquor in this house and not just sherry I'd take a drink without its having the least effect, would take two drinks or three, and it wouldn't slow my mind at all but only make it faster—it's like when I've been drunk and there's been a part of me that's got nothing to do with that, and is still sober, and is angry at me for the control I've lost, over my lack of precision, and is at the same time powerless to do a thing about it.

I get up and turn the television on. The set is new, but it's been built into the old cabinet. The six o'clock newscaster invites me to contemplate the hundreds of accidents that have taken place all across the country so far on this holiday weekend, this Canada Day weekend. He is trying to prevent additional carnage, he says, but I think he finds a perverse pleasure in recounting how all of us are running up the bloody tally. He takes more than appropriate interest in comparing the number of deaths this weekend with the number by Saturday night on other Canada Days, on other long weekends, and in projecting the possible total devastation by the time all of us have finished enjoying three days off work.

It's poured all day in Edmonton and the sewers are backed up. "Sunny Alberta," the newscaster smirks, and I feel defensive. It is sunny there a lot of the time. Even when it's very cold, at least the sun is shining. Not like this pressing, sticky heat, this overcast sky with no rain and no relief.

I wonder if my suite has flooded. I don't feel like phoning Madelyn to find out.

"They sentenced Proulx. He got three years."

"It's not enough," Madelyn said. "He should have gotten life."

It was about five-thirty on a Thursday last November. It had been dark for an hour already, and I found, as I did every year, that those early nightfalls and late sunrises depressed me. It seemed to be dark all the time.

I'd come home from work to make a bite to eat before going back to finish an order I was working on, but Madelyn had caught me on the stairs and insisted that I come up for a glass of wine, that I keep her company while she was making dinner.

"It's not a real murder. It was a domestic dispute. Haven't you ever been that mad?"

"Mad enough to kill? No."

"Come on, Madelyn. Be honest."

"No. And neither have you. You just think you have." She took a small yellow bag of Robin Hood flour from the cupboard over the stove. "Proulx actually did it. He killed his mother. There's no such thing as 'not a real murder'."

"She made him do it."

"That wasn't clear. That wasn't clear at all."

"A person could be driven, by someone like that, to such rage that there'd be no control left. You've seen her picture. Butter wouldn't have melted in her mouth."

She lifted the lid from the saucepan and inhaled the aroma of her stew. I watched her sprinkle two tablespoons of flour into the saucepan and thought: how stupid. She's thirty-five years old and still doesn't know how to make gravy.

She turned to me. She was wearing a frilly pink blouse which didn't suit her hair. "What's bugging you, Diana? Have I done something to offend you?"

"What would you have done?"

"You sound so chilly. Have for weeks. I had to drag you in here for a drink tonight."

"I haven't wanted to bother you. New love and all."

"I promise to lock the door when I don't want to be disturbed. Okay?" She smiled. "I've missed you."

"With Sonny here, the rules have changed."

She pressed her lips together, sighing. "Sonny isn't going to make any difference to our friendship, unless one of us lets him. I hope that doesn't happen. I'm not about to ignore my friends, especially not you, just because there's a man in my life. Sonny knows that, even if you don't."

"I know." I sighed too. "I'm just tired. We've put in so many hours trying to get the new computer running smoothly at the store. It's been driving me crazy. I'm sorry."

It was true. I was irritated and tired from work, but whenever I thought of anywhere I'd like to go for a break from it, to a movie, out for supper, I knew I'd have to go alone. Or go up and ask both Sonny and Madelyn if they wanted to come with me, and then end up feeling like a third wheel all evening. "Besides," I said, looking around the kitchen, "this just doesn't seem like your place any more." I was trying to speak lightly. "It's too clean."

She laughed. "Not by your standards."

"By yours, though. I feel like I'm somewhere else."

She stirred the contents of the saucepan. I could imagine what they looked like.

"I got lucky—Sonny's a good housekeeper." She put the spoon down on the counter. "Are you still having nightmares?"

I shrugged, wishing I'd never told her about them in the first place. I wondered if she'd told him, and at night when I wakened I worried that I'd shouted in my sleep. The house wasn't as private as it used to be. I needed to find a new place to live.

I had to think of a way to tell Madelyn I was leaving without creating an argument. She needed the income from the basement suite, and would not look forward to finding a new tenant.

"Having the same dream over and over again means something. Why don't you talk to someone about it?"

"Come off it, Madelyn. I know what's causing it, and now that they've sentenced Proulx, I'll quit dreaming about him."

"You aren't dreaming about him. You should go and talk to her, that's what you should do. Get it out of your system."

"I don't dream it all that often."

"Often enough. People don't have reruns of their dreams for no reason at all. I don't think you want to kill your mother, no matter how you protest to the contrary. But you've got problems with her and you know it. You'd be a lot happier if you sorted them out."

"I got another unopened letter back from Boston. I have a father who won't communicate with me, Madelyn. My mother is the cause of that." I poured myself a third, or maybe fourth, glass of wine from the bottle of Donini on her kitchen table. Their kitchen table.

Mitchell, on a visit to Edmonton about a year before, had given me Father's address. He'd only discovered it himself a short time

before, by accident. Mother had given him some legal papers to take
care of and Father's address was in them. Mitchell gave me the address
without any hesitation when I asked for it, but he seemed not to understand why I might want it. "He doesn't matter," he said.

"He's your father."

"She's your mother. Haven't noticed you stopping by lately for
tea."

"It's different."

"Of course, it's different. And if anyone deserves the contact,
it's her. Not him. He deserted her, left her stranded."

"She drove him out."

"Shit. We can never talk about this without going over and over
it like a worn record. Let's talk about something else, okay?"

But he didn't, for long. He kept returning to it, to her,
throughout his visit, throughout all of his visits after the first one,
because the purpose of his visits was to get me to come back. And to
show how well he could handle waiters in fancy restaurants.

"Why do you keep writing to him?" Madelyn asked me, pouring
herself a glass of wine from the bottle on the table. "If he wanted to
have some contact with you, he could. He knows where you are now."

"She . . ."

"She doesn't control the mail he opens. She's in Donellon Ont,
and he's in Boston Mass." She said it like that: Ont and Mass. She did
that all the time: Edmonton Ab, she'd say. Tonight that little contrivance
irritated me.

I twisted the glass in my hand and swallowed the wine in my
mouth. "Your theories of individual responsibility don't always hold,
you know."

She put her hand on my wrist. "You know how much I like you.
I think you're great. Best friend I've ever had. But you've got these
huge pieces of anger inside you, and I know you'd be happier if you got
rid of them. Somehow. I just don't understand why you always let him
off the hook and then skewer her with it. You're his daughter, but he
won't open your letters. Why can't you get mad at him?" She went
back to stir her pot, hurriedly, as though she'd forgotten it.

"Imagine how he feels. Of anyone, he knew best what life would
be like for us, for me, when he took off like that. In a town the size of
Donellon . . . He grew up there. Guilt. He'd have a ton of it. All I want
to do is say I understand that."

"Phone him, then. Go visit him."

I shook my head. "I don't want to interfere any more. I don't know how much he's told his new wife, and I'm not trying to mess things up for them. Maybe things are better for him now. I don't want to mess that up by intruding. All I want to do, Madelyn, is tell him it's okay."

I stood, swallowing the last of my wine.

"Where are you going? I want you to stay for dinner."

I shook my head. "Thanks. I have to get back to work."

"We never get a chance to talk." She lifted something out of the saucepan and looked at it. "This gravy has lumps in it."

I didn't say anything.

"I'll get off the subject, honest. I just want you to be happier. I think you're being too open-minded about him and too closed-minded about her."

"She's pretty good at closed-mindedness herself."

"But it eats away at you, more than it did even a year ago. You seem depressed, withdrawn. You haven't gone anyplace but work in months. It's not healthy. I think that if you went and talked with her, you'd feel better. You don't have to be crazy about her. You don't have to concede anything to her. Sometimes you can win by only giving a little."

Her new-found contentment had obviously given her the license and the expertise to tell me how to straighten my life out.

"Is that what you're doing with Sonny? Giving up without giving in?"

"You don't like him, do you? That's what's been bugging you." She didn't seem worried about it.

"There's nothing wrong with him." I sighed and sat down again for a moment. When I got back to the record store was up to me, and I didn't really want to be there anyway. "I'm sorry for what I just said. But I feel like you're betraying everything you said you believed in. You're cooking with wine and bay leaves. You never used to bother with such crap. Your whole life's changed because of him."

She sat down, too, across from me. "Sonny's a good guy. He's willing to make compromises, too."

"They all are. At the beginning. In two months, you'll be making all the compromises."

She shook her head. "There's more to it than that. I'm not afraid, the way I was, about commitments. About being with someone."

"But you're stirring stew and wearing a frilly pink blouse that, if you'll pardon me, doesn't exactly suit you. What happened to independence? Your own house? Your own decisions?"

She flushed. "Nothing. It's still my house. I bought this blouse because I liked it, and I'm sorry if you don't. I'll dye my hair brown before I wear it out in public if you think it'll help." Her eyes were begging me to smile.

I did.

"He's got nothing to do with this blouse, Diana. What I wear is up to me, and what he wears is up to him." She stared into her empty wine glass. Refilled it. "What a load of nonsense all this talk about details seems sometimes. Who wears the pants in the family has become such a damned sidetrack of an issue. All I know is that I love him, and it's one hell of a lot better than being alone. To coin a phrase." She smiled self-consciously. "Please stay for dinner? If you got to know him, you'd understand it better."

I shook my head and pulled my coat from the back of the chair, stood, put it on.

"We'll get together soon." I said. "Maybe we can all go out for dinner or something."

"I knew it! It's the stew, right? If I ordered in a pizza, would you stay?"

I laughed. "It's not the stew. It's work. But I'd recommend you put the gravy through a strainer before you serve it to anyone."

I went out the back door as I heard the front one open. Sonny.

I sat in the car and waited in the dark for a moment before I started it, assessing whether the wine I'd drunk was going to have any major effect on my driving. I wondered what Noel would have said to her. But I could not imagine.

It was a useless game. For years I'd been able to resurrect him in my head, to talk to him, protecting my memory of him that way. But he'd become nothing more than a name to the voice that everyone carries around—the one people talk to when they're talking to themselves. A wise old relative and nothing more.

I resisted, because if I lost that name, that sense of him, I feared I'd lose him completely. But now I'm thinking that the Noel who died was an eighteen year old boy and I am thirty-three. I think of the eighteen, nineteen year old boys who come into the shop to buy records. Would I ask advice of them? Talk to them about anything that mattered to my life? Never.

It's true that Noel was different from most that I see in the store. He was obsessed with his photography, to the exclusion of all else. He did only enough work at school to get by and to satisfy his father, but his marks were far too close to average to reflect his intelligence. He saved his effort on school work until the exams that would count toward his admission to university.

But when he graduated his father was so busy clearing land and selling pieces of it that he wanted Noel to stay. He did, resenting both his inability to get away and his father's sudden interest in making money. Whenever he could, he worked on his photography.

I was the subject of many of his photographs. He'd long since stopped taking pictures of landscapes and cats and dogs, and even of the tails of dead rats, and instead he did a lot of studies in black and white of people like the grocer, the farmer down the road with his noisy, dirty children. When I looked at the photographs of those seven little brats, I was astonished: they reminded me of ones I'd seen in newspapers and magazines of children in far-off countries who needed someone here to send them money every month. I saw something in the subjects that I'd never seen before, some indefinable depth and universality.

Noel was dissatisfied with creating illusions out of what he found around them. He envied *Life* photographers their subject matter.

"What ever happens here?" he asked. "Some rich kid with too much time on her hands gets knocked up and has to leave town. Shit. People in some parts of the world are so busy trying not to starve to death that they'd never have time to even sit down while you explained that situation to them. They'd never understand it. Overpopulation is a fact of life: what difference can one more baby make?"

Another time, he said, "That day Kennedy was shot? You remember the way everyone was standing around here crying? Why? Donellon's over a thousand miles from Dallas. Kennedy wasn't our president. This stupid little town, this country, has to import heroes and tragedies because it can't come up with anything decent of its own."

To Noel, the world that mattered was beyond the boundaries of Donellon, of Ontario, of Canada. Even of North America. He wanted to go to Latin America, to India, to China, to take his pictures. He was drawn by pain and poverty. He hated his father for wanting to get rich, but he wouldn't leave without his father's blessing.

"He wants to be rich like the Guthries, or the Haultains," he mocked. "Wonderful, upright, happy families, eh? Money means comfort, right? God. I can't wait to get out of here."

When he said "Guthries" or "Haultains," I didn't suppose that he included me. I assumed that when he left, he would take me with him. I thought he was waiting until I was finished grade thirteen, so that both of us could go. When I mentioned something along those lines, he nodded, although he never raised the subject of my joining him himself. I didn't notice that until after he was dead.

One afternoon he asked me to wear my bluejeans and a print shirt and he drove me on the tractor to the field beyond their barn and he instructed me to lie down on the rubble near it, my arms here, no here, my leg like this. The straw poked through my blouse and the ground was spring-spongy and a field mouse or something ran by close enough that it brushed against my leg, but I didn't shudder or stir. His face was set, remembering, until he had me posed exactly right, and then he put his mother's death on film.

He was awed by the result, excited by his power, and he tried similar, less dramatic projects after that, attempting to film his memories, the things that had happened in his life when he hadn't had a camera with him. It was never exactly right, of course. Nothing in Donellon ever was. He and Jenny were alike in that—both of them wanted out: Jenny for the glamour of places like Toronto, Noel for a more violent reality.

"Diana. You sleeping?"

"Wish," I say.

Mitchell comes into the room and sits in the chair beside me, the armchair, Mother's chair.

"You aren't going to eat that?" He nods at my plate.

I shake my head. "Go ahead."

I close my eyes again and lean back on the couch, listening to a promo for a program that features a slick black car that flips and rolls the way my mind is doing.

"Westmoreland called a few minutes ago. He wants to talk to me when he comes by later. What did you tell him?"

"Just what you told me. That you think I should stay out of it."

"That's all?"

"And that you thought he should as well."

"Why did you tell him that?"

"You said it, didn't you?"

I open my eyes and watch him stab macaroni with his fork. He's speared about five pale cheesy tubes and is trying for a sixth. Even when he visited me in Edmonton and stuck to fish and salads, he always put as much on his fork as he could possibly get there.

"I didn't say it to him. It should be up to me to decide what I want to tell him. After you leave, he'll still be here and so will I. You don't have to live in the same town." He impales a bit of lettuce with one tine and puts the whole construction in his mouth.

I close my eyes again.

"Besides," he mumbles after a minute, swallowing before he continues, "he's a client."

"I'm sorry. With you telling me to stay out of it and him telling me to stay in it, I blew up."

I can hear him jabbing the plate with his fork. "I'll tell him it was a misunderstanding. It would have been so much easier if he'd never called you."

"I heartily agree with that."

He suddenly inhales. "God."

"What?"

"What if he called Father while he was at it? I wouldn't put it past him." He puts his fork down and leans back in the chair, holding the plate with one hand so that it won't spill.

"Father wouldn't come. Even if he was called."

"I would have said that about you less than a day ago."

"He's remarried. It's a whole different thing. I doubt Westmoreland would call him anyway."

"Why not? He seems to be on some kind of misguided goodwill mission."

"I just don't think he would. He never liked him when he was here, and the way he talks about Mother . . ." I shrug.

He stares at me, mouth open a little, and then he laughs, hard and long. He laughs like Father did, many many years ago. The sound of that laugh makes me desolate.

When he's recovered, he says, "You're crazy. You know that? Westmoreland and Mother? Never." He shakes his head. "Never."

I shrug again and look around the room, stretch. My skin feels scummy, my hair needs washing, my eyes ache from lack of sleep. I want to crawl out of my body.

After a moment he says quietly, "You don't know anything about this place, Diana. You don't belong here. Why don't you just go?" He begins to eat again.

"I won't be here forever."

Into the silence Hilda comes with a full plate. She sees the empty one in his lap and looks at me unhappily.

"Do you want this?" she asks Mitchell.

"Thanks," he says, trading with her, and starts on the second plate.

"You'll get sick, Diana. You've got to eat." She dusts the top of the television set with her apron before she goes back to the kitchen.

I wish that I were her. She's in this house as I am but her rules are defined, her course of action clear. Everything about her life is like that—she has a blueprint for existence. If you don't eat, you'll get sick. If you commit adultery, you'll go to Hell. I envy that simplicity, that certainty. What do you have to give up, to get it? Reasoning, perhaps, but she's not stupid. She's chosen to turn her attention to other matters, to doing the best she can do with the task that is at hand, and left the other, bigger matters to the dictates of other people. God, she calls it, although it's a different, more explicit one than Mother's or Westmoreland's. In the long run, when both of us are dead, what difference will it make? She'll be remembered more kindly. That's one of the things she's gained. She'd never be in the position I'm in. She has all the answers: they're written down somewhere so she can check them if she's ever wondering. I wish that I were her.

Once I asked Madelyn whether she believed in God. She didn't answer me directly. Instead she said, "You know what my dad calls God? He calls him 'the man upstairs'. And when he says that, I say, 'How do you know it's a man'? It makes him mad. 'Damned feminists', he yells. 'Can't ya even leave God alone?'"

I look over at Mitchell. "You still don't think I should go up? The question's academic, of course. I'm only wondering."

He sighs and leans back in his chair. "If I thought you'd go up there peaceably, I'd say, 'Go ahead'. But you won't. I want you to go back to Edmonton." He wipes his lips with his table napkin. "How's Madelyn doing, anyway?"

"Fine. She's met a man she likes a lot."

"Getting married?"

Of course he would expect that. It's the way things are done. Around here. Around this house.

"She hasn't said."

"Well, that's great."

"What's great?"

"Isn't that what you always say when someone finds someone? When someone's getting married?" He looks at me slyly. "Besides, I was beginning to wonder about you two."

"You son of a bitch. Your mother's son."

"I was kidding." He doesn't look contrite.

"You're getting on yourself, Mitchell. There aren't any women in your life."

He shrugs easily. "How would you know? You haven't been here for fifteen years." He glances up at the ceiling. "I've been too busy for anything serious. You and Father left me quite a project to take care of."

I wonder what kind of woman he could bring home who would meet with her approval. I don't think they make them any more. Her approval would be important to him.

The doorbell goes and he stands, pats his belly, stretches. "Stand by, my dear. Comb your hair and clean your nails. We're about to be invaded."

I watch his back as he goes to the front hall, and I'm thinking about what he's suggested about Madelyn and me. How many other people have wondered that about us?

Women have always lived together, shared accommodation, but the gay rights movement has cast a different light on such arrangements. People will think what they think, I guess. But it's a shame, in a way, when what they think is wrong. It takes something away from a friendship I was proud of.

Though it's not physical, what I feel for her, part of my irritation with Sonny is certainly jealousy.

One morning about a month ago, I came out the back door just as she was entering the garage to go to work. She turned, to give a warm and friendly wave, and I was about to respond when I saw that her gesture was directed at the kitchen window, where Sonny was standing. She kindly appended another wave for me. Even then, I recognized what I felt as jealousy.

I needed Madelyn to justify me somehow. As long as both of us were single, it was easier. I admired her. Everything she said about being independent made sense to me, and I was sure we were the same. And now we're not. I don't want to need anyone again. I have to start over, all over again, from the beginning. One more time.

"It's not a loss of freedom," Madelyn said, "but giving freely to make something important work."

She needed him, that's all. I do not understand how affection, friendship, love, can ever be separate from need. I don't think they can. I don't want to be needed. I want nothing to do with need.

Chapter Twelve

Dr. Whittick pokes his head into the den and waves hello, says he'll be back down to visit once he's seen my mother. He's changed less than Westmoreland. His gaunt kind face has acquired a few lines since I left, but that's about it.

Whittick has been the repository for the personal and medical histories of most of Donellon since long before I was born, long before Haultain arrived. He's known of impending births and deaths before those most affected have known, has ministered to the victims of accidents and occasional violent crimes before the next of kin were aware they'd happened. He knows it all, and whether out of fear at this knowledge or respect for it, he's revered by many people in this town.

Jenny was almost as determined that Whittick not know about her pregnancy as she was that her parents not find out. I had trouble believing that this had happened to her, to someone I'd been so close to, to someone so much in control of everything. But I was almost equally surprised that she could know that she was pregnant when neither her father nor Dr. Whittick knew of it.

Neither of us talked of the product: blue booties and pink frilled bonnets never crossed my mind. Pregnancy was dirty, ugly, sinful. There was no joy in it.

She looked helpless, standing there in our driveway where we'd been let off by the school bus. Her blond hair was limp and needed washing. She had pimples on her face. She was at the mercy of her body, of the damage done to it by Geoffrey Hargreaves' lust.

Hers, too, of course, but she didn't mention that.

"I don't know what I can do," I said.

"There must be something. Surely you can think of something? Please?"

She was begging when there was nothing I could give her and before, when I would have given her anything, she never asked.

"You're an adult in a kid's body," she said, clutching at the sleeve of my coat. "You must have at least one idea?"

Her eyes were puffy and red, running tears. Jenny Haultain looked terrible. I began to believe that maybe she really was pregnant.

"What did Geoff say?"

"Him? That bastard? I wouldn't tell him." She snorted, either because of her tears or in spite of them. "If he'd had the guts to walk into Parker's . . . But instead, I had to do it myself. In Toronto. What do I know about buying safes? If he wasn't so bloody gutless . . .

"Jesus, Diana, what am I going to do?"

"I don't know."

"I've tried everything. I've almost killed myself trying to get rid of this. I feel like killing myself."

I shook my head and put my hand out to touch her shoulder. "You can't do that. Don't even think of it." I was motherly. Distant. Maybe afraid I'd catch it if I got too close.

"Why not?"

"What about the school nurse, Mrs. Harper?"

She looked at me, incredulous. "Are you serious?"

I shrugged.

I was sure the problem would go away if she'd just stop talking about it. I couldn't seem to gather its implications together in my head.

She took a deep breath and composed herself, pulling a kleenex from her purse. "I knew you'd be no help," she said after a few moments, turning toward the road, toward her house. "I don't know why I bothered."

She turned back toward me. I tried to keep my eyes from looking at her stomach area. Her jeans didn't seem to fit any differently than they had before.

"You know?" she said. "For once in my life I'd give everything I own to be you."

I shook my head, politely.

I'd promised her that I wouldn't say a word to anyone, but I told Noel two days later. He was developing a roll of film in his kitchen. I liked those quiet evenings at his house, with his father watching television in the living room while Noel worked at the sink with only a red bulb illuminating the room a little. The windows had aluminum foil over them to keep out the light.

Mother reluctantly permitted me to see him, as long as his father was around, as long as we were in a public place. She never missed an opportunity to let me know that she considered Noel beneath my dignity, and when I came home even ten minutes later than I'd said I would, she took away a weekend. I was rarely late.

There were times, with Noel, when I held his full attention. Not frequently, but sometimes. We went to dances at the school, although he didn't like them, and sometimes to a basketball or a football game when Donellon Secondary School was playing.

Afterwards, he'd pull the pickup off the road, the roughness of his jaw hard when I put my cheek against it, against his neck, the sweet cleanness of his shirt a scent I inhaled with pleasure.

Unlike Beak, he was in no hurry, in less of a hurry than I would have liked. He moved slowly, sensuously, seeming to savour each new progression for its sake rather than as a prelude to another. He pulled my blouse up in the cab of the pickup, undid my bra in the darkness, and touched my nipples very gently, then bent and sucked on them, driving me crazy with tenderness and passion as I stroked his head and rubbed the back beneath his shirt. He unbuttoned his shirt as well and pulled it off, then helped me off with mine as though it were a ritual, slowly and seriously placing my clothes in a pile beside us on the seat and then leaning forward he held me, my breasts against the hardness of his chest. And kissed me.

The night I told him about Jenny I waited for his response so long that I wondered if perhaps he'd been so involved in what he was doing that he hadn't heard me. He was working at the counter and I found it peaceful listening to the drip of developing fluid off the negatives as he held them up to examine them. I didn't normally talk to him while he was working but just sat and watched, and felt that I must hold a piece of his awareness just by being there.

After a long time, he said, "What's she going to do?"

"She doesn't know. She's scared."

"Can hardly blame her. What about Geoff?"

"She doesn't want to tell him."

He pursed his lips. "She should. He'll find out sooner or later, but it'll be safe for him by then. He'll think about it for five minutes and then decide it isn't any of his business. She should tell him now."

"She says she can't stand him. She never wants to see him again."

He shrugged.

"What makes me mad is that my mother's been predicting this for years. I kept saying, 'She can take care of herself'. When she finds out, she's going to be delighted. Because she's right."

He turned from the negative to look at me, his dark eyes thoughtful in the dull gleam of red light. "You know, when you told me about Jenny just now, there was this little tone to your voice that sounded like you didn't approve of her, either. Like your mother. What do you think you and I have been doing all this time?"

"I do not sound like my mother," I said, vehement. "And you and I aren't like Jenny and Geoff."

Pregnancy had to do with back seats and Southern Comfort and condoms. It had nothing to do with us. "We wouldn't . . ."

"Of course we would. Given half a chance."

But we were different. I could sense it, the difference, although I couldn't phrase it. What we did was different. Cleaner. More loving.

Mother found out in no time flat, even before Jenny left for Toronto ("because the schooling's better there"). I wasn't permitted to see Noel for several days until the shock wore off.

"You see what happens? I told you, Diana."

"It didn't happen to me."

"I don't like that Fletcher boy. He doesn't have the same background you have, the same kind of upbringing. He's too old for you, too serious. I want you to stay away from him. At your age you should be going out in groups, anyway, not just with one boy."

"I'm sixteen."

"That's exactly what I mean."

"I'm not Jenny Haultain, Mother, and he's not Geoff. He's not like Geoff at all."

"They're all the same," she said, contradicting herself I thought, after she'd just finished telling me that Noel wasn't my kind. If anyone was, it was Geoff. Blue blood by anyone's standards.

"They're all after the same thing."

What did she know about it, about anything? She hadn't even been able to hang onto the one man she had, but had driven him away with her prudish, moralistic, Leavenworth approach to life.

I would do better. I would never, could not even imagine doing so, would not ever put my mother ahead of Noel nor ahead of anyone else in my life, as she had done.

And still did. When Grandmother called, she went to her immediately. Everything else was secondary.

I knew what Noel was after, and it was the perfect print. He was obsessed by it to the exclusion of his schoolwork, to the exclusion of friends and family. When his mind was on his photographs it was as though he'd disappeared into himself, as though I weren't there. People, his father and I, had little effect on him. What made him happy, and what threw him into rages, was his photography. His work—he always called it his "work"—dictated his moods, and too often it wasn't good enough to please him.

Touching me was a sideline, an occasional diversion, and it

would never be more than that. That was all right with me. I had things I wanted to do with my future as well.

Now, I can't remember what they were.

"Telephone, Diana," Hilda says, hurrying into the den and collecting the plate Mitchell left behind him.

I follow her out into the hall mechanically, walking step by careful step, enforcing order. The phone is on the table in the hall where Westmoreland earlier left his hat, across from the foot of the stairs.

Mitchell in the living room looks away as I lift the receiver to my ear. It's Beak.

"Diana," he says quietly. "I've spent the afternoon trying to find a recirculation valve for you. No luck. Can't find one anyplace."

I hesitate, unwilling to voice my dismay.

"I've got almost all of it straightened away now, but that valve should be replaced. I hunted all over, even called up to Hamilton where my wife's visiting her sister but every place I tried was closed for the long weekend. My wife could have brought it back with her."

"Sounds like I'm stuck here forever."

Mitchell looks as displeased with this as I feel.

"Would that be so terrible?" Beak laughs. "No. I'm going to see what I can do with this one. Maybe I can do a patch job that'll last till you get back to Toronto." He pronounces it 'Trawna'. "I'm not guaranteeing anything, understand, but I'll give it a shot."

"Thanks." I can't keep the discouragement out of my voice and I seem to lack the energy to conclude the conversation. I wait for him to finish it, wondering if I have the nerve to ask him to drop me off a bottle of scotch on his way home. He'd do it. I calculate how far that would be out of his way, and how much I'd owe him for the favour. I don't ask.

After a moment's silence he says, "I'm doing the best I can. I know you want it fixed."

I sigh. "I know you are. I didn't meant to sound ungrateful. I'm just . . ."

"I understand." There's another pause. "Diana? I've been working on this damned car for hours. I'm really starved. I could pick you up. We could go over to the Fern, have a burger, talk. It'd do you good to get out for a while. I remember when my aunt . . ."

"I've eaten." I turn my back so I can't see Mitchell and lower my voice. "I really shouldn't leave."

"I figured you might say that, but it never hurts to ask. Right?"

"Thanks, anyway."

"I hope we get some time to talk before you have to go. I'd like to see you."

He isn't ready to end the conversation and I feel no urgency to hang up either. When I do, I'll have to turn and face this house again. He's telling me now how he discovered the problem with the valve, which he doesn't think was caused by the accident, and I'm watching Mitchell who's leaned back and clasped his arms behind his head and closed his eyes. He looks tense. He's listening, but he's also waiting for something.

I sit on the bottom step the way I used to do when I was talking to Jenny or Noel, the telephone cord spanning the vestibule so that I'm out of Mitchell's line of vision. I feel, from the upper floor, the pall of impending death.

"Beak," I interrupt. "I appreciate what you've done. I'll bet you usually close up hours before this."

He's surprised, I think. Draws in his breath. "We try to please our customers." There's a short pause. "Besides . . ."

"Besides?" I'm determined to know what he remembers.

"Like I told you this afternoon. I'll always have this feeling for you. I never figured I'd see you again."

His answer makes me sad. I imagine him standing in his empty service station, the white lights blazing against the dark, uncurtained windows (a foolish vision because it's still light out there, still grey and heavy, but I can't rid myself of it), surrounded by tires and oil cans and vending machines, in his overalls, dirty now and smelling of grease and gasoline as he shows me his soft underside. His surroundings, his life as I imagine it, are even worse than mine are, even less appropriate to this conversation. His wife is probably round and dull as he is and his house is undoubtedly full of dirty kids. And maybe he's always thought that if it had worked out with Diana Guthrie, it might have been different.

Maybe he's lain awake at night, thinking that. The way I've always thought that if Noel had lived, I might be whole. Less lonely. I feel sadness for him, for me, for Mitchell in the living room, sadness gnawing at me deep inside, tearless, persistent, slate-grey.

I tap the coil of the telephone cord with my finger, making it leap like a skipping rope.

"I was thinking about you and Jenny while I was working on your car. You two stood out, right from the beginning. She pulls in here sometimes in that green B.M.W. of hers, when she's up visiting the family, and you know that commercial on t.v. that says 'you're not getting older. You're getting better'? Well that's her. Both of you. I was thinking that this afternoon, that a person could have known it right from the very beginning."

Whittick comes quietly down the stairs behind me and I stand to let him pass into the living room.

"Beak?" I say. "I got this part time job and now I'm manager. I sort of fell into it. It isn't the way you think."

Madelyn hates it when women downplay their accomplishments. She says they do it for effect, to make men feel stronger. That's not my reason here, although Beak could use all the help he can get. But still I'm glad she hasn't overheard.

"I've known you and Jenny a long time. You had it written all over your faces all along. Success."

If Jenny and I are his models for success, he's in worse shape than I thought. I wonder if he remembers that she got pregnant in grade eleven. Maybe he never knew it. He must have.

Maybe it doesn't matter to him one way or the other. Maybe he doesn't see Jenny's pregnancy the way my mother did, as the frayed inner lining of what Noel and I were doing, the side she saw when the cloak was up to hide us from her eyes.

Maybe he thinks her survival of an unwanted pregnancy adds to her courage, her success.

And maybe he doesn't see that we all got what we deserved. Jenny and Geoff. Noel and Diana. Mitchell. Even Beak.

"I'd better go." My hand is moist and my ear aches from the pinch of the receiver against it, but still I clutch at the black earpiece, tap the cord which snakes into the telephone and out to where there's life.

"Me, too, I guess," he says reluctantly. "It's been good talking to you. Really nice."

I nod. "Thanks, Beak." I've been using you. I'm sorry.

"Diana. Wait a minute. Would you do me a favour?"

"What?" I ask him cautiously.

"Please don't call me 'Beak'. No one's called me that since high school."

"Okay." I smile. "I won't."

"I'll call you soon. Let you know how the repair's going."

"Thanks. Again. For everything."

It's not till I've hung up that I realize that I don't know what to call him instead of 'Beak'. I wander into the living room where Whittick and Mitchell are talking low. They glance at me, and Whittick smiles before he turns back to listen to Mitchell.

". . . a personality change in the past few days," he is saying. "Before, it seemed to comfort her when I was up there when she woke up." He holds his hand out and rubs the fingertips against his thumb. "Now she wants to be alone. I figure maybe it's the medication. What have you got her on?"

"A combination of a number of drugs: morphine among others. It's a special recipe." Whittick sighs. "A painkilling elixir."

"Morphine?" Mitchell is surprised. "You're giving Mother morphine?"

Whittick nods. "And cocaine. And alcohol. Everything I can think of."

"But how can you do that? How can she possibly relate to anyone when she's strung out of her mind?" His face is drawn and white, his eyes dark hollows. He's angry, and his anger is increasing by the moment.

"Mitchell," Whittick says gently, leaning over to touch his wrist. "There's no purpose to be served by pain at this point. She wouldn't relate to anyone at all."

I feel something inside me. Dread and horror. Dying is one thing, abstract and fearsome, but pain is something else again. Pain is real. I bow my head and study the ordered pattern of the floorboards, back up slowly and seat myself in the chair across from them.

"There are often personality changes," Whittick goes on, "as the patient comes to terms with dying. Withdrawal is part of it."

"But not from me. Not from people you're closest to, surely." Mitchell sounds close to tears.

I shake my head, suddenly terrified that I'm going to laugh: wildly, inappropriately.

"Mitchell!" I shout. But no, thank God, I haven't shouted after all. "Mitchell," I say again. "Excuse me."

He looks at me impatiently. "What?"

"What's Beak Zimmerman's real name?"

He pauses, shifting gears, inhaling to regain control. "The guy who runs the service station? I didn't know his name was Beak."

Whittick leans back into his chair and answers, "Berkeley. Delivered him myself. Never forget the name of a baby I've delivered." He glances at Mitchell, a professional glance that wonders if his attention is needed further there, but Mitchell is rubbing his eyes with his hands cupped against his face, excluding us.

"'Beak', from 'Berkeley'. That makes sense, I guess." So much for locker room deviations: never could trust Jenny. The subject changed I can almost breathe again, but before I've had a chance to fill my lungs, the doorbell rings.

Hilda answers it and after a moment, her arms laden with packages of food, shows Mother's friends into the living room. My eyes dart involuntarily to the french doors but that would be ridiculous so I sit in the winged back chair with my hands folded in my lap as Whittick and my brother rise.

Westmoreland's behind the five women, coming in as well. But no. He turns and tiptoes up the stairs instead.

All ten of their bespectacled eyes are on me.

"Sit down, ladies," Whittick says expansively. "Sit down. You remember Diana."

"Of course," says one of them as they all arrange themselves on chairs and couches, more familiar with the furniture than I am, so that Whittick can sit down again. Women in Donellon have strange powers. What seems like an innocent ritual, like this one, is only a manifestation. If it weren't for the largesse, the indescribable charity of these women, Whittick and Mitchell would have to remain standing up forever.

I should have stood as well, of course, when they arrived. I'm younger than they are. Ladies stand for older women. The pecking order is defined.

Mitchell greets them politely, sadly, as befits someone so soon to be bereaved, and then he leaves the room: ostensibly to assist Hilda with the parcels. I doubt he'll be back.

Hilda told me this morning how irritated she is with their daily offerings of food—she sees them as an insult. She's running out of freezer space, she says, and she wonders how much food they think one sick woman can eat. When she returns their empty casseroles from time to time so they'll think it's all been eaten and received with proper gratitude, they only fill them up and bring them back again.

"You're looking well," says one of them to me, disapproving of my health.

"Thank you," I reply.

I almost said, I'm sorry.

"I must say . . ."

". . . give her satisfaction . . ."

". . . took a crisis . . ."

". . . alone at a time like this . . ."

". . . before it was too late."

My answer has loosened all of their tongues: Kenyon, Robinson, McAllister, Williams, Gardiner. What WASPish names they all have.

Guthrie. Leavenworth. Westmoreland. Madelyn Panchyshyn.

They're not talking to me, however, but to one another and to Whittick, quietly, sternly. Their conversation buzzes in tight circles.

I can recall all of their names but as I look at them—although they are all different: some taller, some thinner than the others, very different really—I'm not certain which is which. All five wear cotton summer dresses in assorted pastels and floral prints, and white or beige sandals with low heels. This group is firmly entrenched in an age that's passed almost everywhere else. They'd never wear dark shoes in summer, nor would they go shopping without their gloves. Ladies never do. Firmly entrenched: and ready to fire.

All of them wear glasses and have grey hair and very familiar faces, their expressions as usual powdered and impenetrable, but I cannot separate them and my skin prickles with their stern and sombre presence. The house is full of them.

"Our visits improve her spirits. Don't they, Dr. Whittick." The one who spoke first has spoken again, not asking a question but seeking confirmation. She was the librarian and smelled of mentholatum. Mrs. Kenyon. Maybe Mrs. Williams.

"I'm sure they do," he says. "Friends are very important at times like these. It's good of you to come so regularly."

They nod, satisfied.

These five, with Mother as their sixth, form the unyielding backbone of the women's auxiliary at the church. They've known one another since all of them but McAllister had other names, and I've known them forever. Their sons and daughters attended school when I did, although most of them were ahead of me. All of the sons would have been more suitable than Noel Fletcher, to Mother's mind. I think sometimes she thought that my seeing him was a deliberate attempt to cost her face when she was with her friends.

Friends. There was opportunity for that, with all those years, but they never took it.

I can't put names to faces; the years I've been away have welded them into a unit, incomplete right now, completed only by the invisible sixth upstairs. By looking at them I can see that she has aged.

"Mitchell's a good son," says another, "but it's far too much for one person to handle. She's needed us as well."

The six of them friends and now one is dying. Do the others fear for their mortalities? I study them for signs of fear, look for crevices in their iron shell and then look away in case I find them, down at my hands which I open and close, open and then close, imposing order.

"Would you like tea?" I ask suddenly. "Hilda . . . I could make you tea." I can barely talk.

The eyes settle on me. "We have our tea afterward. After we've visited your mother. Then Hilda makes the tea."

Silence after that.

Again the urge to laugh. But not to laugh: to scream. As their talk begins again—they're asking Whittick if her condition's changed since yesterday—I feel it rising in my throat, know it's only determination that keeps it down. Is everyone in this house suppressing screams? Is that the weight I feel?

He says she's about the same as yesterday. No. Not better. He wouldn't be able to say that. And I hear a sound escape from the woman to my left which is the beginning of a whimper.

I imagined that, I think.

Have all of the people in this house been grasped by unseen hands, which find the seams in their flesh and slowly pull their skins off?

I clench my fists and keep the scream inside, quelling through conscious effort my fear that the house may grasp my flesh, and tear and shred my self control away. But once I've felt the scream disperse throughout my body (not gone, but only dispersed, ready to gather again at any moment) I gasp and realize I've been holding my breath.

There are four floorboards between the rugs and the doorway to the hall. If you count the two across the threshold—flesh hold—count the two across the threshold there are all together six. Six boards.

Hysteria. The word has something to do with women. That makes me angry. It's a wonderful word, a perfect word. Why couldn't it be genderless?

I'm hysterical inside. But I won't let it out. If it were genderless, perhaps I would let it out.

I wish I hadn't thought that. I'm on the verge of giggling. I clench my teeth. Concentrate. Concentrate on concentrating. Forget to concentrate.

Noel. Waving to me from across the lawn of the school, off near the trees, standing back far enough from the building that he knows I'll be able to see him through the classroom window on the second floor. He's finished grade thirteen, is working for his father, but he knows where my desk is, what my class rotation schedule is: he knows I'm in Mr. Gregg's English class and that my desk is next to the window. He knows that I can see him, and he's waving to me madly, waving at me to come down, waving me closer to him.

And I am suppressing the urge to giggle, to laugh aloud with pleasure that he wants me there. I would not dream of going, would not dare to raise my hand and ask to leave the room lest Mr. Gregg, in the midst of some iamb or trochee, step over to the window and see what I am up to. I look around the room, barely able to keep my laughter inside, wanting all the others to see what I see: that beautiful, dark-haired, lean young man who wants me out there, with him, in the afternoon sun.

When at last the day is over and I am out and free, he's gone. Later, in the darkness, he tells me that his beckonings were not the playfulness I'd thought, that they were caused by something else.

"I was scared," he says. "Filled with some terrible dread, that something awful was about to happen. I needed you—to come down. I was scared."

"Of what? In the middle of the day, with all that sunlight?"

"I don't know 'of what'. If I'd known, I could have done something about it. Just suddenly terrified."

"But you're all right now?" I say, watching him closely.

"Yeah. I'm all right now."

I reach my arms around his neck then. "And nothing terrible happened, did it?"

He looks over my head, away from me, but reaches around my waist. "No. Nothing terrible happened. Nothing terrible ever happens. Nothing ever happens at all."

When it comes, it's not a scream exactly, more like an incredible hiccough. Whittick turns, and the women look as though they don't remember what I'm doing here.

I put my hand over my mouth and stand, go out toward the hall.

My foot is on the bottom step of the stairs—Diana-six or Diana-seven, fleeing to her bedroom—when I look up and see Westmoreland there at the landing, his eyes squeezed closed and his hand a fist against his mouth. He notices me and drops it, presses it with the other, behind his back.

I remember who I am, and where, and when. I walk down the hall to the den and close myself inside.

Chapter Thirteen

Westmoreland and Mother. Mother and Westmoreland. Is it possible? I spoke more out of curiosity than certainty when I mentioned it earlier to Mitchell. I wanted to know how he'd react. But that squeezed up face with a fist against it, that pain, is more than a professional concern: Timothy Westmoreland is losing more than a parishioner.

Does she love him, too? Is it possible that she feels that way about anyone? I can't imagine her looking at anyone with longing. Can't conceive of her relinquishing enough of her haughtiness to convey genuine affection.

She always spent a good deal of time with Westmoreland. He drove her home from church gatherings, came to tea sometimes on Sunday afternoons, provided consistent support when there were crises. He dropped over when Father was still here and Mrs. Westmoreland was still alive, all four of them sitting and sipping in the living room or in the garden, and so I thought nothing of it when he continued to come alone, when the other two were gone. I thought it his pastoral duty. I assumed he did the same for the other people in his parish.

If it is true, that there is some feeling there, then why have they done nothing about it? It's been more than twenty years since Father left and almost as many since Mrs. Westmoreland died. Surely an appropriate time has passed, even in this community.

Perhaps the attraction started when they were both still married. Maybe a step too soon would have aroused the suspicions of the other women, of the entire congregation, that something had started earlier. Maybe they maintained their distance afterward to protect their reputations, and because of their own involvement could not tell how long an appropriate waiting time might be. Maybe they erred for so long on the side of caution, both of them alone for so many years, that their desire to "do something about it" waned. That theory appeals to me. It makes perfect sense in this town and suits the twisted sense of propriety that my mother's always had.

How many different ways are there to destroy love, to leave it unsatiated, to let it cool? The options there are endless. And how many ways are there to make it work? None, I don't believe. I haven't seen it happen. Staying with someone is tolerance and need. It cannot remain genuine, complete and satisfied, unless—like Hilda and her religion—some logic, some self-knowledge, some power to reason, is relinquished.

There is no point in attempting to make anything work. There's always so much pain before it's over, like Westmoreland's pain that he can't admit or share with anyone, like mine with Noel, and Jenny's with Geoff, and Beak's with me. Circles and more circles. This above all—to thine own self be true. Nothing else is ever worth the effort.

Maybe it was the contact with God in him that Mother wanted, the chance to patch into the ultimate connection. But Westmoreland is riddled with humanness. The closer she got to him, the more she'd know it. Did she check her reflection in the mirror before she went to church? Did she blush during the communion if his hand accidently brushed hers? Does my mother know if there is a join in that stiff band of white he wears around his neck?

I lie on my back in the darkness of the den, a crack of light under the door letting in the murmers of the women who are coming down the stairs from visiting her. I wonder if she's lain alone at night and wanted him along the length of her, the way I have the memory of Noel. I draw circles in the air with my index finger, my back against the couch, tracing circles and thinking of us all, wanting but never consummated: Mother, Westmoreland, Beak. Completed, it would be no better. Madelyn. Sonny. Me. Standing alone in our circles.

Mitchell. I lower my hand. If she wants anyone, if anyone can bring her comfort, it's the clergyman, not Mitchell. He's got nothing he can offer her, no way to win her. He can't have her.

I roll and face the back of the couch, trying to get comfortable against the sheet and pillow that Hilda's left here for me, a light blanket still folded where she left it on the chair, but my skin is oily in this heat and the people outside the room insinuate themselves, even through one small crack at the base of the door. Mother's presence squeezes them and me. My mind is relentless, even after all these hours, still awake and racing.

Noel, I feel you closer than I have in years, just being in this house. What am I going to say to her if I go up there. What can I possibly say?

Noel's been dead for sixteen years. Almost half my life.

He brought his father's revolver and put it on the ground

between us before he set the tripod firmly in the earth.

"Stand there."

"Noel, you've done enough with death."

But I did as he'd told me, watching him tilt back to adjust the lens and focus, watching his shoulders and his thighs.

"Why does your father need a gun?"

"For killing animals in pain. It's a merciful gun." He laughed, mocking. "Move back a little."

His father had done nothing right for months, but Noel still couldn't bring himself to leave him. He was trapped in Donellon like Mitchell is, by a dependent single parent.

Except that Noel resented every moment of it, while Mitchell seems to feed himself on being needed. I wonder if he'll get fat again when she dies. I wonder if he'll realize then the futility of everything he's done for all these years. It wouldn't be like him, to become aware of that.

Some people reinvent the past, recalling it not the way it was, but the way it needed to have been in order for them to have arrived in the crevasses where they're caught. Mitchell is one of those, and it will probably never come to him that his mother would have felt the same way about him as she does if he'd chosen to settle in Toronto or Ottawa, or even in Boston, when he had finished law school. She could quite easily have found other people to arrange the cleanups of her garden, the repaintings of her house. Hilda could have handled that for her. So could Westmoreland. Mitchell is superfluous.

I looked at the black iron between us. I was almost unmindful of the camera by then, so used to being its subject, so used to the results which always seemed to be focussed on something else.

"Is it loaded?"

"Of course it isn't loaded. Pick it up."

I did. It was much heavier than I'd expected and I wanted to put it down again.

"No. Don't do that. Stand up and hold it against your head."

"Are you crazy?"

"Maybe I am. Depends on your definition. Against your head."

"You're sure it isn't loaded."

"I'm sure." He moved his legs far apart to support himself as he adjusted dials and twisted knobs in order to make it the way he wanted it to be. "You know what my dad wants to do now?"

"What?"

"Build a house like yours. He doesn't like it when I say that—he says the one he's planning is entirely different. But it's not. Adults are totally screwed up."

I laughed. "You're right about that."

"We'll be just like them in twenty years."

"Oh, no, we won't. Not if I have anything to say about it."

"You don't, and we will."

I shook my head. "No way."

"Hold it against your head. That's right. You're about to kill yourself."

I laughed nervously. He seemed to be very far away from me, inaccessible. I was afraid of angering him. "Why would I want to do that?"

"Just do it. Squeeze the trigger."

I stared at him, my lip between my teeth. "You do it. I'll take the picture."

"I'm the photographer." He straightened against the darkening sky and looked at me. "Do you trust me, that it's not loaded?"

I wished I could see his eyes more clearly. "I trust you. I just don't like it—any of it: the way it feels, the idea of it, none of it."

"It's only a picture, like the others. It means nothing. Come on, Diana, it's getting dark." He sounded so business-like and self-controlled. I wished he'd stop all this and come over to me, hold me, that he would reassure me that I knew him.

I closed my eyes, my finger on the trigger and the gun was pulled toward my face because of the weight, not toward the side as I'd always imagined it would be. My arm ached with the strain of holding it so long.

"No one would kill himself standing up," I said at last, lowering myself onto the grass.

He changed the camera angle.

Clicks. His and mine.

"Again."

I fired. Click.

"Do it again. It's almost right."

But I put the gun down on the grass, tired of pleasing him. I pushed it as far away from me as I could reach. I loathed the way it felt.

"No more. I can't."

He sighed, exasperated. Almost immediately he shrugged and straightened. "It'll do. The light's not right, anyway."

I watched him putting his things away, wrapping his cameras in their cases to keep them from the dew. He talked while he worked.

He said, "Everyone starts out the same. Determined to be different. But it never turns out that way. They all . . . we all, we'll get caught up in mortgage payments and kids and at the end . . . Well, I suppose the only thing I hope is that we don't remember at the end how we started out, all the things we meant to do with our lives."

I was quiet. His bleakness would pass—it always had before. He'd put his things away and come to me, and when we were holding each other it would be better.

Beyond us the skin of the pond rippled with a draft of warm air which spent itself before it reached the rushes. A raven, large and dark and distinct despite its great height spiralled down the circle of sky in long, slow arcs, then soared over the crowns of the trees and disappeared into the dusk.

Everything was quiet then, and still: dark green. The light was almost gone.

Our eyes were on one another's eyes but his were still bleak, and almost fierce, not really looking at me but through me, at some point beyond. There was no weakness in those eyes, not ever. I coaxed with my eyes, trying to pull him closer as we loosened the clasps and buttons which kept us separate and let the clothing drop onto the ground beside us. Standing naked in the grasses I explored his familiar body slowly, my eyes following my hands as they moved across the long angle of his collarbone and the thick dark hair of his chest and down, over the deep soft curves of his hips.

Slowly as though memorizing he touched me too, cupping my breasts and then running his hands softly over the down of my belly and around the backs of my legs, drawing his hands up and pulling me toward him.

Together we lay down upon the grasses which were thick and soft as though a place had been prepared for us.

Still slow, I sensed what he wanted and moved to that, and I urged him to do the same for me, to touch where the touch was needed, bringing one another pleasure to get it back that way again. As the darkness grew and covered us from everything but one another, my mind seemed to extend into his and at last I felt him move out of himself and bring himself to me. The strokes grew even more direct and accurate, the want more certain, tangible, demanding. His need for me increased. I needed him.

His body was against my body, his skin against my skin, and he was close but not enough, not nearly close enough. I wanted to contain him. Silently, urgently, he moved and I felt him against me, felt him move and could not wait—I'd never known such need.

The light hit us suddenly, directly.

"Diana!"

We leapt at Mother's voice so near. He twisted up away.

"My Lord." She snapped the flashlight out again. "Diana. Oh, my Lord."

I rolled fast to find my clothes, rushing into my jeans, the underthings forgotten, scrambling in my haste and panic. Noel had moved away, was nowhere near me.

"Noel!"

That last time I spoke to you, and you heard: you did not respond.

"Noel Fletcher!" She was shouting. "Fletcher! You bastard . . ." She whispered the word at first, then repeated it, louder, shouted it again.

Stunned, I waited for you to suck in breath at the way that she had spoken. But you were gone, you did not respond as I covered my nakedness in shame, at me, at her, lowered hidden from my mother who was still shouting words that could not be coming from that mouth, her mouth, my mother's mouth. I struggled into my jeans and shirt at last, shirt buttons still undone I stood, tripping on a pant leg that would not come straight, and stumbled toward her.

I did not follow you, but her, and she was off ahead of me, silent now, her flashlight poking ahead of her as she strode toward the house, with me behind her completing my dressing as I went, shoving my forgotten underwear into the pocket of my jeans. I didn't know where you had gone, didn't even think of you but only of my shame, our shame, until I was at home, in my room, waiting while she poured the bath.

As it filled she walked back and forth between the bathroom, bright and steaming, and my cool dark room.

I watched her, watched myself, as though from the outside, saving what I saw to tell you later when I saw you.

She was caught in detail, telling me to scrub myself, over and over again to scrub myself, every inch of me. As though I could wash you away, as though I wanted to wash you away. Her voice was full of loathing. She avoided touching me. She moved around me as though I were a pariah, contaminated, evil.

"And when you're finished, go back to your room. And stay there, Diana. And stay there. You should stay there forever you little, stupid . . . " But here in the house she stopped herself.

"What do you think you were doing out there? Do you think it is a stupid little game, what you were doing there? My God. Just stay there, in your room, do you hear me?"

Impotent to deal with what she'd seen, she started, came to my room every few minutes for hours to make another start: "How could you have done this to me?", and could not finish, and came again: "Do you think it's easy, raising both of you alone? Do you?" and left deflated, her rage increased each time until I became aware at last of the impotence of her. There was nothing she could say or do that would exact her retribution.

I never answered her. I did not speak. I allied myself with you.

I was planning how I would get out of the house, as soon as she stopped coming, how I would come to you in the darkness, my knuckles banging softly on your window, to assure you that I had nothing to do with her, nor she with me. We would be different, you and I. We couldn't help but be. I would tell you that I should have stayed beside you when she found us. I should not have gone with her.

Waiting for her to come back, very late, I fell asleep.

And at some point during that long night, you took the gun out to the barn and you loaded it. You sat and pressed it against your temple. Did you sit for a long moment thinking, before you squeezed? Or did you do it quickly, to get it done with, before you could reconsider?

Did you wonder how your father would react? Did you contemplate that there might follow a whole year of silence and inactivity? Did you guess that others would harvest his crops that fall, would plant for him the following spring, that they would bring him food which he would barely touch, that they would clean his house and do his laundry while he tried to die?

Did you consider the weakness of your parent, which you knew, the weakness of our parents?

Lacking your courage, your father resigned himself to living, stuck with life against his will.

And in the moment before you splashed your blood on straw, did you think of me? We were old enough to leave Donellon, to go away together.

Did you think of me, or him?

You left no note to anyone. You should have fixed the blame.

She came to my room in the morning, just after I'd fallen asleep it seemed for I woke suddenly, alert, as though I hadn't been asleep at all. I thought that she would carry on from the insignificant place she'd left off the last time she'd been in.

She said it fast and flat. "Noel is dead, Diana. He killed

himself." Her face was grim, grey, drawn. She seemed uncertain what to do next. There was a little silence before she added, perfunctorily, as one might to a perfect stranger, "With his father's gun. I'm sorry."

And then she left, closing the door again, and when she had gone I sat, staring at the door, and staring at the door. I shook my head, slowly, over and over again. I opened my mouth wide, and the scream started low, deep, and gushed up into my throat and out and came and came and filled the house, poured out the windows. The screaming was hideous, so hideous that I couldn't believe that the sound was coming from me.

After Whittick had come I stopped screaming. Every motion was made from numbness. Even after the tiny yellow pill wore off, still I moved as though a great impenetrable barrier were there, between me and the place in which my body was moving, breathing, living.

I turned aside Hilda's gestures of sympathy, her offers of food, her attempts to reach me. Mother offered none of those gestures. She seemed to be avoiding me.

The funeral was on Thursday. Late on Wednesday night, she knocked on my door. I was lying on my bed in my pyjamas, staring at my chemistry book which was open on the pillow.

"What?"

The door behind me opened.

I glanced back at her, away again.

She was wearing a dressing gown I hadn't seen in years, flannel, plaid, unbecoming. Her face was haggard.

"Hilda can drive you to the funeral," she said.

I moved to sit up on the bed, pulling my knees up to my chin. She was gazing out the window.

"I'm not going."

She looked over at me. "I think you should."

"He hated everyone in Donellon. I'm not going there, to stand with them. He wouldn't want me to." I began to cry, tears running down my cheeks. She took a step forward but I shook my head, warning her away. She stopped. I did nothing to stop the tears, did not reach for a handkerchief to wipe them away. I wanted her to see them, to see that they had nothing to do with her. To see that they were mine.

"Why don't you say you're sorry?"

"What on earth for?"

"If you hadn't come, he wouldn't have . . . He would never have done that if you hadn't come."

"Don't be ridiculous, Diana," she said sharply.

"He did it because you came."

"Don't be stupid," she said, tired. She looked tired.

I said, swallowing first, "I am not being stupid."

"Of course you are."

"I'm not."

Stupid words, childish words that led back into one another again and could find no resolution. We broke them off.

I was cold, passionately cold, deliberately cold, for the year before I left. My grades were good that final year of school. I came home immediately after school to study, helped Hilda with the cleaning and the kitchen, and showed Mother with my eloquent, elaborate politeness, that it had nothing to do with her. I would not let her close enough to tell me she was pleased with my marks, with my punctuality, with my tidiness. I didn't cry at my grandmother's funeral.

I've ignored her with equal commitment since. For what? Because she didn't have the courage to put her arms around me? Because she was incapable of saying what she meant, incapable of even feeling what she ought to feel? Is that why I've hated her so long?

My hands are pressed against my eyes. The house is still, the visitors gone, but this is worse, this weight of her and Noel, the scummy crust of skin my envelope too small, my pounding head. I must get up, away.

And I am up and through the living room, tea cups and little plates scattered around the room—Where is Hilda? Is nothing the way it should be?—and to the french doors. Locked. I pull, slow down enough to unlock them and thrust them open, running down the lawn and into the darkness of the trees, stumbling over the brush and roots that would never let themselves be memorized until I break, break through, to the lighter darkness of the clearing and the pond.

And running tear my clothes from my skin, caked in oil and peeling inside out, I run into the water, plunge, hold my breath and swim below the surface, strong strokes, pulling hard, pulling, pulling hard against them. Against Mother who didn't care, she wanted him dead, she wanted him killed, she killed him: pulling the words, trying to draw them back to me, back to where they've been so long. But they won't stay there. They won't stay there any more.

I pound and thrash the water, smash ineffective, smash and smash again until I'm too tired to go on. Too tired to move. Too tired.

He loaded the gun. He lifted it. And then he killed himself. He did it. I didn't matter enough to him to stop that.

I float face down, wanting to stay that way but my breath's too fast, too soon I must raise my head and gasp lungful after lungful from the air.

I stand, naked and cold and weeping, drag my body through the cool black water, my feet in silken mud, to the edge, and move shivering up the bank. On my knees I pull myself along the grasses and grope until I find my clothes to use them as a towel. I weep for him, rock, mourning him, rock in the grasses where we lay all those years ago. And I weep for something else, for something gone, that isn't him at all.

I've never needed anyone but Noel Fletcher, and he did not need me. He killed himself. He chose to kill himself. I had nothing to do with it. And I've never cared for anyone since him.

I'm exactly like her. She made me what I am, in her own image. I don't know how she did that, or how I let it happen.

When I waken, I've had the dream again. She was sitting in the garden, the flowers in her lap, the garden scissors at her knee. I stepped forward to reach for those scissors, to pick them up, to use them. And then I woke up.

In the pale light, I close my eyes and push myself back into it. I let myself step forward, watching to see what I will do. This time I will let myself take those scissors, will kill her if I want to. I will finish the dream, and let myself be done with it.

I want to gather all of it this time, to gather all of the detail. The leaves are full on the trees, but new, and the sun is warm. I would guess that it is June. The lawn is freshly cut, my father's work. The dress I'm wearing is one I wore the year I started school, and the hand that is reaching for the scissors, my hand, belongs to a small child. If I look up, I will see that she's smiling at me gently. She will take the scissors from me so that I won't hurt myself. I wonder if it's dream or memory.

The sky is yellow-pink and I stand for a moment at the water's edge warmed by the early sun, and watch the mist through the trees from the rose-grey of the water. The sun warmth, scents of mud and grass and spruce-gum tantalize and comfort, and I cannot duplicate them in my suite no matter how many plants I buy.

Over the trees I see the gables of a house that wasn't there before. Fletcher built it.

I turn back toward the house that I grew up in, walking slowly though the trees until I reach the lawn. There's a feeling of Sunday here. I know the day immediately. Sundays in Edmonton do not distinguish themselves this way.

Mitchell's standing inside the french doors as I walk up the lawn toward the house. He must have pulled them shut, or Hilda did, sometime during the dark, for I don't remember closing them when I ran out, any more than I recall drawing my clothes on before I slept last night.

He doesn't look as though he's had any sleep at all and I wonder where he's been—sitting beside her bed all night and waiting for her to open her eyes at last, to thank him for giving up his life for her? I think he knows she's never going to do that.

"I thought maybe you'd left," he says as I pull one door open and step in.

"Without a car?"

He stands away to let me pass him and then catches my arm to hold me. "Where are you going?"

"Upstairs."

"Upstairs."

"Right. I'm going upstairs."

He meets my eyes and studies them and I don't look away. He drops my arm. "She's sleeping."

"I'll wait until she wakes up."

He turns away toward the kitchen, his back a posture of defeat, and I start toward the stairs. On the bottom step I pause as I did last night, and look up. But there's no one there. I put my hand on the bannister and slowly tiptoe up to the dusk of the upper hall. Here in the shadows Grandmother used to sit, to frighten me intentionally I thought, or at least to catch me off my guard. To catch me doing something I should not be doing. She's dead.

The nurse opens the guest room door and looks out at me, her hair disheveled, but still she wears her uniform. Huge scarecrow. I put my finger to my lips and nod and she closes the door again.

My bedroom door is closed. I open it and look around; nothing is missing after all. I remember Hilda's saying she changed my sheets last week and indeed the room looks as though I'd just stepped out of it for a moment—a little girl who'll be be right back. And sure enough, I'm here.

I leave the door open, some light from that window cast into the hall to brighten it a little, and raise my hand to knock at the door of the room across, raise my knuckles instinctively because I was never allowed inside without knocking first, but I change my mind and twist the handle, letting myself in silently.

It cannot be Mother who is lying in that bed all pale and thin against the pillows, her eyes closed and her chest barely moving, her skin seamed, knotted and drawn at the neck, her hair in a plait along her shoulder. This isn't the woman of the vision, nor even of my more recent memory. This is Grandmother.

But, more closely now, as I tiptoe across the rug and still she doesn't stir, I see that it is Mother and I wipe the perspiration from my hands onto my jeans. In thirty, forty, fifty years, will that be the reflection that looks back at me from the mirror, a hand mirror that I hold up to my face as I lie dying in some bed: if I should dare to look?

Her breath comes slowly. Her mouth opens, closes, and again there is the sound of air through her nostrils, even.

On the dresser there is a photo, far enough away that Mother can't possibly see it, and I pick it up from between the pill bottles. I don't remember seeing it before, this only photograph that she's chosen to keep in her room.

She looks too small for that bed.

It is a black and white. Father and Mother sit in the lawn swing, each of them with a child leaning against the knee. They look normal, like any family, really, and I can't see anything in those faces to say what was to come.

I don't remember its being taken, but I sense that it's right, it's accurate. It used to be this way before dinner, perhaps, on a Sunday, with Grandmother wheeling around inside, waiting impatiently for us to finish with the foolishness so she could have her meal.

I am caught suddenly by Mitchell, a boy of five or so with his father's arm around his waist: caught because I didn't notice him at first. Which means that he's accurate as well. The boy is pudgy, stocky, definitely that. But not nearly as fat as I'd remembered.

I wonder who took the picture. Noel reconstructed the past as he remembered it, but this is not a reconstruction. I would have made Mitchell fatter, my father sadder, Mother more severe. And myself? I would have stood her away from them, to one side, apart. Aware but disconnected. But there I am, with Mother's hand on my hip.

Perhaps Hilda held the camera, nodding nervously, worried about the chicken unattended in the oven but unable to decline my father's request. What does she think of all of us? Why did she change my sheets?

"Well."

I'm startled by her voice, not nearly as weak as I'd thought it would be, and my hand jerks as I look over the frame of the photograph at her. Her eyes look back at me, my eyes: cold and blue.

I turn to replace the photograph on the top of the dresser.

"Not like that," she says. "Turn it a little toward me."

Which means that she can see it, or enough of it to nudge her memory. I adjust it the way she's asked.

"I didn't think you were going to come up," she says as I step closer to the bed.

I smile. "I wasn't sure myself."

I want to ask her if she's glad I did, but don't. The silence grows. She's looking at me carefully and I have fixed my eyes on a bedpost but I see out of the corner of my eye that she suddenly seems to grapple with some pain, and fights it down. There's a shot glass full of a red liquid on the bedside table and I look down at it, at her.

She nods, and I raise it toward her, wondering if I'll have to pour it in her mouth but she pushes herself up onto her elbow, takes it with the other hand, and trembling a little, drinks it. Grimaces. Lies back against the pillow as I take the glass from her hand and put it empty on the table.

She's wearing a cotton nightgown of pale blue, utilitarian, no lace, and the plait is closed near her head and again at its thin tip with brown elastic bands. She's so thin. She's so much weaker than I ever thought she could be. But still she has no aura of helplessness about her.

She's a victim, of this illness. Is it the first time in her life she's been a victim? I would have said so, yesterday.

But what if Madelyn was right about her? What if she was helpless all that time, and knew it, and was covering it up with bravado, with performance? What if there was nothing she could do to change her mother, my father, me, or Mitchell? To change any of her circumstances? What if her only skill was her consummate talent for putting up a good front, for maintaining a stiff upper lip? Then what have I been fighting all these years?

"I've been at the pond."

She closes her eyes for a moment, and then nods, wrestling perhaps with the same memories as I. I look down at the translucent skin of her thin hand, at the veins, and remember Grandmother's hand squeezing mine.

Is her memory of that night as terrible as mine? Did she feel the same rage at him as I have felt at her?

There's no way I'll ever find out.

"Mother?"

She opens her eyes.

"I want to know one thing. Why did you come to the pond, that night?"

She shakes her head, closes her eyes again. "Mitchell." Swallows. "Mitchell said there was a gun." Shakes her head again. "I don't want to talk about that. Just sit down and tell me what you're doing. Please. Don't talk about that any more."

I sit in the chair beside her bed, turning it back from where Seabring or Mitchell has placed it so that the window is visible from it as well, turn it so I'm looking at the bed. As matter-of-factly as I can, I describe what I've been doing since I left here, tell her about Rosen and Madelyn, and even Sonny. As I'm talking I'm wondering whether she knows any of this already, whether Mitchell has told her some of it.

And I'm thinking about what she said—that Mitchell was the one who caused her to come to the pond. He must have been sneaking around in the bushes in another attempt to ingratiate himself with her. The gun was a prop for his tattle-telling as much as it was for the photographs. I'm sure he wasn't trying to save my life.

"I suppose if she does get married, I'll have to move again."

She's raised herself once more onto an elbow and I can see the effort that costs her for her whole body has begun to tremble.

"Aren't you coming home?"

I stare at her. Home? This is not home. Edmonton is home.

"I like it there, Mother. I've been there my whole adult life."

"But it's cold there. I've seen the television, read the papers—it gets terribly cold out there."

I smile. Has she been following my weather that carefully? "It makes us tough."

I imagine taking her into my arms. She would be too slight to have been the weight I've carried all these years. Too slight. There are tears on my cheeks and when I look up I see them on hers as well.

"I'm sorry," I whisper.

"So am I."

We're uncomfortable even with this small gesture, but I touch her hand, cool. She doesn't move it to respond, but rests back against the pillows.

"Do you want me to sit here, for a little while?'

She shakes her head. "I'm tired. Come back a little later if you want to." She glances at me and then closes her eyes. "You don't think I'll be here in a little while, do you?"

I swallow, hard. Swallow again. "I'm sure that if you decide to be, you will."

She smiles a little. "I'll be here." Opens her eyes. "Is the Reverend Westmoreland here?"

"Mother," I say gently, "it's five o'clock in the morning."

She nods, and almost immediately is sleeping.

I lean back against the chair and let the tears run down my face, weeping now not because she's dying but for the distance between us that cannot be breached any more than this. For all of the distances.

Sunday Afternoon

Epilogue

"Madelyn. It's me." I stand in the Sunday feeling of the vestibule, wood panels glowing from the sunlight through the windows on the landing. The women, changed and repowdered, have all come back to the living room but they are quieter today. They are eavesdropping on my conversation at the moment. Westmoreland is here as well, leaning back in the armchair, hands clasped over his black-shirted chest.

"Diana. How are you?" She says away from the receiver, to Sonny, "It's Diana."

"I'm all right."

Showered and wearing clean clothes, I do feel better.

"How is it going? Your mother?"

"She's stable, I guess. Not good."

Miss Seabring passes me on her way from the dining room table to the front door which she opens, going out into the sunlight for her walk. Even in dying there is routine.

"I'm glad you called, Diana. I wanted to phone you last night, but I didn't want to intrude."

"Don't worry about intruding."

I'm glad she didn't call last night.

"Okay," she says, not certain that I mean it, "I won't. Sounds like you might be there for a while."

"I don't know. I guess so. I suppose I'll have to call Rosen and make arrangements."

"He called here this morning. Sounds completely lost without you. I think he's afraid you're never going to come back." Madelyn's fond of Rosen.

"Tell him I'll be back." He'll get along without me for a while. The store practically runs itself. "Any water in my suite? I heard there was a flood."

"There was. Is. But we're dry." She's proud of that. It's her basement, after all. My suite. Her basement.

"My plants could probably use some water."

She laughs, and the tension's gone. "I'll take care of it."

"Thanks. I'll give you a call in a couple of days. Say hello to

Sonny."

She says she will.

I've barely hung up when the telephone rings.

"I got it fixed."

"That's great, Beak. Berkeley."

"It's a temporary repair, but it'll get you back to Toronto. I'm going to bring it around in a few minutes, and I wondered if you could give me a lift back home again."

I look back at the living room. "I suppose I could." I'm suspicious of his motives, with his wife out of town, but after what he's done for me I can hardly refuse to drive him home.

"Maybe you'd consider stopping in for a drink, maybe staying for dinner? We could have some time to visit."

There, I draw the line. I lower my voice. "My mother . . . I really couldn't leave. I hope you haven't gone to any trouble."

"No. Don't think about it. It was going to be potluck anyway. Sara got in about an hour ago. Didn't have time to shop." He pauses. "You're sure?"

"I am. Thanks, anyway." I'm glad that I refused, even if Sara is at home. I couldn't bear it now, his kids complaining (three or four of them: I don't remember what he said), and their parents nagging that they'll eat what they've been served, and Beak stepping over toys to serve the drinks, and hauling out old yearbooks to remind me that I met his wife in high school.

"Well, then," he says more slowly, "I'll just get Sara to follow me over in the van. She can drive me back."

"I don't mind driving you back. I don't want to put her to any trouble."

"She won't mind."

If that's true, she must be cut from the same cloth as he is.

"How much do I owe you for the car?"

"The rental company will take care of it."

"They might not. And it'll be weeks if they do. I think it'd be better if I paid you now, so you could forget about it."

"I'd really be insulted if you paid me," he says quietly after a moment. "After Sara, and Melanie, you're about the most important woman in my life. Let me be a hero for once, okay?"

"Who's Melanie?"

"My daughter."

I consider this. "Okay."

"I'll be there in fifteen minutes."

I walk back into the living room where all of them have been listening to my conversation to fill the void. Like a delegation they came here after church, Mother's friends first and a little later Westmoreland. Hilda's going to have to feed the vigil and she's busy, contented, in the kitchen. Mitchell's upstairs with Mother, trying to coax some lunch into her.

Westmoreland's head is sunk and he looks tired and grey. I study him for a minute and then go through to the dining room and get out a shining glass and the polished decanter full of sherry. I fill the glass almost to the brim and carry it carefully into the living room, stand in front of him. He raises his head and I hold the glass toward him, stricken suddenly with the image of a communion rail between us, but he smiles gratefully and takes the glass from me.

"Anyone else?" I ask.

All of the women decline. They've come distinct in my mind at last—Miss McAllister's the one who's been talking about the bridge they'll play when Mother's up and about and the rest of them are irritated with her as usual. They try, unsuccessfully, to silence her with glares and yet they too discuss their gardens and the tea next Thursday afternoon.

They will go on, they seem to be asserting. Any fears, any weaknesses, will be concealed from one another—even though all of them are feeling exactly the same way. They won't share, these friends, not anything but baking. I don't like these women, particularly, and I'm not fond of my mother, either.

Women are not all sisters, Madelyn, no matter what you think. So I'm grateful for our friendship.

Mitchell comes down and says something quietly to Westmoreland. He puts his glass down on the lace doily beside him, nods, and goes upstairs, excusing himself from the women first.

Mitchell looks exhausted and I'm surprised when he sits down with the rest of us. All of us are waiting for one final visit, one last visit to the dying woman, and then another, and another. To what end? What is there left to say? What was ever said in the first place? Nothing. These women, individually and alone, are merely preparing themselves to follow her casket to the grave, to participate in Donellon's final ceremony.

Hilda brings in a plate of sandwiches and I take a quarter of a chicken-salad and a sprig of parsley, chewing one bite slowly and then putting the sandwich on the linen table napkin on the small table beside me. I had an egg and a piece of toast about two hours ago, so Hilda doesn't look concerned that I'm not eating now. The other women take one quarter each on this round. Mitchell takes three and a pickle.

The doorbell rings.

"Where are you going?" Mitchell asks, leaping to his feet and setting his sandwiches down.

"My car."

He waits behind me in the hall as I open the door. I glance back at the tableau: Friends and Relatives Waiting for The End.

"Can I change my mind?"

"Sure." Beak grins at me. "That'd be great. We'll bring you back whenever you want. Come on. I want you to meet Sara. You'll probably remember her . . ."

"Diana," Mitchell says hard behind me. "She's very ill."

"It's okay, Mitchell. I've seen her."

"You can't do this . . . You can't run off again."

"I'll be back. You know where I am if you need me."

I walk down the steps toward the van where Beak is yelling at his children (three) in the back to shove over, and pulling his wife from the front to meet me.

I put out my hand to shake Sara Zimmerman's and then shake my head as she indicates that she's going to climb into the back, and let me have the front. She ignores my protests and gets in with her kids.

I climb into the passenger seat, and turn to offer a wave to Mitchell. But he's disappeared, and the front door's closed. Beak closes my door and gives it a little pat of satisfaction with his hand. I smile at him through the open window, and he smiles back.

I'll only be gone an hour or two.

I'm just curious, that's all.